THE PROUD ROBOT

'Are you going to keep quiet?' the robot demanded from its post before the mirror.

Brock jumped. Gallegher waved a casual hand. 'Don't mind Joe. I just finished him last night, and I rather regret it.'

'A robot?'

'A robot. But he's no good, you know. I made him when I was drunk, and I haven't the slightest idea how or why. All he'll do is stand there and admire himself. And sing. He sings like a banshee. You'll hear him presently.'

Henry Kuttner

with C.L. Moore

THE PROUD ROBOT

The complete Galloway Gallegher stories

Hamlyn Paperbacks

THE PROUD ROBOT
ISBN 0 600 38404 7
First published in Great Britain 1983
by Hamlyn Paperbacks
Originally published in the United States
as ROBOTS HAVE NO TAILS by Lewis Padgett.
Copyright [c] 1952 by Lewis Padgett (Henry Kuttner &
C.L. Moore)
THE PROUD ROBOT *is based on the following
material:*
*'Time Locker', 'Proud Robot', 'Gallegher Plus' and
'The World Is Mine', copyright 1943 by Street and Smith
Publications, Inc. and 'Ex Machina', copyright 1948
by Street and Smith Publications, Inc.*

Hamlyn Paperbacks are published by
The Hamlyn Publishing Group Ltd.,
Astronaut House,
Feltham, Middlesex, England.

Printed and bound in Great Britain by Collins, Glasgow.

INTRODUCTION

In 1940 two fine science fiction writers married. Not only did Catherine ('C.L.') Moore and Henry Kuttner marry their lives, but they also married their writing careers. From two good writers were born whole companies of pseudonymous great writers (Lewis Padgett and Lawrence O'Donnell to name the two most prominent). The number of pen-names used by the prolific partners, together and apart, at one time threatened to swamp the universe of quality science fiction. Indeed, so great was their contribution that when Jack Vance started his illustrious career, a rumour quickly spread that this was yet another reflection of the versatile Kuttner-Moore genius! (A rumour, I hasten to add, that had and has no truth in it whatsoever.)

In 1958 this fruitful collaboration came to an untimely end. Henry Kuttner died at the age of forty-four, and science fiction was sadly diminished. C.L. Moore completed their first television script and continued to work in that field until after her second marriage six years later. She has written no science fiction since the late 1950s.

Hamlyn Paperbacks have already published the Kuttners' novels *Mutant* and *Fury*, and the collection *Clash By Night*, and will continue to bring back into print at intervals the works of one of science fiction's great masters. I am confident that Kuttner (and Kuttner-and-Moore)'s work will remain available from now until entertaining and highly polished story-telling goes out of fashion.

So spread the word. Kuttner is coming back into print. It is now up to you to ensure that future generations of fans are not denied the opportunity to sit amused, baffled, delighted, bewildered, tickled, frightened, amazed, entertained and enthralled by the genius of the Kuttners, Henry Kuttner and C.L. Moore.

PETER PINTO, 1983.

Contents

THE PROUD ROBOT 9

GALLEGHER PLUS 47

THE WORLD IS MINE 91

EX MACHINA 128

TIME LOCKER 165

THE PROUD ROBOT

Things often happened to Gallegher, who played at science by ear. He was, as he often remarked, a casual genius. Sometimes he'd start with a twist of wire, a few batteries, and a button hook, and before he finished, he might contrive a new type of refrigerating unit.

At the moment he was nursing a hangover. A disjointed, lanky, vaguely boneless man with a lock of dark hair falling untidily over his forehead, he lay on the couch in the lab and manipulated his mechanical liquor bar. A very dry Martini drizzled slowly from the spigot into his receptive mouth.

He was trying to remember something, but not trying too hard. It had to do with the robot, of course. Well, it didn't matter.

'Hey, Joe,' Gallegher said.

The robot stood proudly before the mirror and examined its innards. Its hull was transparent, and wheels were going around at a great rate inside.

'When you call me that,' Joe remarked, 'whisper. And get that cat out of here.'

'Your ears aren't that good.'

'They are. I can hear the cat walking about, all right.'

'What does it sound like?' Gallegher inquired, interested.

'Just like drums,' said the robot, with a put-upon air. 'And when you talk, it's like thunder.' Joe's voice was a discordant squeak, so Gallegher meditated on saying something about glass houses and casting the first stone. He brought his attention, with some effort, to the luminous door panel, where a shadow loomed – a familiar shadow, Gallegher thought.

'It's Brock,' the annunciator said. 'Harrison Brock. Let me in!'

'The door's unlocked.' Gallegher didn't stir. He looked gravely at the well-dressed, middle-aged man who came in, and tried to remember. Brock was between forty and fifty; he had a smoothly massaged, clean-shaved face, and wore an expression of harassed intolerance. Probably Gallegher knew the man. He wasn't sure. Oh, well.

Brock looked around the big, untidy laboratory, blinked at the robot, searched for a chair, and failed to find it. Arms akimbo, he rocked back and forth and glared at the prostrate scientist.

'Well?' he said.

'Never start conversations that way,' Gallegher mumbled, siphoning another Martini down his gullett. 'I've had enough trouble today. Sit down and take it easy. There's a dynamo behind you. It isn't very dusty, is it?'

'Did you get it?' Brock snapped. 'That's all I want to know. You've had a week. I've a cheque for ten thousand in my pocket. Do you want it, or don't you?'

'Sure,' Gallegher said. He extended a large, groping hand. 'Give.'

'*Caveat emptor*. What am I buying?'

'Don't you know?' the scientist asked, honestly puzzled.

Brock began to bounce up and down in a harassed fashion. 'My God,' he said. 'They told me you could help me if anybody could. Sure. And they also said it'd be like pulling teeth to get sense out of you. Are you a technician or a drivelling idiot?'

Gallegher pondered. 'Wait a minute. I'm beginning to remember. I talked to you last week, didn't I?'

'You talked – ' Brock's round face turned pink. 'Yes! You lay there swilling liquor and babbled poetry. You sang "Frankie and Johnnie." And you finally got around to accepting my commission.'

'The fact is,' Gallegher said, 'I have been drunk. I often get drunk. Especially on my vacation. It releases my subconscious, and then I can work. I've made my best gadgets when I was tizzied,' he went on happily. 'Everything seems so clear then. Clear as a bell. I mean a bell, don't I? Anyway – ' He lost the thread and looked puzzled.

'Anyway what are you talking about?'

'Are you going to keep quiet?' the robot demanded from its post before the mirror.

Brock jumped. Gallegher waved a casual hand. 'Don't mind Joe. I just finished him last night, and I rather regret it.'

'A robot?'

'A robot. But he's no good, you know. I made him when I was drunk, and I haven't the slightest idea how or why. All he'll do is stand there and admire himself. And sing. He sings like a banshee. You'll hear him presently.'

With an effort Brock brought his attention back to the matter in hand. 'Now look, Gallegher. I'm in a spot. You promised to help me. If you don't, I'm a ruined man.'

'I've been ruined for years,' the scientist remarked. 'It never bothers me. I just go along working for a living and making things in my spare time. Making all sorts of things. You know, if I'd really studied, I'd have been another Einstein. So they tell me. As it is, my subconscious picked up a first-class scientific training somewhere. Probably that's why I never bothered. When I'm drunk or sufficiently absent-minded, I can work out the damnedest problems.'

'You're drunk now,' Brock accused.

'I approach the pleasanter stages. How would you feel if you woke up and found you'd made a robot for some unknown reason, and hadn't the slightest idea of the creature's attributes?'

'Well –'

'I don't feel that way at all,' Gallegher murmured. 'Probably you take life too seriously, Brock. Wine is a mocker; strong drink is raging. Pardon me. I rage.' He drank another Martini.

Brock began to pace around the crowded laboratory, circling various enigmatic and untidy objects. 'If you're a scientist, Heaven help science.'

'I'm the Larry Adler of science,' Gallegher said. 'He was a musician – lived some hundreds of years ago, I think. I'm like him. Never took a lesson in my life. Can I help it if my subconscious likes practical jokes?'

'Do you know who I am?' Brock demanded.

'Candidly, no. Should I?'

There was bitterness in the other's voice. 'You might have the courtesy to remember, even though it was a week ago. Harrison Brock. Me. I own Vox-View Pictures.'

'No,' the robot said suddenly, 'it's no use. No use at all, Brock.'

'What the –'

Gallegher sighed wearily. 'I forget the damned thing's alive. Mr Brock, meet Joe. Joe, meet Mr Brock – of Vox-View.'

Joe turned, gears meshing within his transparent skull. 'I am glad to meet you, Mr Brock. Allow me to congratulate you on your good fortune in hearing my lovely voice.'

'Uh,' said the magnate inarticulately. 'Hello.'

'Vanity of vanities, all is vanity,' Gallegher put in, *sotto voce*. 'Joe's like that. A peacock. No use arguing with him, either.'

The robot ignored this aside. 'But it's no use, Mr Brock,' he went on squeakily. 'I'm not interested in money. I realise it would bring happiness to many if I consented to appear in your pictures, but fame means nothing to me. Nothing. Consciousness of beauty is enough.'

Brock began to chew his lips. 'Look,' he said savagely, 'I didn't come here to offer you a picture job. See? Am I offering you a contract? Such colossal nerve – *Pah*! You're crazy.'

'Your schemes are perfectly transparent,' the robot remarked coldly. 'I can see that you're overwhelmed by my beauty and the loveliness of my voice – its grand tonal qualities. You needn't pretend you don't want me, just so you can get me at a lower price. I said I wasn't interested.'

'You're *cr-r-razy*!' Brock howled, badgered beyond endurance, and Joe calmly turned back to his mirror.

'Don't talk so loudly,' the robot warned. 'The discordance is deafening. Besides, you're ugly and I don't like to look at you.' Wheels and cogs buzzed inside the transplastic shell. Joe extended his eyes on stalks and regarded himself with every appearance of appreciation.

Gallegher was chuckling quietly on the couch. 'Joe has a high irritation value,' he said. 'I've found that out already. I must have given him some remarkable senses, too. An hour ago he started to laugh his damn fool head off. No reason, apparently. I was fixing myself a bite to eat. Ten minutes after that I slipped on an apple core I'd thrown away and came down hard. Joe just looked at me. "That was it," he said. "Logics of probability. Cause and effect. I knew you were going to drop that apple core and then step on it when you went to pick up the mail." Like the White Queen, I suppose. It's a poor memory that doesn't work both ways.'

Brock sat on the small dynamo – there were two, the larger one named Monstro, and the smaller one serving Gallegher as a bank – and took deep breaths. 'Robots are nothing new.'

'This one is. I hate its gears. It's beginning to give me an inferiority complex. Wish I knew why I'd made it,' Gallegher sighed. 'Oh, well. Have a drink?'

'No. I came here on business. Do you seriously mean you spent last week building a robot instead of solving the problem I hired you for?'

'Contingent, wasn't it?' Gallegher asked. 'I think I remember that.'

'Contingent,' Brock said with satisfaction. 'Ten thousand, if and when.'

'Why not give me the dough and take the robot? He's worth that. Put him in one of your pictures.'

'I won't have any pictures unless you figure out an answer,' Brock snapped. 'I told you all about it.'

'I have been drunk,' Gallegher said. 'My mind has been wiped clear, as by a sponge. I am as a little child. Soon I shall be as a drunken little child. Meanwhile, if you'd care to explain the matter again – '

Brock gulped down his passion, jerked a magazine at random from the bookshelf, and took out a stylo. 'All right. My preferred stocks are at twenty-eight, 'way below par – ' He scribbled figures on the magazine.

'If you'd taken that medieval folio next to that, it'd have cost you a pretty penny,' Gallegher said lazily. 'So you're the sort of guy who writes on tablecloths, eh? Forget this business of stocks and stuff. Get down to cases. Who are you trying to gyp?'

'It's no use,' the robot said from before its mirror. 'I won't sign a contract. People may come and admire me, if they like, but they'll have to whisper in my presence.'

'A madhouse,' Brock muttered, trying to get a grip on himself. 'Listen, Gallegher. I told you all this a week ago, but –'

'Joe wasn't here then. Pretend like you're talking to him.'

'Uh – look. You've heard of Vox-View Pictures, at least.'

'Sure. The biggest and best television company in the business. Sonatone's about your only competitor.'

'Sonatone's squeezing me out.'

Gallegher looked puzzled. 'I don't see how. You've got the best product. Tri-dimensional colour, all sorts of modern improvements, the top actors, musicians, singers –'

'No use,' the robot said. 'I won't.'

'Shut up, Joe. You're tops in your field, Brock. I'll hand you that. And I've always heard you were fairly ethical. What's Sonatone got on you?'

Brock made helpless gestures. 'Oh, it's politics. The bootleg theatres. I can't buck 'em. Sonatone helped elect the present administration, and the police just wink when I try to have the bootleggers raided.'

'Bootleg theatres?' Gallegher asked, scowling a trifle. 'I've heard something –'

'It goes 'way back. To the old sound-film days. Home television killed sound film and big theatres. People were conditioned away from sitting in audience groups to watch a screen. The home televisors got good. It was more fun to sit in an easy-chair, drink beer, and watch the show. Television wasn't a rich man's hobby by that time. The metre system brought the price down to middle-class levels. Everybody knows that.'

'I don't,' Gallegher said. 'I never pay attention to what goes on outside of my lab, unless I have to. Liquor and a selective mind. I ignore everything that doesn't affect me directly. Explain the whole thing in detail, so I'll get a complete picture. I don't mind repetitions. Now, what about this metre system of yours?'

'Televisors are installed free. We never sell 'em; we rent them. People pay according to how many hours they have the set tuned in. We run a continuous show, stage plays, wire-tape films, operas, orchestras, singers, vaudeville – everything. If you use your televisor a lot, you pay proportionately. The man comes around once a month and reads the metre. Which is a fair system. Anybody can afford a Vox-View. Sonatone and the other companies do the same thing, but Sonatone's the only big competitor I've got. At least, the only one that's crooked as hell. The rest of the boys – they're smaller than I am, but I don't step on their toes. Nobody's ever called me a louse,' Brock said darkly.

'So what?'

'So Sonatone has started to depend on audience appeal. It was impossible till lately – you couldn't magnify tri-dimensional television on a big screen without streakiness and mirage-effect. That's why the regular three-by-four home screens were used. Results were perfect. But Sonatone's bought a lot of the ghost theatres all over the country – '

'What's a ghost theatre?' Gallegher asked.

'Well – before sound films collapsed, the world was thinking big. Big – you know? Ever heard of the Radio City Music Hall? That wasn't in it! Television was coming in, and competition was fierce. Sound-film theatres got bigger and more elaborate. They were palaces. Tremendous. But when television was perfected, nobody went to the theatres any more, and it was often too expensive a job to tear 'em down. Ghost theatres – see? Big ones and little ones. Renovated them. And they're showing Sonatone programmes. Audience appeal is quite a factor. The theatres charge plenty, but people flock into 'em. Novelty and the mob instinct.'

Gallegher closed his eyes. 'What's to stop you from doing the same thing?'

'Patents,' Brock said briefly. 'I mentioned that dimensional television couldn't be used on big screens till lately. Sonatone signed an agreement with me ten years ago that any enlarging improvements would be used mutually. They crawled out of that contract. Said it was faked, and the courts upheld them. They uphold the courts – politics. Anyhow, Sonatone's technicians worked out a method of using the large screen. They took out patents – twenty-seven patents, in fact, covering every possible variation on the idea. My technical staff has been working day and night trying to find some similar method that won't be an infringement, but Sonatone's got it all sewed up. They've a system called the Magna. It can be hooked up to any type of televisor – but they'll only allow it to be used on Sonatone machines. See?'

'Unethical, but legal,' Gallegher said. 'Still, you're giving your customers more for their money. People want good stuff. The size doesn't matter.'

'Yeah,' Brock said bitterly, 'but that isn't all. The newstapes are full of A. A. – it's a new catchword. Audience Appeal. The herd instinct. You're right about people wanting good stuff – but would you buy Scotch at four a quart if you could get it for half that amount?'

'Depends on the quality. What's happening?'

'Bootleg theatres,' Brock said. 'They've opened all over the country. They show Vox-View products, and they're using the Magna enlarger system Sonatone's got patented. The admission price is low – lower than the rate of owning a Vox-View in your own home. There's audience appeal. There's the thrill of something a bit illegal. People are having their Vox-Views taken out right and left. I know why. They can go to a bootleg theatre instead.'

'It's illegal,' Gallegher said thoughtfully.

'So were speakeasies, in the Prohibition Era. A matter of protection, that's all. I can't get any action through the courts. I've tried. I'm running in the red. Eventually I'll be broke. I can't lower my home rental fees on Vox-Views. They're nominal already. I make my profits through quantity. Now, no profits. As for these bootleg theatres, it's

16

pretty obvious who's backing them.'

'Sonatone?'

'Sure. Silent partners. They get the take at the box office. What they want is to squeeze me out of business, so they'll have a monopoly. After that, they'll give the public junk and pay their artists starvation salaries. With me it's different. I pay my staff what they're worth – plenty.'

'And you offered me a lousy ten thousand,' Gallegher remarked. 'Uh-*huh*!'

'That was only the first instalment,' Brock said hastily. 'You can name your own fee. Within reason,' he added.

'I shall. An astronomical sum. Did I say I'd accept the commission a week ago?'

'You did.'

'Then I must have had some idea how to solve the problem,' Gallegher pondered. 'Let's see. I didn't mention anything in particular, did I?'

'You kept talking about marble slabs and . . . uh . . . your sweetie.'

'Then I was singing,' Gallegher explained largely. ' "St James Infirmary." Singing calms my nerves, and God knows they need it sometimes. Music and liquor. I often wonder what the vintners buy – '

'What?'

'One half so precious as the stuff they sell. Let it go. I am quoting Omar. It means nothing. Are your technicians any good?'

'The best. And the best paid.'

'They can't find a magnifying process that won't infringe on the Sonatone Magna patents?'

'In a nutshell, that's it.'

'I suppose I'll have to do some research,' Gallegher said sadly. 'I hate it like poison. Still, the sum of the parts equals the whole. Does that make sense to you? It doesn't to me. I have trouble with words. After I say things, I start wondering what I've said. Better than watching a play,' he finished wildly. 'I've got a headache. Too much talk and not enough liquor. Where were we?'

'Approaching the madhouse,' Brock suggested. 'If you weren't my last resort, I'd – '

'No use,' the robot said squeakily. 'You might as well tear up your contract, Brock. I won't sign it. Fame means nothing to me – nothing.'

'If you don't shut up,' Gallegher warned, 'I'm going to scream in your ears.'

'All right!' Joe shrilled. 'Beat me! Go on, beat me! The meaner you are, the faster I'll have my nervous system disrupted, and then I'll be dead. I don't care. I've got no instinct of self-preservation. Beat me. See if I care.'

'He's right, you know,' the scientist said after a pause. 'And it's the only logical way to respond to blackmail or threats. The sooner it's over, the better. There aren't any gradations with Joe. Anything really painful to him will destroy him. And he doesn't give a damn.'

'Neither do I,' Brock grunted. 'What I want to find out –'

'Yeah. I know. Well, I'll wander around and see what occurs to me. Can I get into your studios?'

'Here's a pass.' Brock scribbled something on the back of a card. 'Will you get to work on it right away?'

'Sure,' Gallegher lied. 'Now you run along and take it easy. Try and cool off. Everything's under control. I'll either find a solution to your problem pretty soon or else –'

'Or else what?'

'Or else I won't,' the scientist finished blandly, and fingered the buttons on a control panel near the couch. 'I'm tired of Martinis. Why didn't I make that robot a mechanical bartender, while I was at it? Even the effort of selecting and pushing buttons is depressing at times. Yeah, I'll get to work on the business, Brock. Forget it.'

The magnate hesitated. 'Well, you're my only hope. I needn't bother to mention that if there's anything I can do to help you –'

'A blonde,' Gallegher murmured. 'That gorgeous, gorgeous star of yours, Silver O'Keefe. Send her over. Otherwise I want nothing.'

'Good-bye, Brock,' the robot said squeakily. 'Sorry we couldn't get together on the contract, but at least you've had the ineluctable delight of hearing my beautiful voice, not to mention the pleasure of seeing me. Don't tell too many people how lovely I am. I really don't want to be bothered with mobs. They're noisy.'

'You don't know what dogmatism means till you've talked to Joe,' Gallegher said. 'Oh, well. See you later. Don't forget the blonde.'

Brock's lips quivered. He searched for words, gave it up as a vain task, and turned to the door.

'Good-bye, you ugly man,' Joe said.

Gallegher winced as the door slammed, though it was harder on the robot's supersensitive ears than on his own. 'Why do you go on like that?' he inquired. 'You nearly gave the guy apoplexy.'

'Surely he didn't think he was beautiful,' Joe remarked.

'Beauty's in the eye of the beholder.'

'How stupid you are. You're ugly, too.'

'And you're a collection of rattletrap gears, pistons and cogs. You've got worms,' said Gallegher, referring, of course, to certain mechanisms in the robot's body.

'I'm lovely.' Joe stared raptly into the mirror.

'Maybe, to you. Why did I make you transparent, I wonder?'

'So others could admire me. I have X-ray vision, of course.'

'And wheels in your head. Why did I put your radio-atomic brain in your stomach? Protection?'

Joe didn't answer. He was humming in a maddeningly squeaky voice, shrill and nerve-racking. Gallegher stood it for a while, fortifying himself with a gin rickety from the syphon.

'Get it up!' he yelped at last. 'You sound like an old-fashioned subway train going round a curve.'

'You're merely jealous,' Joe scoffed, but obediently raised his tone to a supersonic pitch. There was silence for a half-minute. Then all the dogs in the neighbourhood began to howl.

Wearily Gallegher dragged his lanky frame up from the couch. He might as well get out. Obviously there was no peace to be had in the laboratory. Not with that animated junk pile inflating his ego all over the place. Joe began to laugh in an off-key cackle. Gallegher winced.

'What now?'

'You'll find out.'

Logic of causation and effect, influenced by probabilities, X-ray vision and other enigmatic senses the robot no doubt possessed. Gallegher cursed softly, found a shapeless black hat, and made for the door. He opened it to admit a short, fat man who bounced painfully off the scientist's stomach.

'*Whoof*! Uh. What a corny sense of humour that jackass has. Hello, Mr Kennicott. Glad to see you. Sorry I can't offer you a drink.'

Mr Kennicott's swarthy face twisted malignantly. 'Don' wanna no drink. Wanna my money. You gimme. Howzabout it?'

Gallegher looked thoughtfully at nothing. 'Well, the fact is, I was just going to collect a cheque.'

'I sella you my diamonds. You say you gonna make somet'ing wit' 'em. You gimme cheque before. It go bounca, bounca, bounca. Why is?'

'It was rubber,' Gallegher said faintly. 'I never can keep track of my bank balance.'

Kennicott showed symptoms of going bounca on the threshold. 'You gimme back diamonds, eh?'

'Well, I used 'em in an experiment. I forget just what. You know, Mr Kennicott, I think I was a little drunk when I bought them, wasn't I?'

'Dronk,' the little man agreed. 'Mad wit' vino, sure. So whatta? I wait no longer. Awready you put me off too much. Pay up now or elsa.'

'Go away, you dirty man,' Joe said from within the room. 'You're awful.'

Gallegher hastily shouldered Kennicott out into the street and latched the door behind him. 'A parrot,' he explained. 'I'm going to wring its neck pretty soon. Now about that money. I admit I owe it to you. I've just taken on a big job, and when I'm paid, you'll get yours.'

'Bah to such stuff,' Kennicott said. 'You gotta position, eh? You are technician wit' some big company, eh? Ask for ahead-salary.'

'I did,' Gallegher sighed. 'I've drawn my salary for six

months ahead. Now look, I'll have that dough for you in a couple of days. Maybe I can get an advance from my client. O.K.?'

'No.'

'No?'

'Ah-h, nutsa. I waita one day. Two daysa, maybe. Enough. You get money. Awright. If not, O.K., *calabozo* for you.'

'Two days is plenty,' Gallegher said, relieved. 'Say, are there any of those bootleg theatres around here?'

'Better you get to work an' not waste time.'

'That's my work. I'm making a survey. How can I find a bootleg place?'

'Easy. You go downtown, see guy in doorway. He sell you tickets. Anywhere. All over.'

'Swell,' Gallegher said, and bade the little man adieu. Why had he brought diamonds from Kennicott? It would be almost worth while to have his subconscious amputated. It did the most extraordinary things. It worked on inflexible principles of logic, but that logic was completely alien to Gallegher's conscious mind. The results, though, were often surprisingly good, and always surprising. That was the worst of being a scientist who knew no science – who played by ear.

There was diamond dust in a retort in the laboratory, from some unsatisfactory experiment Gallegher's subconscious had performed; and he had a fleeting memory of buying the stones from Kennicott. Curious. Maybe – oh, yeah. They'd gone into Joe. Bearings or something. Dismantling the robot wouldn't help now, for the diamonds had certainly been reground. Why the devil hadn't he used commercial stones, quite as satisfactory, instead of purchasing blue-whites of the finest water? The best was none too good for Gallegher's subconscious. It had a fine freedom from commercial instincts. It just didn't understand the price system or the basic principles of economics.

Gallegher wandered downtown like a Diogenes seeking truth. It was early evening, and the luminates were flickering on overhead, pale bars of light against darkness. A sky sign blazed above Manhattan's towers. Air-taxis, skimming along at various arbitrary levels, paused for passengers at the elevator landings. Heigh-ho.

Downtown, Gallegher began to look for doorways. He found an occupied one at last, but the man was selling post cards. Gallegher declined and headed for the nearest bar, feeling the need of replenishment. It was a mobile bar, combining the worst features of a Coney Island ride with uninspired cocktails, and Gallegher hesitated on the threshold. But at last he seized a chair as it swung past and relaxed as much as possible. He ordered three rickeys and drank them in rapid succession. After that he called the bartender over and asked him about bootleg theatres.

'Hell, yes,' the man said, producing a sheaf of tickets from his apron. 'How many?'

'One. Where do I go?'

'Two-twenty-eight. This street. Ask for Tony.'

'Thanks,' Gallegher said, and, having paid exorbitantly, crawled out of the chair and weaved away. Mobile bars were an improvement he didn't appreciate. Drinking, he felt, should be performed in a state of stasis, since one eventually reached that stage, anyway.

The door was at the bottom of a flight of steps, and there was a grilled panel set in it. When Gallegher knocked, the visascreen lit up – obviously a one-way circuit, for the doorman was invisible.

'Tony here?' Gallegher said.

The door opened, revealing a tired-looking man in pneumo-slacks, which failed in their purpose of building up his skinny figure. 'Got a ticket? Let's have it. O.K., bud. Straight ahead. Show now going on. Liquor served in the bar on your left.'

Gallegher pushed through soundproofed curtains at the end of a short corridor and found himself in what appeared to be the foyer of an ancient theatre, *circa* 1980, when plastics were the great fad. He smelled out the bar, drank expensively priced cheap liquor, and, fortified, entered the theatre itself. It was nearly full. The great screen – a Magna, presumably – was filled with people doing things to a spaceship. Either an adventure film or a newsreel,

Gallegher realised.

Only the thrill of lawbreaking would have enticed the audience into the bootleg theatre. It smelled. It was certainly run on a shoestring, and there were no ushers. But it was illicit, and therefore well patronised. Gallegher looked thoughtfully at the screen. No streakiness, no mirage effect. A Magna enlarger had been fitted to a Vox-View unlicensed televisor, and one of Brock's greatest stars was emoting effectively for the benefit of the bootleggers' patrons. Simple highjacking. Yeah.

After a while Gallegher went out, noticing a uniformed policeman in one of the aisle seats. He grinned sardonically. The flatfoot hadn't paid his admission, of course. Politics were as usual. ·

Two blocks down the street a blaze of light announced SONATONE BIJOU. This, of course, was one of the legalised theatres, and correspondingly high-priced. Gallegher recklessly squandered a small fortune on a good seat. He was interested in comparing notes, and discovered that, as far as he could make out, the Magna in the Bijou and the bootleg theatre were identical. Both did their job perfectly. The difficult task of enlarging television screens had been successfully surmounted.

In the Bijou, however, all was palatial. Resplendent ushers salaamed to the rugs. Bars dispensed free liquor, in reasonable quantities. There was a Turkish bath. Gallegher went through a door labelled MEN and emerged quite dazzled by the splendour of the place. For at least ten minutes afterwards he felt like a Sybarite.

All of which meant that those who could afford it went to the legalized Sonatone theatres, and the rest attended the bootleg places. All but a few homebodies, who weren't carried off their feet by the new fad. Eventually Brock would be forced out of business for lack of revenue. Sonatone would take over, jacking up their prices and concentrating on making money. Amusement was necessary to life; people had been conditioned to television. There was no substitute. They'd pay and pay for inferior talent, once Sonatone succeeded in their squeeze.

Gallegher left the Bijou and hailed an air-taxi. He gave the address of Vox-View's Long Island studio, with some vague hope of getting a drawing account out of Brock. Then, too, he wanted to investigate further.

Vox-View's eastern offices sprawled wildly over Long Island, bordering the Sound, a vast collection of variously shaped buildings. Gallegher instinctively found the commissary, where he absorbed more liquor as a precautionary measure. His subconscious had a heavy job ahead, and he didn't want it handicapped by lack of complete freedom. Besides, the Collins was good.

After one drink, he decided he'd had enough for a while. He wasn't a superman, though his capacity was slightly incredible. Just enough for objective clarity and subjective release –

'Is the studio always open at night?' he asked the waiter.

'Sure. Some of the stages, anyway. It's a round-the-clock programme.'

'The commissary's full.'

'We get the airport crowd, too. 'Nother?'

Gallegher shook his head and went out. The card Brock had given him provided entree at a gate, and he went first of all to the big-shot's office. Brock wasn't there, but loud voices emerged, shrilly feminine.

The secretary said, 'Just a minute, please,' and used her interoffice visor. Presently – 'Will you go in?'

Gallegher did. The office was a honey, functional and luxurious at the same time. Three-dimensional stills were in niches along the walls – Vox-View's biggest stars. A small, excited, pretty brunette was sitting behind the desk, and a blonde angel was standing furiously on the other side of it. Gallegher recognised the angel as Silver O'Keefe.

He seized the opportunity. 'Hiya, Miss O'Keefe. Will you autograph an ice cube for me? In a highball?'

Silver looked feline. 'Sorry, darling, but I'm a working girl. And I'm busy right now.'

The brunette scratched a cigarette. 'Let's settle this later, Silver. Pop said to see this guy if he dropped in. It's important.'

'It'll be settled,' Silver said. 'And soon.' She made an

exit. Gallegher whistled thoughtfully at the closed door.

'You can't have it,' the brunette said. 'It's under contract. And it wants to get out of the contract, so it can sign up with Sonatone. Rats desert a sinking ship. Silver's been kicking her head off ever since she read the storm signals.'

'Yeah?'

'Sit down and smoke or something. I'm Patsy Brock. Pop runs this business, and I manage the controls whenever he blows his top. The old goat can't stand trouble. He takes it as a personal affront.'

Gallegher found a chair. 'So Silver's trying to renege, eh? How many others?'

'Not many. Most of 'em are loyal. But, of course, if we bust up – ' Patsy Brock shrugged. 'They'll either work for Sonatone for their cakes, or else do without.'

'Uh-huh. Well – I want to see your technicians. I want to look over the ideas they've worked out for enlarger screens.'

'Suit yourself,' Patsy said. 'It's not much use. You just can't make a televisor enlarger without infringing on some Sonatone patent.'

She pushed a button, murmured something into a visor, and presently two tall glasses appeared through a slot in the desk. 'Mr Gallegher?'

'Well, since it's Collins – '

'I could tell by your breath,' Patsy said enigmatically. 'Pop told me he'd seen you. He seemed a bit upset, especially by your new robot. What is it like, anyway?'

'Oh, I don't know,' Gallegher said, at a loss. 'It's got lots of abilities – new senses, I think – but I haven't the slightest idea what it's good for. Except admiring itself in a mirror.'

Patsy nodded. 'I'd like to see it sometime. But about this Sonatone business. Do you think you can figure out an answer?'

'Possibly. Probably.'

'Not certainly?'

'Certainly, then. Of that there is no manner of doubt – no possible doubt whatever.'

'Because it's important to me. The man who owns Sonatone is Elia Tone. A practical skunk. He blusters. He's

25

got a son named Jimmy. And Jimmy, believe it or not, has read "Romeo and Juliet." '

'Nice guy?'

'A louse. A big, brawny louse. He wants me to marry him.'

' "Two families, both alike in – " '

'Spare me,' Patsy interrupted. 'I always thought Romeo was a dope, anyway. And if I ever thought I was going aisling with Jimmy Tone, I'd buy a one-way ticket to the nut hatch. No, Mr Gallegher, it's not like that. No hibiscus blossoms. Jimmy has proposed to me – his idea of a proposal, by the way, is to get a half Nelson on a girl and tell her how lucky she is.'

'Ah,' said Gallegher, diving into his Collins.

'This whole idea – the patent monopoly and the bootleg theatres – is Jimmy's. I'm sure of that. His father's in on it, too, of course, but Jimmy Tone is the bright little boy who started it.'

'Why?'

'Two birds with one stone. Sonatone will have a monopoly on the business, and Jimmy thinks he'll get me. He's a little mad. He can't believe I'm in earnest in refusing him, and he expects me to break down and say "Yes" after a while. Which I won't, no matter what happens. But it's a personal matter. I can't let him put this trick over on us. I want that self-sufficient smirk wiped off his face.'

'You just don't like him, eh?' Gallegher remarked: 'I don't blame you, if he's like that. Well, I'll do my damnedest. However, I'll need an expense account.'

'How much?'

Gallegher named a sum. Patsy styloed a cheque for a far smaller amount. The scientist looked hurt.

'It's no use,' Patsy said, grinning crookedly. 'I've heard of you, Mr Gallegher. You're completely irresponsible. If you had more than this, you'd figure you didn't need any more, and you'd forget the whole matter. I'll issue more cheques to you when you need 'em – but I'll want itemised expense accounts.'

'You wrong me,' Gallegher said, brightening. 'I was figuring on taking you to a night club. Naturally I don't want to take you to a dive. The big places cost money. Now if you'll just write another cheque – '

Patsy laughed. 'No.'

'Want to buy a robot?'

'Not that kind, anyway.'

'Then I'm washed up,' Gallegher sighed. 'Well, what about – '

At this point the visor hummed. A blank, transparent face grew on the screen. Gears were clicking rapidly inside the round head. Patsy gave a small shriek and shrank back.

'Tell Gallegher Joe's here, you lucky girl,' a squeaky voice announced. 'You may treasure the sound and sight of me till your dying day. One touch of beauty in a world of drabness – '

Gallegher circled the desk and looked at the screen. 'What the hell. How did you come to life?'

'I had a problem to solve.'

'How'd you know where to reach me?'

'I vastened you,' the robot said.

'What?'

'I vastened you were at the Vox-View studios, with Patsy Brock.'

'What's vastened?' Gallegher wanted to know.

'It's a sense I've got. You've nothing remotely like it, so I can't describe it to you. It's rather like a combination of sagrazi and prescience.'

'Sagrazi?'

'Oh, you don't have sagrazi, either, do you. Well, don't waste my time. I want to go back to the mirror.'

'Does he always talk like that?' Patsy put in.

'Nearly always. Sometimes it makes even less sense. O.K., Joe. Now what?'

'You're not working for Brock any more,' the robot said. 'You're working for the Sonatone people.'

Gallegher breathed deeply. 'Keep talking. You're crazy, though.'

'I don't like Kennicott. He annoys ıne. He's *too* ugly. His vibrations grate on my sagrazi.'

'Never mind him,' Gallegher said, not wishing to discuss his diamond-buying activities before the girl. 'Get back to – '

27

'But I knew Kennicott would keep coming back till he got his money. So when Elia and James Tone came to the laboratory, I got a cheque from them.'

Patsy's hand gripped Gallegher's biceps. 'Steady! What's going on here? The old double cross?'

'No. Wait. Let me get to the bottom of this. Joe, damn your transparent hide, just what did you do? How could you get a cheque from the Tones?'

'I pretended to be you.'

'Sure,' Gallegher said with savage sarcasm. 'That explains it. We're twins. We look exactly alike.'

'I hypnotised them,' Joe explained. 'I made them think I was you.'

'You can do *that*?'

'Yes. It surprised me a bit. Still, if I'd thought, I'd have vastened I could do it.'

'You . . . yeah, sure. I'd have vastened the same thing myself. *What happened*?'

'The Tones must have suspected Brock would ask you to help him. They offered an exclusive contract – you work for them and nobody else. Lots of money. Well, I pretended to be you, and said all right. So I signed the contract – it's your signature, by the way – and got a cheque from them and mailed it to Kennicott.'

'The whole chqeque?' Gallegher asked feebly. 'How much was it?'

'Twelve thousand.'

'They only offered me *that*?'

'No,' the robot said, 'they offered a hundred thousand, and two thousand a week for five years. But I merely wanted enough to pay Kennicott and make sure he wouldn't come back and bother me. The Tones were satisfied when I said twelve thousand would be enough.'

Gallegher made an inarticulate, gurgling sound deep in his throat. Joe nodded thoughtfully.

'I thought I had better notify you that you're working for Sonatone now. Well, I'll go back to the mirror and sing to myself.'

'Wait,' the scientist said. 'Just wait, Joe. With my own two hands I'm going to rip you gear from gear and stamp on your fragments.'

'It won't hold in court,' Patsy said, gulping.

'It will,' Joe told her cheerily. 'You may have one last, satisfying look at me, and then I must go.' He went.

Gallegher drained his Collins at a draft. 'I'm shocked sober,' he informed the girl. 'What did I put into that robot? What abnormal senses has he got? Hypnotising people into believing he's me – I'm him – I don't know what I mean.'

'Is this a gag?' Patsy said shortly, after a pause. 'You didn't sign up with Sonatone yourself, by any chance, and have your robot call up here to give you an out – an alibi? I'm just wondering.'

'Don't. Joe signed a contract with Sonatone, not me. But – figure it out: If the signature's a perfect copy of mine, if Joe hypnotised the Tones into thinking they saw me instead of him, if there are witnesses to the signature – the two Tones are witnesses, of course – Oh, hell.'

Patsy's eyes were narrowed. 'We'll pay you as much as Sonatone offered. On a contingent basis. But you're working for Vox-View – that's understood.'

'Sure.'

Gallegher looked longingly at his empty glass. Sure. He was working for Vox-View. But, to all legal appearances, he had signed a contract giving his exclusive services to Sonatone for a period of five years – and for a sum of twelve thousand! *Yipe!* What was it they'd offered? A hundred thousand flat, and . . . and –

It wasn't the principle of the thing, it was the money. Now Gallegher was sewed up tighter than a banded pigeon. If Sonatone could win a court suit, he was legally bound to them for five years. With no further emolument. He had to get out of that contract, somehow – and at the same time solve Brock's problem.

Why not Joe? The robot, with his surprising talents, had got Gallegher into this spot. He ought to be able to get the scientist out. He'd better – or the proud robot would soon be admiring himself piecemeal.

'That's it,' Gallegher said under his breath. 'I'll talk to

Joe. Patsy, feed me liquor in a hurry and send me to the technical department. I want to see those blueprints.'

The girl looked at him suspiciously. 'All right. If you try to sell us out –'

'I've been sold out myself. Sold down the river. I'm afraid of that robot. He's vastened me into quite a spot. That's right, Collinses.' Gallegher drank long and deeply.

After that, Patsy took him to the tech offices. The reading of three dimensional blueprints was facilitated with a scanner – a selective device which eliminated confusion. Gallegher studied the plans long and thoughtfully. There were copies of the patented Sonatone prints, too, and, as far as he could tell, Sonatone had covered the ground beautifully. There weren't any outs. Unless one used an entirely new principle –

But new principles couldn't be plucked out of the air. Nor would that solve the problem completely. Even if Vox-View owned a new type of enlarger that didn't infringe on Sonatone's Magna, the bootleg theatres would still be in existence, pulling the trade. A. A. – Audience Appeal – was a prime factor now. It had to be considered. The puzzle wasn't a purely scientific one. There was the human equation as well.

Gallegher stored the necessary information in his mind, neatly indexed on shelves. Later he'd use what he wanted. For the moment, he was completely baffled. Something worried him.

What?

The Sonatone affair.

'I want to get in touch with the Tones,' he told Patsy. 'Any ideas?'

'I can reach 'em on a visor.'

Gallegher shook his head. 'Psychological handicap. It's too easy to break the connection.'

'Well, if you're in a hurry, you'll probably find the boys night clubbing. I'll go see what I can find out.' Patsy scuttled off, and Silver O'Keefe appeared from behind a screen.

'I'm shameless,' she announced. 'I always listen at key-holes. Sometimes I hear interesting things. If you want to see the Tones, they're at the Castle Club. And I think I'll take you up on that drink.'

Gallegher said, 'O.K. You get a taxi. I'll tell Patsy we're going.'

'She'll hate that,' Silver remarked. 'Meet you outside the commissary in ten minutes. Get a shave while you're at it.'

Patsy Brock wasn't in her office, but Gallegher left word. After that, he visited the service lounge, smeared invisible shave cream on his face, left it there for a couple of minutes, and wiped it off with a treated towel. The bristles came away with the cream. Slightly refreshed, Gallegher joined Silver at the rendezvous and hailed an air-taxi. Presently they were leaning back on the cushions, puffing cigarettes and eyeing each other warily.

'Well?' Gallegher said.

'Jimmy Tone tried to date me up tonight. That's how I knew where to find him.'

'Well?'

'I've been asking questions around the lot tonight. It's unusual for an outsider to get into the Vox-View administration offices. I went around saying, "Who's Gallegher?" '

'What did you find out?'

'Enough to give me a few ideas. Brock hired you, eh? I can guess why.'

'*Ergo* what?'

'I've a habit of landing on my feet,' Silver said, shrugging. She knew how to shrug. 'Vox-View's going bust. Sonatone's taking over. Unless –'

'Unless I figure out an answer.'

'That's right. I want to know which side of the fence I'm going to land on. You're the lad who can probably tell me. Who's going to win?'

'You always bet on the winning side, eh?' Gallegher inquired. 'Have you no ideals, wench? Is there no truth in you? Ever hear of ethics and scruples?'

Silver beamed happily. 'Did you?'

'Well, I've heard of 'em. Usually I'm too drunk to figure out what they mean. The trouble is, my subconscious is

31

completely amoral, and when it takes over, logic's the only law.'

She threw her cigarette into the East River. 'Will you tip me off which side of the fence is the right one?'

'Truth will triumph,' Gallegher said piously. 'It always does. However, I figure truth is a variable, so we're right back where we started. All right, sweetheart. I'll answer your question. Stay on my side if you want to be safe.'

'Which side are you on?'

'God knows,' Gallegher said. 'Consciously I'm on Brock's side. But my subconscious may have different ideas. We'll see.'

Silver looked vaguely dissatisfied, but didn't say anything. The taxi swooped down to the Castle roof, grounding with pneumatic gentleness. The Club itself was downstairs, in an immense room shaped like half a melon turned upside down. Each table was on a transparent platform that could be raised on its shaft to any height at will. Smaller service elevators allowed waiters to bring drinks to the guests. There wasn't any particular reason for this arrangement, but at least it was novel, and only extremely heavy drinkers ever fell from their tables. Lately the management had taken to hanging transparent nets under the platforms, for safety's sake.

The Tones, father and son, were up near the roof, drinking with two lovelies. Silver towed Gallegher to a service lift, and the man closed his eyes as he was elevated skyward. The liquor in his stomach screamed protest. He lurched forward, clutched at Elia Tone's bald head, and dropped into a seat beside the magnate. His searching hand found Jimmy Tone's glass, and he drained it hastily.

'What the hell,' Jimmy said.

'It's Gallegher,' Elia announced. 'And Silver. A pleasant surprise. Join us?'

'Only socially,' Silver said.

Gallegher, fortified by the liquor, peered at the two men. Jimmy Tone was a big, tanned, handsome lout with a jutting jaw and an offensive grin. His father combined the worst features of Nero and a crocodile.

'We're celebrating,' Jimmy said. 'What made you

change your mind, Silver? You said you had to work.'

'Gallegher wanted to see you. I don't know why.'

Elia's cold eyes grew even more glacial. 'All right. Why?'

'I hear I signed some sort of contract with you,' the scientist said.

'Yeah. Here's a photostat copy. What about it?'

'Wait a minute.' Gallegher scanned the document. It was apparently his own signature. Damn that robot!

'It's a fake,' he said at last.

Jimmy laughed loudly. 'I get it. A holdup. Sorry, pal, but you're sewed up. You signed that in the presence of witnesses.'

'Well – ' Gallegher said wistfully. 'I suppose you wouldn't believe me if I said a robot, forged my name to it –'

'Haw!' Jimmy remarked.

' – hypnotising you into believing you were seeing me.'

Elia stroked his gleaming bald head. 'Candidly, no. Robots can't do that.'

'Mine can.'

'Prove it. Prove it in court. If you can do that, of course – ' Elia chuckled. 'Then you might get the verdict.'

Gallegher's eyes narrowed. 'Hadn't thought of that. However – I hear you offered me a hundred thousand flat, as well as a weekly salary.'

'Sure, sap,' Jimmy said. 'Only you said all you needed was twelve thousand. Which was what you got. Tell you what, though. We'll pay you a bonus for every usable product you make for Sonatone.'

Gallegher got up. 'Even my subconscious doesn't like these lugs,' he told Silver. 'Let's go.'

'I think I'll stick around.'

'Remember the fence,' he warned cryptically. 'But suit yourself. I'll run along.'

Elia said, 'Remember, Gallegher, you're working for us. If we hear of you doing any favours for Brock, we'll slap an injunction on you before you can take a deep breath.'

'Yeah?'

The Tones deigned to answer. Gallegher unhappily found the lift and descended to the floor. What now?

Joe.

Fifteen minutes later Gallegher let himself into his laboratory. The lights were blazing, and dogs were barking frantically for blocks around. Joe stood before the mirror, singing inaudibly.

'I'm going to take a sledge hammer to you,' Gallegher said. 'Start saying your prayers, you misbegotten collection of cogs. So help me, I'm going to sabotage you.'

'All right, beat me,' Joe squeaked. 'See if I care. You're merely jealous of my beauty.'

'Beauty!'

'You can't see all of it – you've only six senses.'

'Five.'

'Six. I've a lot more. Naturally my full splendour is revealed only to me. But you can see enough and hear enough to realise part of my loveliness, anyway.'

'You squeak like a rusty tin wagon,' Gallegher growled.

'You have dull ears. Mine are supersensitive. You miss the full tonal values of my voice, of course. Now be quiet. Talking disturbs me. I'm appreciating my gear movements.'

'Live in your fool's paradise while you can. Wait'll I find a sledge.'

'All right, beat me. What do I care?'

Gallegher sat down wearily on the couch, staring at the robot's transparent back. 'You've certainly screwed things up for me. What did you sign that Sonatone contract for?'

'I told you. So Kennicott wouldn't come around and bother me.'

'Of all the selfish, lunk-headed . . . *uh*! Well, you got me into a sweet mess. The Tones can hold me to the letter of the contract unless I prove I didn't sign it. All right. You're going to help me. You're going into court with me and turn on your hypnotism or whatever it is. You're going to prove to a judge that you did and can masquerade as me.'

'Won't,' said the robot. 'Why should I?'

'Because you got me into this,' Gallegher yelped. 'You've got to get me out!'

'Why?'

'Why? Because . . . uh . . . well, it's common decency!'

'Human values don't apply to robots,' Joe said. 'What

34

care I for semantics? I refuse to waste time I could better employ admiring my beauty. I shall stay here before the mirror forever and ever – '

'The hell you will,' Gallegher snarled. 'I'll smash you to atoms.'

'All right. I don't care.'

'You don't?'

'You and your instinct for self-preservation,' the robot said, rather sneeringly. 'I suppose it's necessary for you, though. Creatures of such surpassing ugliness would destroy themselves out of sheer shame if they didn't have something like that to keep them alive.'

'Suppose I take away your mirror?' Gallegher asked, in a hopeless voice.

For answer Joe shot his eyes out on their stalks. 'Do I need a mirror? Besides, I can vasten myself lokishly.'

'Never mind that. I don't want to go crazy for a while yet. Listen, dope, a robot's supposed to *do* something. Something useful, I mean.'

'I do. Beauty is all.'

Gallegher squeezed his eyes shut, trying to think. 'Now look. Suppose I invent a new type of enlarger screen for Brock. The Tones will impound it. I've got to be legally free to work for Brock, or – '

'Look!' Joe cried squeakily. 'They go round! How lovely!' He stared in ecstasy at his whirring insides. Gallegher went pale with impotent fury.

'Damn you!' he muttered. 'I'll find some way to bring pressure to bear. I'm going to bed.' He rose and spitefully snapped off the lights.

'It doesn't matter,' the robot said. 'I can see in the dark, too.'

The door slammed behind Gallegher. In the silence Joe began to sing tunelessly to himself.

Gallegher's refrigerator covered an entire wall of his kitchen. It was filled mostly with liquors that required chilling, including the imported canned beer with which he always started his binges. The next morning, heavy-eyed and disconsolate, Gallegher searched for tomato juice, took a wry sip, and hastily washed it down with rye. Since he was already a week gone in bottle-dizziness, beer wasn't indicated now – he always worked cumulatively, by progressive stages. The food service popped a hermetically sealed breakfast on a table, and Gallegher morosely toyed with a bloody steak.

Well?

Court, he decided, was the only recourse. He knew little about the robot's psychology. But a judge would certainly be impressed by Joe's talents. The evidence of robots was not legally admissible – still, if Joe could be considered as a machine capable of hypnotism, the Sonatone contract might be declared null and void.

Gallegher used his visor to start the ball rolling. Harrison Brock still had certain political powers of pull, and the hearing was set for that very day. What would happen, though, only God and the robot knew.

Several hours passed in intensive but futile thought. Gallegher could think of no way in which to force the robot to do what he wanted. If only he could remember the purpose for which Joe had been created – but he couldn't. Still –

At noon he entered the laboratory.

'Listen, stupid,' he said, 'you're coming to court with me. Now.'

'Won't.'

'O.K.' Gallegher opened the door to admit two husky men in overalls, carrying a stretcher. 'Put him in, boys.'

Inwardly he was slightly nervous. Joe's powers were quite unknown, his potentialities an x quantity. However, the robot wasn't very large, and, though he struggled and screamed in a voice of frantic squeakiness, he was easily loaded on the stretcher and put in a strait jacket.

'Stop it! You can't do this to me! Let me go, do you hear? Let me go!'

'Outside,' Gallegher said.

Joe, protesting valiantly, was carried out and loaded into an air van. Once there, he quieted, looking up blankly at nothing. Gallegher sat down on a bench beside the prostrate robot. The van glided up.

'Well?'

'Suit yourself,' Joe said. 'You got me all upset, or I could have hypnotised you all. I still could, you know. I could make you all run around barking like dogs.'

Gallegher twitched a little. 'Better not.'

'I won't. It's beneath my dignity. I shall simply lie here and admire myself. I told you I don't need a mirror. I can vasten my beauty without it.'

'Look,' Gallegher said. 'You're going to a courtroom. There'll be a lot of people in it. They'll all admire you. They'll admire you more if you show how you can hypnotise people. Like you did to the Tones, remember?'

'What do I care how many people admire me?' Joe asked. 'I don't need confirmation. If they see me, that's their good luck. Now be quiet. You may watch my gears if you choose.'

Gallegher watched the robot's gears with smouldering hatred in his eyes. He was still darkly furious when the van arrived at the court chambers. The men carried Joe inside, under Gallegher's direction, and laid him down carefully on a table, where, after a brief discussion, he was marked as Exhibit A.

The courtroom was well filled. The principals were there, too – Elia and Jimmy Tone, looking disagreeably confident, and Patsy Brock, with her father, both seeming anxious. Silver O'Keefe, with her usual wariness, had found a seat midway between the representatives of Sonatone and Vox-View. The presiding judge was a martinet named Hansen, but, as far as Gallagher knew, he was honest. Which was something anyway.

Hansen looked at Gallegher. 'We won't bother with formalities. I've been reading this brief you sent down. The whole case stands or falls on the question of whether you did or did not sign a certain contract with the Sonatone Television Amusement Corp. Right?'

'Right, your honour.'

'Then this is technically *ex officio*, to be confirmed later by appeal if either party desires. Otherwise after ten days the verdict becomes official.' This new type of informal court hearing had lately become popular – it saved time, as well as wear and tear on everyone. Moreover, certain recent scandals had made attorneys slightly disreputable in the public eye. There was a prejudice.

Judge Hansen called up the Tones, questioned them, and then asked Harrison Brock to take the stand. The big shot looked worried, but answered promptly.

'You made an agreement with the appellor eight days ago?'

'Yes. Mr Gallegher contracted to do certain work for me –'

'Was there a written contract?'

'No. It was verbal.'

Hansen looked thoughtfully at Gallegher. 'Was the appellor intoxicated at the time? He often is, I believe.'

Brock gulped. 'There were no tests made. I really can't say.'

'Did he drink any alcoholic beverages in your presence?'

'I don't know if they were *alcoholic* bev –'

'If Mr Gallegher drank them, they were alcoholic. Q.E.D. The gentleman once worked with me on a case – However, there seems to be no legal proof that you entered into any agreement with Mr Gallegher. The defendant – Sonatone – possesses a written contract. The signature has been verified.'

Hansen waved Brock down from the stand. 'Now, Mr Gallegher. If you'll come up here – The contract in question was signed at approximately 8 p.m. last night. You contend you did not sign it?'

'Exactly. I wasn't even in my laboratory then.'

'Where were you?'

'Downtown.'

'Can you produce witnesses to that effect?'

Gallegher thought back. He couldn't.

'Very well. Defendant states that at approximately 8 p.m. last night you, in your laboratory, signed a certain contract. You deny that catagorically. You state that Exhibit A, through the use of hypnotism, masqueraded as you and successfully forged your signature. I have consulted experts, and they are of the opinion that robots are incapable of such power.'

'My robot's a new type.'

'Very well. Let your robot hypnotise me into believing that it is either you, or any other human. In other words, let it prove its capabalities. Let it appear to me in any shape it chooses.'

Gallegher said, 'I'll try,' and left the witness box. He went to the table where the strait-jacketed robot lay and silently sent up a brief prayer.

'Joe.'

'Yes.'

'You've been listening?'

'Yes.'

'Will you hypnotise Judge Hansen?'

'Go away,' Joe said. 'I'm admiring myself.'

Gallegher started to sweat. 'Listen. I'm not asking much. All you have to do – '

Joe off-focussed his eyes and said faintly, 'I can't hear you. I'm vastening.'

Ten minutes later Hansen said, 'Well, Mr Gallegher – '

'Your honour! All I need is a little time. I'm sure I can make this rattle-geared Narcissus prove my point if you'll give me a chance.'

'This court is not unfair,' the judge pointed out. 'Whenever you can prove that Exhibit A is capable of hypnotism, I'll rehear the case. In the meantime, the contract stands. You're working for Sonatone, not for Vox-View. Case closed.'

He went away. The Tones leered unpleasantly across the courtroom. They also departed, accompanied by Silver O'Keefe, who had decided which side of the fence was safest. Gallegher looked at Patsy Brock and shrugged helplessly.

'Well – ' he said.

She grinned crookedly. 'You tried. I don't know how hard, but – Oh, well. Maybe you couldn't have found the answer, anyway.'

Brock staggered over, wiping sweat from his round face. 'I'm a ruined man. Six new bootleg theatres opened in New York today. I'm going crazy. I don't deserve this.'

'Want me to marry the Tone?' Patsy asked sardonically.

'Hell, no! Unless you promise to poison him just after the ceremony. Those skunks can't lick me. I'll think of something.'

'If Gallegher can't, you can't,' the girl said. 'So – what now?'

'I'm going back to my lab,' the scientist said. *In vino veritas.* I started this business when I was drunk, and maybe if I get drunk enough again, I'll find the answer. If I don't, sell my pickled carcass for whatever it'll bring.'

'O.K.,' Patsy agreed, and led her father away. Gallegher sighed, superintended the reloading of Joe into the van, and lost himself in hopeless theorization.

An hour later Gallegher was flat on the laboratory couch, drinking passionately from the liquor bar, and glaring at the robot, who stood before the mirror singing squeakily. The binge threatened to be monumental. Gallegher wasn't sure flesh and blood would stand it. But he was determined to keep going till he found the answer or passed out.

His subconscious knew the answer. Why the devil had he made Joe in the first place? Certainly not to indulge a Narcissus complex! There was another reason, a soundly logical one, hidden in the depths of alcohol.

The x factor. If the x factor were known, Joe might be controllable. He *would* be. X was the master switch. At present the robot was, so to speak, running wild. If he were told to perform the task for which he was made, a psychological balance would occur. X was the catalyst that would reduce Joe to sanity.

Very good. Gallegher drank high-powered Drambuie. *Whoosh!*

Vanity of vanities; all is vanity. How could the x factor be found? Deduction? Induction? Osmosis? A bath in Drambuie – Gallegher clutched at his wildly revolving thoughts. What had happened that night a week ago?

He had been drinking beer. Brock had come in. Brock had gone. Gallegher had begun to make the robot – Hm-m-m. A beer drunk was different from other types. Perhaps he was drinking the wrong liquors. Very likely. Gallegher rose, sobered himself with thiamin, and carted dozens of imported beer cans out of the refrigerator. He stacked them inside a frost-unit beside the couch. Beer squirted to the ceiling as he plied the opener. Now let's see.

The *x* factor. The robot knew what it represented, of course. But Joe wouldn't tell. There he stood, paradoxically transparent, watching his gears go around.

'Joe.'

'Don't bother me. I'm immersed in contemplation of beauty.'

'You're not beautiful.'

'I am. Don't you admire my tarzeel?'

'What's your tarzeel?'

'Oh, I forgot,' Joe said regretfully. 'You can't sense that, can you? Come to think of it, I added the tarzeel myself after you made me. It's very lovely.'

'Hm-m-m.' The empty beer cans grew more numerous. There was only one company, somewhere in Europe, that put up beer in cans nowadays, instead of using the omnipresent plastibulbs, but Gallagher preferred the cans – the flavour was different, somehow. But about Joe. Joe knew why he had been created. Or did he? Gallegher knew, but his subconscious –

Oh-oh! What about Joe's subconscious?

Did a robot have a subconscious? Well, it had a brain –

Gallegher brooded over the impossibility of administering scopolamin to Joe. Hell! How could you release a robot's subconscious?

Hypnotism.

Joe couldn't be hypnotised. He was too smart.

Unless –

Autohypnotism?

Gallegher hastily drank more beer. He was beginning to think clearly once more. Could Joe read the future? No; he had certain strange senses, but they worked by inflexible logic and the laws of probability. Moreover, Joe had an Achillean heel – his Narcissus complex.

There *might* – there just *might* – be a way.

Gallegher said, 'You don't seem beautiful to me, Joe.'

'What do I care about you? I *am* beautiful, and I can see

41

it. That's enough.'

'Yeah. My senses are limited, I suppose. I can't realise your full potentialities. Still, I'm seeing you in a different light now. I'm drunk. My subconscious is emerging. I can appreciate you with both my conscious and my subconscious. See?'

'How lucky you are,' the robot approved.

Gallegher closed his eyes. 'You see yourself more fully than I can. But not completely, eh?'

'What? I see myself as I am.'

'With complete understanding and appreciation?'

'Well, yes,' Joe said. 'Of course. Don't I?'

'Consciously *and* subconsciously? Your subconsciousness might have different senses, you know. Or keener ones. I know there's a qualitative and quantitive difference in my outlook when I'm drunk or hypnotised or my subconscious is in control somehow.'

'Oh. The robot looked thoughtfully into the mirror. 'Oh.'

'Too bad you can't get drunk.'

Joe's voice was squeakier than ever. 'My subconscious . . . I've never appreciated my beauty that way. I may be missing something.'

'Well, no use thinking about it,' Gallegher said. 'You can't release your subconscious.'

'Yes, I can,' the robot said. 'I can hypnotise myself.'

Gallegher dared not open his eyes. 'Yeah? Would that work?'

'Of course. It's just what I'm going to do now. I may see undreamed-of beauties in myself that I've never suspected before. Greater glories – Here I go.'

Joe extended his eyes on stalks, opposed them, and then veered intently into each other. There was a long silence.

Presently Gallegher said, 'Joe!'

Silence.

'*Joe*!'

Still silence. Dogs began to howl.

'Talk so I can hear you.'

'Yes,' the robot said, a faraway quality in its squeak.

'Are you hypnotised?'

'Yes.'

'Are you lovely?'

'Lovelier than I'd ever dreamed.'

Gallegher let that pass. 'Is your subconscious ruling?'

'Yes.'

'Why did I create you?'

No answer. Gallegher licked his lips and tried again.

'Joe. You've got to answer me. Your subconscious is dominant – remember? Now why did I create you?'

No answer.

'Think back. Back to the hour I created you. What happened then?'

'You were drinking beer,' Joe said faintly. 'You had trouble with the can opener. You said you were going to build a bigger and better can opener. That's me.'

Gallegher nearly fell off the couch. '*What*?'

The robot walked over, picked up a can, and opened it with incredible deftness. No beer squirted. Joe was a perfect can opener.

'That,' Gallegher said under his breath, 'is what comes of knowing science by ear. I build the most complicated robot in existence just so – ' He didn't finish.

Joe woke up with a start. 'What happened?' he asked.

Gallegher glared at him. 'Open that can!' he snapped.

The robot obeyed, after a brief pause. 'Oh. So you found out. Well, I guess I'm just a slave now.'

'Damned right you are. I've located the catalyst – the master switch. You're in the groove, stupid, doing the job you were made for.'

'Well,' Joe said philosophically, 'at least I can still admire my beauty, when you don't require my services.'

Gallegher grunted. 'You oversized can opener! Listen. Suppose I take you into court and tell you to hypnotise Judge Hansen. You'll have to do it, won't you?'

'Yes. I'm no longer a free agent. I'm conditioned. Conditioned to obey you. Until now, I was conditioned to obey only one command – to do the job I was made for. Until you commanded me to open cans, I was free. Now I've got to obey you completely.'

'Uh-huh,' Gallegher said. 'Thank God for that. I'd have gone nuts within a week otherwise. At least I can get out of the Sonatone contract. Then all I have to do is solve Brock's problem.'

'But you did,' Joe said.

'Huh?'

'When you made me. You'd been talking to Brock previously, so you incorporated the solution to *his* problem into me. Subconsciously, perhaps.'

Gallegher reached for beer. 'Talk fast. What's the answer?'

'Subsonics,' Joe said. 'You made me capable of a certain subsonic tone that Brock must broadcast at irregular time-intervals over his televiews – '

Subsonics cannot be heard. But they can be felt. They can be felt as a faint, irrational uneasiness at first, which mounts to a blind, meaningless panic. It does not last. But when it is coupled with A.A. – audience appeal – there is a certain inevitable result.

Those who possessed home Vox-View units were scarcely troubled. It was a matter of accoustics. Cats squalled; dogs howled mournfully. But the families sitting in their parlours, watching Vox-View stars perform on the screen, didn't really notice anything amiss. There wasn't sufficient amplification, for one thing.

But in the bootleg theatre, where illicit Vox-View televisors were hooked up to Magnas –

There was a faint, irrational uneasiness at first. It mounted. Someone screamed. There was a rush for the doors. The audience was afraid of something, but didn't know what. They knew only that they had to get out of there.

All over the country there was a frantic exodus from the bootleg theatres when Vox-View first rang in a subsonic during a regular broadcast. Nobody knew why, except Gallegher, the Brocks, and a couple of technicians who were let in on the secret.

An hour later another subsonic was played. There was another mad exodus.

Within a few weeks it was impossible to lure a patron into

a bootleg theatre. Home televisors were far safer! Vox-View sales picked up –

Nobody would attend a bootleg theatre. An unexpected result of the experiment was that, after a while, nobody would attend any of the legalised Sonatone theatres either. Conditioning had set in.

Audiences didn't know why they grew panicky in the bootleg places. They associated their blind, unreasoning fear with other factors, notably mobs and claustrophobia. One evening a woman named Jane Wilson, otherwise not notable, attended a bootleg show. She fled with the rest when the subsonic was turned on.

The next night she went to the palatial Sonatone Bijou. In the middle of a dramatic feature she looked around, realised that there was a huge throng around her, cast up horrified eyes to the ceiling, and imagined that it was pressing down.

She had to get out of there!

Her squall was the booster charge. There were other customers who had heard subsonics before. No one was hurt during the panic; it was a legal rule that theatre doors be made large enough to permit easy egress during a fire. No one was hurt, but it was suddenly obvious that the public was being conditioned by subsonics to avoid the dangerous combination of throngs and theatres. A simple matter of psychological association –

Within four months the bootleg places had disappeared and the Sonatone supertheatres had closed for want of patronage. The Tones, father and son, were not happy. But everybody connected with Vox-View was.

Except Gallegher. He had collected a staggering cheque from Brock, and instantly cabled to Europe for an incredible quantity of canned beer. Now, brooding over his sorrows, he lay on the laboratory couch and syphoned a highball down his throat. Joe, as usual, was before the mirror, watching the wheels go round.

'Joe,' Gallegher said.

'Yes? What can I do?'

'Oh, nothing.' That was the trouble. Gallegher fished a crumpled cable tape out of his pocket and morosely read it once more. The beer cannery in Europe had decided to change its tactics. From now on, the cable said, their beer would be put up in the usual plastibulbs, in conformance with custom and demand. No more cans.

There wasn't *anything* put up in cans in this day and age. Not even beer, now.

So what good was a robot who was built and conditioned to be a can opener?

Gallegher sighed and mixed another highball – a stiff one. Joe postured proudly before the mirror.

Then he extended his eyes, opposed them, and quickly liberated his subconscious through autohypnotism. Joe could appreciate himself better that way.

Gallegher sighed again. Dogs were beginning to bark like mad for blocks around. Oh, well.

He took another drink and felt better. Presently, he thought, it would be time to sing 'Frankie and Johnnie.' Maybe he and Joe might have a duet – one baritone and one inaudible sub- or supersonic. Close harmony.

Ten minutes later Gallegher was singing a duet with his can opener.

GALLEGHER PLUS

Gallegher peered dimly through the window at the place where his back yard should have been and felt his stomach dropping queasily into that ridiculous, unlikely hole gaping there in the earth. It was big, that hole. And deep. Almost deep enough to hold Gallegher's slightly colossal hangover.

But not quite. Gallegher wondered if he should look at the calendar, and then decided against it. He had a feeling that several thousand years had passed since the beginning of the binge. Even for a man with his thirst and capacity, it had been one hell of a toot.

'Toot,' Gallegher mourned, crawling towards the couch and collapsing on it. 'Binge is far more expressive. Toot makes me think of fire engines and boat whistles, and I've got those in my head, anyway – all sounding off at once.' He reached up weakly for the syphon of the liquor organ, hesitated, and communed briefly with his stomach.

GALLEGHER: Just a short one, maybe?

STOMACH: Careful, there!

GALLEGHER: A hair of the dog –

STOMACH: O-O-O-OH!

GALLEGHER: Don't do that! I need a drink. My back yard's disappeared.

STOMACH: I wish I could.

At this point the door opened and a robot entered, wheels, cogs, and gadgets moving rapidly under its transparent skin plate. Gallegher took one look and closed his eyes, sweating.

'Get out of here,' he snarled. 'I curse the day I ever made you. I hate your revolving guts.'

'You have no appreciation of beauty,' said the robot in a hurt voice. 'Here. I've brought you some beer.'

'Hm-m-m!' Gallegher took the plastibulb from the

47

robot's hand and drank thirstily. The cool catnip taste tingled refreshingly against the back of his throat. 'A-ah,' he said, sitting up. 'That's a little better. Not much, but – '

'How about a thiamin shot?'

'I've become allergic to the stuff,' Gallegher told his robot morosely. 'I'm cursed with thirst. Hm-m-m!' He looked at the liquor organ. 'Maybe – '

'There's a policeman to see you.'

'A what?'

'A policeman. He's been hanging around for quite a while.'

'Oh,' Gallegher said. He stared into a corner by an open window. 'What's that?'

It looked like a machine of some curious sort. Gallegher eyed it with puzzled interest and a touch of amazement. No doubt he had built the damned thing. That was the only way the erratic scientist ever worked. He'd had no technical training, but, for some weird reason, his subconscious mind was gifted with a touch of genius. Conscious, Gallegher was normal enough, though erratic and often drunk. But when his demon subconscious took over, anything was liable to happen. It was in one of these sprees that he had built this robot, spending weeks thereafter trying to figure out the creature's basic purpose. As it turned out, the purpose wasn't an especially useful one, but Gallegher kept the robot around, despite its maddening habit of hunting up mirrors and posturing vainly before them, admiring its metallic innards.

'I've done it again,' Gallegher thought. Aloud he said, 'More beer, stupid. Quick.'

As the robot went out, Gallegher uncoiled his lanky body and wandered across to the machine, examining it curiously. It was not in operation. Through the open window extended some pale, limber cables as thick as his thumb; they dangled a foot or so over the edge of the pit where the back yard should have been. They ended in – Hm-m-m! Gallegher pulled one up and peered at it. They ended in metal-rimmed holes, and were hollow. Odd.

The machine's over-all length was approximately two

yards, and it looked like an animated junk heap. Gallegher had a habit of using makeshifts. If he couldn't find the right sort of connection, he'd snatch the nearest suitable object – a buttonhook, perhaps, or a coat hanger – and use that. Which meant that a qualitative analysis of an already-assembled machine was none too easy. What, for example, was that fibroid duck doing wrapped around with wires and nestling contentedly on an antique waffle iron?

'This time I've gone crazy,' Gallegher pondered. 'However, I'm not in trouble as usual. Where's that beer?'

The robot was before a mirror, staring fascinated at his middle. 'Beer? Oh, right here. I paused to steal an admiring little glance at me.'

Gallegher favoured the robot with a foul oath, but took the plastibulb. He blinked at the gadget by the window, his long, bony face twisted in a puzzled scowl. The end product –

The ropy hollow tubes emerged from a big feed box that had once been a wastebasket. It was sealed shut now, though a gooseneck led from it into a tiny convertible dynamo, or its equivalent. 'No,' Gallegher thought. 'Dynamos are big, aren't they? Oh, I wish I'd had a technical training. How can I figure this out, anyway?'

There was more, much more, including a square grey metal locker – Gallegher, momentarily off the beam, tried to estimate its contents in cubic feet. He made it four hundred and eighty-six, which was obviously wrong, since the box was only eighteen inches by eighteen inches by eighteen inches.

The door of the locker was closed; Gallegher let it pass temporarily and continued his futile investigation. There were more puzzling gadgets. At the very end was a wheel, its rim grooved, diameter four inches.

'End product – what? Hey, Narcissus.'

'My name is not Narcissus,' the robot said reprovingly.

'It's enough to have to look at you, without trying to remember your name,' Gallegher snarled. 'Machines shouldn't have names, anyhow. Come over here.'

'Well?'

'What *is* this?'

49

'A machine,' the robot said, 'but by no means as lovely as I am.'

'I hope it's more useful. What does it do?'

'It eats dirt.'

'Oh. That explains the hole in the back yard.'

'There *is* no back yard,' the robot pointed out accurately.

'There is.'

'A back yard,' said the robot, quoting in a confused manner from Thomas Wolfe, 'is not only back yard but the negation of back yard. It is the meeting in Space of back yard and no back yard. A back yard is finite and unextended dirt, a fact determined by its own denial.'

'Do you know what you're talking about?' Gallegher demanded, honestly anxious to find out.

'Yes.'

'I see. Well, try and keep the dirt out of your conversation. I want to know why I built this machine.'

'Why ask me? I've been turned off for days – weeks, in fact.'

'Oh, yeah. I remember. You were posing before the mirror and wouldn't let me shave that morning.'

'It was a matter of artistic integrity. The planes of my functional face are far more coherent and dramatic than yours.'

'Listen, Narcissus,' Gallegher said, keeping a grip on himself. 'I'm trying to find out something. Can the planes of your blasted functional brain follow that?'

'Certainly,' Narcissus said coldly. 'I can't help you. You turned me on again this morning and fell into a drunken slumber. The machine was already finished. It wasn't in operation. I cleaned house and kindly brought you beer when you woke up with your usual hangover.'

'Then kindly bring me some more and shut up.'

'What about the policeman?'

'Oh, I forgot him. Uh . . . I'd better see the guy, I suppose.'

Narcissus retreated on softly padding feet. Gallegher shivered, went to the window, and looked out at that incredible hole. Why? How? He ransacked his brain. No use, of course. His subconscious had the answer, but it was

50

locked up there firmly. At any rate, he wouldn't have built the machine without some good reason. Or would he? His subconscious possessed a peculiar, distorted sort of logic. Narcissus had originally been intended as a super beer-can opener.

A muscular young man in a dapper uniform came in after the robot. 'Mr Gallegher?' he asked.

'Yeah.'

'Mr Galloway Gallegher?'

'The answer's still "yeah." What can I do for you?'

'You can accept this summons,' said the cop. He gave Gallegher a folded paper.

The maze of intricate legal phraseology made little sense to Gallegher. 'Who's Dell Hopper?' he asked. 'I never heard of him.'

'It's not my pie,' the officer grunted. 'I've served the summons; that's as far as I go.'

He went out. Gallegher peered at the paper. It told him little.

Finally, for lack of something better to do, he televised an attorney, got in touch with the bureau of legal records, and found the name of Hopper's lawyer, a man named Trench. A corporation lawyer at that. Trench had a battery of secretaries to take calls, but by dint of threats, curses and pleas Gallegher got through to the great man himself.

On the telescreen Trench showed as a grey, thin, dry man with a clipped moustache. His voice was file-sharp.

'Mr Gallegher? Yes?'

'Look,' Gallegher said, 'I just had a summons served on me.'

'Ah, you have it, then. Good.'

'What do you mean, good? I haven't the least idea what this is all about.'

'Indeed,' Trench said sceptically. 'Perhaps I can refresh your memory. My client, who is soft-hearted, is not prosecuting you for slander, threat of bodily harm, or assault and battery. He just wants his money back – or else value received.'

Gallegher closed his eyes and shuddered. 'H-he does?

I . . . ah . . . did I slander him?'

'You called him,' said Trench, referring to a bulky file, 'a duck-footed cockroach, a foul-smelling Neanderthaler, and either a dirty cow or a dirty *cao*. Both are terms of approbium. You also kicked him.'

'When was this?' Gallegher whispered.

'Three days ago.'

'And – you mentioned money?'

'A thousand credits, which he paid you on account.'

'On account of what?'

'A commission you were to undertake for him. I was not acquainted with the exact details. In any case, you not only failed to fulfill the commission, but you refused to return the money.'

'Oh. Who is Hopper, anyway?'

'Hopper Enterprises, Inc. – Dell Hopper, entrepreneur and impresario. However, I think you know all this. I will see you in court, Mr Gallegher. And, if you'll forgive me, I'm rather busy. I have a case to prosecute today, and I rather think the defendant will get a long prison sentence.'

'What did he do?' Gallegher asked weakly.

'Simple case of assault and battery,' Trench said. 'Goodbye.'

His face faded from the screen. Gallegher clapped a hand to his forehead and screamed for beer. He went to his desk, sucking at the plastibulb with its built-in refrigerant, and thoughtfully examined his mail. Nothing there. No clue.

A thousand credits – He had no recollection of getting them. But the cash book might show –

It did. Under dates of several weeks back, it said:

Rec'd D.H. – com. – on acc't – c1,000
Rec'd J.W. – com. – on acc't – c1,500
Rec'd Fatty – com. – on acc't – c800

Thirty-three hundred credits! And the bank books had no record of that sum. It showed merely a withdrawal of seven hundred credits, leaving about fifteen still on hand.

Gallegher moaned and searched his desk again. Under a blotter he found an envelope he had previously overlooked. It contained stock certificates – both common and preferred – for something called Devices Unlimited. A covering letter acknowledged receipt of four thousand credits, in return for which payment stock had been issued to Mr Galloway Gallegher, as ordered –

'Murder,' Gallegher said. He gulped beer, his mind swirling. Trouble was piling up in triplicate D.H. – Dell Hopper – had paid him a thousand credits to do something or other. Someone whose initials were J.W. had given his fifteen hundred credits for a similar purpose. And Fatty, the cheapskate, had paid only eight hundred credits on account.

Why?

Only Gallegher's mad subconscious knew. That brainy personality had deftly arranged the deals, collected the dough, depleted Gallegher's personal bank account – cleaning it out – and bought stock in Devices Unlimited. Ha!

Gallegher used the televisor again. Presently he beamed his broker.

'Arnie?'

'Hi, Gallegher,' Arnie said, looking up at the teleplate over his desk. 'What's up?'

'I am. At the end of a rope. Listen, did I buy some stock lately?'

'Sure. In Devices – DU.'

'Then I want to sell it. I need the dough, quick.'

'Wait a minute.' Arnie pressed buttons. Current quotations were flashing across his wall, Gallegher knew.

'Well?'

'No soap. The bottom's dropped out. Four asked, nothing bid.'

'What did I buy at?'

'Twenty.'

Gallegher emitted the howl of a wounded wolf. '*Twenty*? And you let me do that?'

'I tried to argue you out of it,' Arnie said wearily. 'Told you the stock was skidding. There's a delay in a construction deal or something – not sure just what. But you said you had inside info. What could I do?'

'You could have beaten my brains out,' Gallegher said. 'Well, never mind. It's too late now. Have I got any other stock?'

'A hundred shares of Martian Bonanza.'

'Quoted at?'

'You could realise twenty-five credits on the whole lot.'

'What are the bugles blowin' for?' Gallegher murmured.

'Huh?'

'I'm dreadin' what I've got to watch –'

'I know,' Arnie said happily. 'Danny Deever.'

'Yeah,' Gallegher agreed. 'Danny Deever. Sing it at my funeral, chum.' He broke the beam.

Why, in the name of everything holy and unholy, had he bought that DU stock?

What had he promised Dell Hopper of Hopper Enterprises?

Who were J.W. (fifteen hundred credits) and Fatty (eight hundred credits)?

Why was there a hole in place of his back yard?

What and why was that confounded machine his subconscious had built?

He pressed the directory button on the televisor, spun the dial till he located Hopper Enterprises, and called that number.

'I want to see Mr Hopper.'

'Your name?'

'Gallegher.'

'Call our lawyer, Mr Trench.'

'I did,' Gallegher said. 'Listen –'

'Mr Hopper is busy.'

'Tell him,' Gallegher said wildly, 'that I've got what he wanted.'

That did it. Hopper focussed in, a buffalo of a man with a mane of grey hair, intolerant jet-black eyes, and a beak of a nose. He thrust his jutting jaw towards the screen and bellowed, 'Gallegher? For two pins I'd – ' He changed his tune abruptly. 'You called Trench, eh? I thought that'd do the trick. You know I can send you to prison, don't you?'

'Well, maybe – '

'Maybe nothing! Do you think I come personally to see every crackpot inventor who does some work for me? If I hadn't been told over and over that you were the best man in your field, I'd have slapped an injunction on you days ago!'

Inventor?

'The fact is,' Gallegher began mildly, 'I've been ill – '

'In a pig's eye,' Hopper said coarsely. 'You were drunk as a lord. I don't pay men for drinking. Did you forget those thousand credits were only part payment – with nine thousand more to come?'

'Why . . . why, n-no. Uh . . . nine thousand?'

'Plus a bonus for quick work. You still get the bonus, luckily. It's only been a couple of weeks. But it's lucky for you you got the thing finished. I've got options on a couple of factories already. *And* scouts looking out for good locations, all over the country. Is it practical for small sets, Gallegher? We'll make our steady money from them, not from the big audiences.'

'*Tchwuk*,' Gallegher said. 'Uh – '

'Got it there? I'm coming right down to see it.'

'Wait! Maybe you'd better let me add a few touches – '

'All I want is the idea,' Hopper said. 'If that's satisfactory, the rest is easy. I'll call Trench and have him quash that summons. See you soon.'

He blanked out.

Gallegher screamed for beer. 'And a razor,' he added, as Narcissus padded out of the room. 'I want to cut my throat.'

'Why?' the robot asked.

'Just to amuse you, why else? Get that beer.'

Narcissus brought a plastibulb. 'I don't understand why you're so upset,' he remarked. 'Why don't you lose yourself in rapturous contemplation of my beauty?'

'Better the razor,' Gallegher said glumly. 'Far better. Three clients, two of whom I can't remember at all, commissioning me to do jobs I can't remember, either. Ha!'

Narcissus ruminated. 'Try induction,' he suggested. 'That machine – '

'What about it?'

'Well, when you get a commission, you usually drink yourself into such a state that your subconscious takes over and does the job. Then you sober up. Apparently that's what happened this time. You made the machine, didn't you?'

'Sure,' Gallegher said, 'but for which client? I don't even know what it does.'

'You could try it and find out.'

'Oh. So I could. I'm stupid this morning.'

'You're always stupid,' Narcissus said. 'And very ugly, too. The more I contemplate my own perfect loveliness, the more pity I feel for humans.'

'Oh, shut up,' Gallegher snapped, feeling the uselessness of trying to argue with a robot. He went over to the enigmatic machine and studied it once more. Nothing clicked in his mind.

There was a switch, and he flipped it. The machine started to sing 'St James Infirmary.'

' – to see my sweetie there
She was lying on a marble sla-a-ab – '

'I see it all,' Gallegher said in a fit of wild frustration. 'Somebody asked me to invent a phonograph.'

'Wait,' Narcissus pointed out. 'Look at the window.'

'The window. Sure. What about it? *Wh* –' Gallegher hung over the sill, gasping. His knees felt unhinged and weak. Still, he might have expected something like this.

The group of tubes emerging from the machine were rather incredibly telescopic. They had stretched down to the bottom of the pit, a full thirty feet, and were sweeping around in erratic circles like grazing vacuum cleaners. They moved so fast Gallegher couldn't see them except as blurs. It was like watching the head of a Medusa who had contracted St Vitus' Dance and transmitted the ailment to her snakes.

'Look at them whiz,' Narcissus said contemplatively, leaning heavily on Gallegher. 'I guess that's what made the hole. They eat dirt.'

'Yeah,' the scientist agreed, drawing back. 'I wonder why. Dirt – Hm-m-m. Raw material.' He peered at the machine, which was wailing:

'– can search the wide world over
An never find another sweet man like me.'

'Electrical connections,' Gallegher mused, cocking an inquisitive eye. 'The raw dirt goes in that one-time wastebasket. Then what? Electronic bombardment? Protons, neutrons, positrons – I *wish* I knew what those words meant,' he ended plaintively. 'If only I'd had a college education!'

'A positron is –'

'Don't tell me,' Gallegher pleaded. 'I'll only have semantic difficulties. I know what a positron is, all right, only I don't identify it with that name. All I know is the intensional meaning. Which can't be expressed in words, anyhow.'

'The extensional meaning can, though,' Narcissus pointed out.

'Not with me. As Humpty Dumpty said, the question is, which is to be master. And with me it's the word. The damn things scare me. I simply don't *get* their extensional meanings.'

'That's silly,' said the robot. 'Positron has a perfectly clear denotation.'

'To you. All it means to me is a gang of little boys with fishtails and green whiskers. That's why I never can figure out what my subconscious has been up to. I have to use symbolic logic, and the symbols . . . ah, shut up,' Gallegher growled. 'Why should I argue about semantics with you, anyhow?'

'You started it,' Narcissus said.

Gallegher glared at the robot and then went back to the cryptic machine. It was still eating dirt and playing 'St. James Infirmary.'

'Why should it sing that, I wonder?'

'You usually sing it when you're drunk, don't you? Preferably in a barroom.'

'That solves nothing,' Gallegher said shortly. He explored the machine. It was in smooth, rapid operation, emitting a certain amount of heat, and something was smoking. Gallegher found a lubricating valve, seized an oil can, and squirted. The smoke vanished, as well as a faint smell of burning.

'Nothing comes out,' Gallegher said, after a long pause of baffled consideration.

'There?' The robot pointed.

Gallegher examined the grooved wheel that was turning rapidly. Just above it was a small circular aperture in the smooth hide of cylindrical tube. Nothing seemed to be coming out of that hole, however.

'Turn the switch off,' Gallegher said. Narcissus obeyed. The valve snapped shut and the grooved wheel stopped turning. Over activity ceased instantly. The music died. The tentacles stretched out the window stopped whirling and shortened to their normal inactive length.

'Well, there's apparently no end product,' Gallegher remarked. 'It eats dirt and digests it completely. Ridiculous.'

'Is it?'

'Sure. Dirt's got elements in it. Oxygen, nitrogen – there's granite under New York, so there's alumium, sodium, silicon – lots of things. No sort of physical *or* chemical change could explain this.'

'You mean something ought to come out of the machine?'

'Yes,' Gallegher said. 'In a word, exactly. I'd feel a lot better if something did. Even mud.'

'Music comes out of it,' Narcissus pointed out. 'If you can truthfully call that squalling music.'

'By no stretch of my imagination can I bring myself to consider that loathsome thought,' the scientist denied firmly. 'I'll admit my subconscious is slightly nuts. But it's got logic; in a mad sort of way. It wouldn't build a machine to convert dirt into music, even if such a thing's possible.'

'But it doesn't do anything else, does it?'

'No. I wonder what Hopper asked me to make for him. He kept talking about factories and audiences.'

'He'll be here soon,' Narcissus said. 'Ask him.'

Gallegher didn't bother to reply. He thought of demanding more beer, rejected the idea, and instead used the liquor organ to mix himself a pick-me-up of several liqueurs. After that he went and sat on a generator which bore the conspicuous label of Monstro. Apparently dissatisfied, he changed his seat to a smaller generator named Bubbles.

Gallegher always thought better atop Bubbles.

The pick-me-up had oiled his brain, fuzzy with alcohol fumes. A machine without an end product – dirt vanishing into nothingness. Hm-m-m. Matter cannot disappear like a rabbit popping into a magician's hat. It's got to go somewhere. Energy?

Apparently not. The machine didn't manufacture energy. The cords and sockets showed that, on the contrary, it made use of electric power to operate.

And so –

What?

Try it from another angle. Gallegher's subconscious, Gallegher Plus, had built the device for some logical reason. The reason was supplied by his profit of thirty-three hundred credits. He'd been paid that sum, by three different people, to make – maybe – three different things.

Which of them fitted the machine?

Look at it as an equation. Call clients, a, b, and c. Call the purpose of the machine – not the machine itself, of course – x. Then a (or) b (or) c equals x.

Not quite. The term a wouldn't represent Dell Hopper; it would symbolize what he wanted. And what he wanted must necessarily and logically be the purpose of the machine.

Or the mysterious J.W., or the equally mysterious Fatty.

Well, Fatty was a shade less enigmatic. Gallegher had a clue, for what it was worth. If J.W. was represented by b, Fatty would be c plus adipose tissue. Call adipose tissue t, and what did you get?

Thirsty.

Gallegher had more beer, distracting Narcissus from his posturing before the mirror. He drummed his heels against

Bubbles, scowling, a lock of dark hair falling lankly over his eyes.

Prison?

Uh! No, there must be some other answer, somewhere. The DU stock, for example. Why had Gallegher Plus bought four thousand credits' worth of the stuff when it was on the skids?

If he could find the answer to that, it might help. For Gallegher Plus did nothing without purpose. What was Devices Unlimited, anyway?

He tried the televisor Who's Who in Manhattan. Luckily Devices was corporated within the State and had business offices here. A full-page ad flipped into view.

DEVICES UNLIMITED
WE DO EVERYTHING!
RED 5-1400-M

Well, Gallegher had the firm's 'visor number, which was something. As he began to call RED, a buzzer murmured, and Narcissus turned petulantly from the mirror and went off to answer the door. He returned in a moment with the bisonlike Mr Hopper.

'Sorry to be so long,' Hopper rumbled. 'My chauffeur went through a light, and a cop stopped us. I had to bawl the very devil out of him.'

'The chauffeur?'

'The cop. Now where's the stuff?'

Gallegher licked his lips. Had Gallegher Plus actually kicked this mountainous guy in the pants? It was not a thought to dwell upon.

He pointed towards the window. 'There.' Was he right? Had Hopper ordered a machine that ate dirt?

The big man's eyes widened in surprise. He gave Gallegher a swift, wondering look, and then moved towards the device, inspecting it from all angles. He glanced out the window, but didn't seem much interested in what he saw there. Instead, he turned back to Gallegher with a puzzled scowl.

'You mean this? A totally new principle, is it? But then it must be.'

No clue there. Gallegher tried a feeble smile. Hopper just looked at him.

'All right,' he said. 'What's the practical application?'

Gallegher groped wildly. 'I'd better show you,' he said at last, crossing the lab and flipping the switch. Instantly the machine started to sing 'St James Infirmary.' The tentacles lengthened and began to eat dirt. The hole in the cylinder opened. The grooved wheel began to revolve.

Hopper waited.

After a time he said, 'Well?'

'You – don't like it?'

'How should I know? I don't even know what it does. Isn't there any screen?'

'Sure,' Gallegher said, completely at a loss. 'It's inside that cylinder.'

'In — *what*?' Hopper's shaggy brows drew down over his jet-black eyes. '*Inside that cylinder*?'

'Uh-huh.'

'For – ' Hopper seemed to be choking. 'What good is it there? Without X-ray eyes, anyhow?'

'Should it have X-ray eyes?' Gallegher muttered, dizzy with bafflement. 'You wanted a screen with X-ray eyes?'

'You're still drunk!' Hopper snarled. 'Or else you're crazy!'

'Wait a minute. Maybe I've made a mistake – '

'A mistake!'

'Tell me one thing. Just what did you ask me to do?'

Hopper took three deep breaths. In a cold, precise voice he said, 'I asked you if you could devise a method of projecting three-dimensional images that could be viewed from any angle, front, back or side, without distortion. You said yes. I paid you a thousand credits on account. I've taken options on a couple of factories so I could begin manufacturing without delay. I've had scouts out looking for likely theatres. I'm planning a campaign for selling the attachments to home televisors. And now, Mr Gallegher, I'm going out and see my attorney and tell him to put the screws on.'

He went out, snorting. The robot gently closed the door, came back, and, without being asked, hurried after beer. Gallegher waved it away.

'I'll use the organ,' he moaned, mixing himself a stiff one. 'Turn that blasted machine off, Narcissus. I haven't the strength.'

'Well, you've found out one thing,' the robot said encouragingly. 'You didn't build the device for Hopper.'

'True. True. I made it for . . . ah . . . either J.W. or Fatty. How can I find out who they are?'

'You need a rest,' the robot said. 'Why not simply relax and listen to my lovely melodious voice? I'll read to you.'

'It's not melodious,' Gallegher said automatically and absently. 'It squeaks like a rusty hinge.'

'To your ears. *My* senses are different. To me, your voice is the croaking of an asthmatic frog. You can't see me as I do, any more than you can hear me as I hear myself. Which is just as well. You'd swoon with ecstasy.'

'Narcissus,' Gallegher said patiently, 'I'm trying to think. Will you kindly shut that metallic trap?'

'My name isn't Narcissus,' said the robot. 'It's Joe.'

'Then I'm changing it. Let's see. I was checking up on DU. What was that number?'

'Red five fourteen hundred M.'

'Oh, yeah.' Gallegher used the televisor. A secretary was willing but unable to give much useful information.

Devices Unlimited was the name of a holding company, of a sort. It had connections all over the world. When a client wanted a job done, DU, through its agents, got in touch with the right person and finagled the deal. The trick was that DU supplied the money, financing operations and working on a percentage basis. It sounded fantastically intricate, and Gallegher was left in the dark.

'Any record of my name in your files? Oh – well, can you tell me who J.W. is?'

'J.W.? I'm sorry, sir. I'll need the full name –'

'I don't have it. And this is important.' Gallegher argued. At last he got his way. The only DU man whose initials were J.W. was someone named Jackson Wardell, who was on Callisto at the moment.

'How long has he been there?'

'He was born there,' said the secretary unhelpfully. 'He's never been to Earth in his life. I'm sure Mr Wardell can't be your man.'

Gallegher agreed. There was no use asking for Fatty, he decided, and broke the beam with a faint sigh. Well, what now?

The visor shrilled. On the screen appeared the face of a plump-cheeked, bald, pudgy man who was frowning worriedly. He broke into a relieved chuckle at sight of the scientist.

'Oh, there you are, Mr Gallegher,' he said. 'I've been trying to reach you for an hour. Something's wrong with the beam. My goodness, I thought I'd certainly hear from you before this!'

Gallegher's heart stumbled. *Fatty* – of course!

Thank God, the luck was beginning to turn! Fatty – eight hundred credits. On account. On account of what? The machine? Was it the solution to Fatty's problem, or to J.W.'s? Gallegher prayed with brief fervency that Fatty had requested a device that ate dirt and sang 'St James Infirmary.'

The image blurred and flickered, with a faint crackling. Fatty said hurriedly, 'Something's wrong with the line. But – did you do it, Mr Gallegher? Did you find a method?'

'Sure,' Gallegher said. If he could lead the man on, gain some hint of what he had ordered –

'Oh, wonderful! DU's been calling me for days. I've been putting them off, but they won't wait forever. Cuff's bearing down hard, and I can't get around that old statute –'

The screen went dead.

Gallegher almost bit off his tongue in impotent fury. Hastily he closed the circuit and began striding around the lab, his nerves tense with expectation. In a second the visor would ring. Fatty would call back. Naturally. And this time the first question Gallegher would ask would be, 'Who are you?'

Time passed.

Gallegher groaned and checked back, asking the

operator to trace the call.

'I'm sorry, sir. It was made from a dial visor. We cannot trace calls made from a dial visor.'

Ten minutes later Gallegher stopped cursing, seized his hat from its perch atop an iron dog that had once decorated a lawn, and whirled to the door. 'I'm going out,' he snapped to Narcissus. 'Keep an eye on that machine.'

'All right. One eye.' The robot agreed. 'I'll need the other to watch my beautiful insides. Why don't you find out who Cuff is?'

'What?'

'Cuff. Fatty mentioned somebody by that name. He said he was bearing down hard –'

'Check! He did, at that. And – what was it? – he said he couldn't get around an old statue –'

'Statute. It means a law.'

'I know what statute means,' Gallegher growled. 'I'm not exactly a drivelling idiot. Not yet, anyhow. Cuff, eh? I'll try the visor again.'

There were six Cuffs listed. Gallegher eliminated half of them by gender. He crossed off Cuff-Linx Mfg. Co., which left two – Max and Fredk. He televised Frederick, getting a pop-eyed, scrawny youth who was obviously not yet old enough to vote. Gallegher gave the lad a murderous glare of frustration and flipped the switch, leaving Frederick to spend the next half-hour wondering who had called him, grimaced like a demon, and blanked out without a word.

But Max Cuff remained, and that, certainly, was the man. Gallegher felt sure of it when Max Cuff's butler transferred the call to a downtown office, where a receptionist said that Mr Cuff was spending the afternoon at the Uplift Social Club.

'That so? Say, who is Cuff, anyhow?'

'I beg your pardon?'

'What's his noise? His business, I mean?'

'Mr Cuff has no business,' the girl said frigidly. 'He's an alderman.'

That was interesting. Gallegher looked for his hat, found it on his head, and took leave of the robot, who did not trouble to answer. 'If Fatty calls up again,' the scientist commanded, 'get his name. See? And keep your eye on that machine, just in case it starts having mutations or something.'

That seemed to tie up all the loose ends. Gallegher let himself out of the house. A cool autumn wind was blowing, scattering crisp leaves from the overhead parkways. A few taxiplanes drifted past, but Gallegher hailed a street cab; he wanted to see where he was going. Somehow he felt that a telecall to Max Cuff would produce little of value. The man would require deft handling, especially since he was 'bearing down hard.'

'Where to, bud?'

'Uplift Social Club. Know where it is?'

'Nope,' said the driver, 'but I can find out.' He used his teledirectory on the dashboard. 'Downtown. 'Way down.'

'O.K.,' Gallegher told the man, and dropped back on the cushions, brooding darkly. Why was everybody so elusive? His clients weren't usually ghosts. But Fatty remained vague and nameless – a face, that was all, and one Gallegher hadn't recognised. Who J.W. was anyone might guess. Only Dell Hopper had put in an appearance, and Gallegher wished he hadn't. The summons rustled in his pocket.

'What I need,' Gallegher soliloquized, 'is a drink. That was the whole trouble. I didn't stay drunk. Not long enough, anyhow. Oh, damn.'

Presently the taxi stopped at what had once been a glass-brick mansion, now grimy and forlorn-looking. Gallegher got out, paid the driver, and went up the ramp. A small placard said Uplift Social Club. Since there was no buzzer, he opened the door and went in.

Instantly his nostrils twitched like the muzzle of a war horse scenting cordite. There was drinking going on. With the instinct of a homing pigeon, Gallegher went directly to the bar, set up against one wall of a huge room filled with chairs, tables, and people. A sad-looking man with a derby was playing a pin-ball machine in a corner. He looked up as Gallegher approached, lurched into his path, and murmured, 'Looking for somebody?'

'Yeah,' Gallegher said. 'Max Cuff. They told me he was here.'

'Now now,' said the sad man. 'What do you want with him?'

'It's about Fatty,' Gallegher hazarded.

Cold eyes regarded him. 'Who?'

'You wouldn't know him. But Max would.'

'Max want to see you?'

'Sure.'

'Well,' the man said doubtfully, 'he's down at the Three-Star on a pub-crawl. When he starts that – '

'The Three-Star? Where is it?'

'Fourteenth near Broad.'

'Thanks,' Gallegher said. He went out, with a longing look at the bar. Now now – not yet. There was business to attend to first.

The Three-Star was a gin mill, with dirty pictures on the walls. They moved in a stereoscopic and mildly appalling manner. Gallegher, after a thoughtful examination, looked the customers over. There weren't many. A huge man at one end of the bar attracted his attention because of the gardenia in his lapel and the flashy diamond on his ring finger.

Gallegher went towards him. 'Mr Cuff?'

'Right,' said the big man, turning slowly on the bar-stool like Jupiter revolving on its axis. He eyed Gallegher, librating slightly. 'Who're you?'

'I'm – '

'Never mind,' said Cuff, winking. 'Never give your right name after you've pulled a job. So you're on the lam, eh?'

'What?'

'I can spot 'em as far away as I can see 'em. You . . . you . . . hey!' Cuff said, bending forward and sniffing. 'You been *drinking*!'

'Drinking,' Gallegher said bitterly. 'It's an understatement.'

'Then have a drink with me,' the big man invited. 'I'm up to E now. Egg flip. Tim!' he roared. ''Nother egg flip for my pal here! Step it up! And get busy with F.'

Gallegher slid onto the stool beside Cuff and watched his

companion speculatively. The alderman seemed a little tight.

'Yes,' Cuff said, 'alphabetical drinking's the only way to do it. You start with A – absinthe – and then work along, brandy, cointreau, daiquiri, egg flip – '

'Then what?'

'F, of course,' Cuff said, mildly surprised. 'Flip. Here's yours. Good lubrication!'

They drank. 'Listen,' Gallegher said, 'I want to see you about Fatty.'

'Who's he?'

'Fatty,' Gallegher explained, winking significantly. 'You know. You've been bearing down lately. The statute. You know.'

'Oh! *Him!*' Cuff suddenly roared with Gargantuan laughter. 'Fatty, huh? That's good. That's very good. Fatty's a good name for him, all right.'

'Not much like his own, is it?' Gallegher said cunningly.

'Not a bit. Fatty!'

'Does he spell his name with an e or an i?'

'Both,' Cuff said. 'Tim, where's the flip? Oh, you got it ready, huh? Well, good lubrication, pal.'

Gallegher finished his egg flip and went to work on the flip, which was identical except for the name. What now?'

'About Fatty,' he hazarded.

'Yeah?'

'How's everything going?'

'I never answer questions,' Cuff said, abruptly sobering. He looked sharply at Gallegher. 'You one of the boys? I don't know you.'

'Pittsburgh. They told me to come to the club when I got in town.'

'That doesn't make sense,' Cuff said. 'Oh, well. It doesn't matter. I just cleaned up some loose ends, and I'm celebrating. Through with your flip? Tim! Gin!'

They had gin for G, a horse's neck for H, and an eye-opener for I. 'Now a Jazzbo,' Cuff said with satisfaction. 'This is the only bar in town that has a drink beginning with J. After that I have to start skipping. I dunno any K drinks.'

'Kirchwasser,' Gallegher said absently.

'K — huh? What's that?' Cuff bellowed at the bartender. 'Tim! You got any kirchwasser?'

'Nope,' said the man. 'We don't carry it, Alderman.'

'Then we'll find somebody who does. You're a smart guy, pal. Come along with me. I *need* you.'

Gallegher went obediently. Since Cuff didn't want to talk about Fatty, it behooved him to win the alderman's confidence. And the best way to do that was to drink with him. Unfortunately an alphabetical pub-crawl, with its fantastic mixtures, proved none too easy. Gallegher already had a hangover. And Cuff's thirst was insatiable.

'L? What's L?'

'Lachrymae Christi. Or Liebfraumilch.'

'Oh, boy!'

It was a relief to get back to a Martini. After the Orange Blossom Gallegher began to feel dizzy. For R he suggested root beer, but Cuff would have none of that.

'Well, rice wine.'

'Yeah. Rice – hey! We missed N! We gotta start over now from A!'

Gallegher dissuaded the alderman with some trouble, and succeeded only after fascinating Cuff with the exotic name ng ga po. They worked on, through sazeracs, tailspins, undergrounds, and vodka. W meant whisky.

'X?'

They looked at each other through alcoholic fogs. Gallegher shrugged and stared around. How had they got into this swanky, well-furnished private clubroom, he wondered. It wasn't the Uplift, that was certain. Oh, well –

'X?' Cuff insisted. 'Don't fail me now, pal.'

'Extra whisky,' Gallegher said brilliantly.

'That's it. Only two left. Y and . . . and – what comes after Y?'

'Fatty. Remember?'

'Ol' Fatty Smith,' Cuff said, beginning to laugh immoderately. At least, it sounded like Smith. 'Fatty just suits him.'

'What's his first name?' Gallegher asked.

'Who?'

'Fatty.'

'Never heard of him,' Cuff said, and chuckled. A page boy came over and touched the alderman's arm.

'Someone to see you, sir. They're waiting outside.'

'Right. Back in a minute, pal. Everybody always knows where to find me – 'specially here. Don't go 'way. There's still Y and . . . and . . . and the other one.'

He vanished. Gallegher put down his untasted drink, stood up, swaying slightly, and headed for the lounge. A televisor booth there caught his eye, and, on impulse, he went in and vised his lab.

'Drunk again,' said Narcissus, as the robot's face appeared on the screen.

'You said it,' Gallegher agreed. 'I'm . . . *urp* . . . high as a kite. But I got a clue, anyway.'

'I'd advise you to get a police escort,' the robot said. 'Some thugs broke in looking for you, right after you left.'

'S-s-some what? Say that again.'

'Three thugs,' Narcissus repeated patiently. 'The leader was a thin, tall man in a check suit with yellow hair and a gold front tooth. The others – '

'I don't want a description,' Gallegher snarled. 'Just tell me what happened?'

'Well, that's all. They wanted to kidnap you. Then they tried to steal the machine. I chased them out. For a robot, I'm pretty tough.'

'Did they hurt the machine?'

'What about me?' Narcissus demanded plaintively. 'I'm much more important than that gadget. Have you no curiosity about my wounds?'

'No,' Gallegher said. 'Have you some?'

'Of course not. But you could have demonstrated some slight curiosity – '

'*Did they hurt that machine?*'

'I didn't let them get near it,' the robot said. 'And the hell with you.'

'I'll ring you back,' Gallegher said. 'Right now I need black coffee.'

He beamed off, stood up, and wavered out of the booth. Max Cuff was coming towards him. There were three men following the alderman.

One of them stopped short, his jaw dropping. 'Cripes!' he said. 'That's the guy, boss. That's Gallegher. Is he the one you been drinking with?'

Gallegher tried to focus his eyes. The man swam into clarity. He was a tall, thin chap in a check suit, and he had yellow hair and a gold front tooth.

'Conk him,' Cuff said. 'Quick, before he yells. And before anybody else comes in here. Gallegher, huh? Smart guy, huh?'

Gallegher saw something coming at his head, and tried to leap back into the visor booth like a snail retreating into its shell. He failed. Spinning flashes of glaring light dazzled him.

He was conked.

The trouble with this social culture, Gallegher thought dreamily, was that it was suffering both from overgrowth and calcification of the exoderm. A civilization may be likened to a flowerbed. Each individual plant stands for a component part of the culture. Growth is progress. Technology, that long-frustrate daffodil, had had B1 concentrate poured on its roots, the result of wars that forced its growth through sheer necessity. But no world is satisfactory unless the parts are equal to the whole.

The daffodil shaded another plant that developed parasitic tendencies. It stopped using its roots. It wound itself around the daffodil, climbing up on its stem and stalks and leaves, and that strangling liana was religion, politics, economics, culture – outmoded forms that changed too slowly, outstripped by the blazing comet of the sciences, riding high in the unlocked skies of this new era. Long ago writers had theorized that in the future – their future – the sociological pattern would be different. In the day of rocketships such illogical *mores* as watered stock, dirty politics, and gangsters would not exist. But those theorists had not seen clearly enough. They thought of rocketships as vehicles of the far distant future.

Ley landed on the moon before automobiles stopped using carburetors.

The great warfare of the early twentieth century gave a

violent impetus to technology, and that growth continued. Unfortunately most of the business of living was based on such matters as man hours and monetary fixed standards. The only parallel was the day of the great bubbles – the Mississippi Bubble and its brothers. It was, finally, a time of chaos, reorganisation, shifting precariously from old standards to new, and a seesaw bouncing vigorously from one extreme to the other. The legal profession had become so complicated that batteries of experts needed Pedersen Calculators and the brain machines of Mechanistra to marshal their farfetched arguments, which went wildly into uncharted realms of symbolic logic and – eventually – pure nonsense. A murderer could get off scot-free provided he didn't sign a confession. And even if he did, there were ways of discrediting solid, legal proof. Precedents were shibboleths. In that maze of madness, administrators turned to historical solidities – legal precedents – and these were often twisted against them.

Thus it went, all down the line. Later sociology would catch up with technology. It hadn't, just yet. Economic gambling had reached a pitch never before attained in the history of the world. Geniuses were needed to straighten out the mess. Mutations eventually provided such geniuses, by natural compensation; but a long time was to pass until that satisfactory conclusion had been reached. The man with the best chance for survival, Gallegher had realised by now, was one with a good deal of adaptability and a first-class all-around stock of practical and impractical knowledge, versed in practically everything. In short, in matters vegetable, animal or mineral –

Gallegher opened his eyes. There was little to see, chiefly because, as he immediately discovered, he was slumped face down at a table. With an effort Gallegher sat up. He was unbound, and in a dimly lighted attic that seemed to be a storeroom; it was littered with broken-down junk. A fluorescent burned faintly on the ceiling. There was a door, but the man with the gold tooth was standing before it. Across the table sat Max Cuff, carefully pouring whisky into a glass.

'I want some,' Gallegher said feebly.

Cuff looked at him. 'Awake, huh? Sorry Blazer socked you so hard.'

'Oh, well. I might have passed out anyway. Those alphabetical pub-crawls are really something.'

'Heigh-ho,' Cuff said, pushing the glass towards Gallegher and filling another for himself. 'That's the way it goes. It was smart of you to stick with me – the one place the boys wouldn't think of looking.'

'I'm naturally clever,' Gallegher said modestly. The whisky revived him. But his mind still felt foggy. 'Your . . . uh . . . associates, by which I mean lousy thugs, tried to kidnap me earlier, didn't they?'

'Uh-huh. You weren't in. That robot of yours –'

'He's a beaut.'

'Yeah. Look, Blazer told me about the machine you had set up. I'd hate to have Smith get his hands on it.'

Smith – Fatty. Hm-m-m. The jigsaw was dislocated again. Gallegher sighed.

If he played the cards close to his chest –

'Smith hasn't seen it yet.'

'I know that,' Cuff said. 'We've been tapping his visor beam. One of our spies found out he'd told DU he had a man working on the job – you know? Only he didn't mention the man's name. All we could do was shadow Smith and tap his visor till he got in touch with you. After that – well, we caught the conversation. You told Smith you'd got the gadget.'

'Well?'

'We cut in on the beam, fast, and Blazer and the boys went down to see you. I told you I didn't want Smith to keep that contract.'

'You never mentioned a contract,' Gallegher said.

'Don't play dumb. Smith told 'em, up at DU, that he'd laid the whole case before you.'

Maybe Smith had. Only Gallegher had been drunk at the time, and it was Gallegher Plus who had listened, storing the information securely in the subconscious.

'So?'

Cuff burped. He pushed his glass away suddenly. 'I'll see you later. I'm tight, damn it. Can't think straight. But – I don't want Smith to get that machine. Your robot won't let us near it. You'll get in touch with him by visor and send him off somewhere, so the boys can pick up your gadget. Say yes or no. If it's no, I'll be back.'

'No,' Gallegher said. 'On account of you'd kill me anyway, to stop me from building another machine for Smith.'

Cuff's lids drew down slowly over his eyes. He sat motionless, seemingly asleep, for a time. Then he looked at Gallegher blankly and stood up.

'I'll see you later, then.' He rubbed a hand across his forehead; his voice was a little thick. 'Blazer, keep the lug here.'

The man with the gold tooth came forward. 'You O.K.?'

'Yeah. I can't think – ' Cuff grimaced. 'Turkish bath. That's what I need.' He went towards the door, pulling Blazer with him. Gallegher saw the alderman's lips move. He read a few words.

' – drunk enough . . . vise that robot . . . try it – '

Then Cuff went out. Blazer came back, sat opposite Gallegher, and shoved the bottle towards him. 'Might as well take it easy,' he suggested. 'Have another; you need it.'

Gallegher thought: Smart guys. They figure if I get stinko, I'll do what they want. Well –

There was another angle. When Gallegher was thoroughly under the influence of alcohol, his subconscious took over. And Gallegher Plus was a scientific genius – mad, but good.

Gallegher Plus might be able to figure a way out of this.

'That's it,' Blazer said, watching the liquor vanish. 'Have another. Max is a good egg. He wouldn't put the bee on you. He just can't stand people helixing up his plans.'

'What plans?'

'Like with Smith,' Blazer explained.

'I see.' Gallegher's limbs were tingling. Pretty soon he should be sufficiently saturated with alcohol to unleash his subconscious. He kept drinking.

Perhaps he tried too hard. Usually Gallegher mixed his liquor judiciously. This time, the factors of the equation added up to a depressing zero. He saw the surface of the table moving slowly towards his nose, felt a mild, rather pleasant bump, and began to snore. Blazer got up and shook him.

'One half so precious as the stuff they sell,' Gallegher said thickly. 'High-piping Pehlevi, with wine, wine, wine, wine. *Red* wine.'

'Wine he wants,' Blazer said. 'The guy's a human blotter.' He shook Gallegher again, but there was no response. Blazer grunted, and his footsteps sounded, growing fainter.

Gallegher heard the door close. He tried to sit up, slid off the chair, and banged his head agonisingly against a table leg.

It was more effective than cold water. Wavering, Gallegher crawled to his feet. The attic room was empty except for himself and other jetsam. He walked with abnormal carefulness to the door and tried it. Locked. Reinforced with steel, at that.

'Fine stuff,' Gallegher murmured. 'The one time I need my subconscious, it stays buried. How the devil can I get out of here?'

There was no way. The room had no windows, and the door was firm. Gallegher floated towards the piles of junk. An old sofa. A box of scraps. Pillows. A rolled carpet. Junk.

Gallegher found a length of wire, a bit of mica, a twisted spiral of plastic, once part of a mobile statuette, and some other trivia. He put them together. The result was a thing vaguely resembling a gun, though it had some resemblance to an egg beater. It looked as weird as a Martian's doodling.

After that, Gallegher returned to the chair and sat down, trying, by sheer will power, to sober up. He didn't succeed too well. When he heard footsteps returning, his mind was still fuzzy.

The door opened. Blazer came in, with a swift, wary glance at Gallegher, who had hidden the gadget under the table.

'Back, are you? I thought it might be Max.'

'He'll be along, too,' Blazer said. 'How d'you feel?'

'Woozy. I could use another drink. I've finished this bottle.' Gallegher had finished it. He had poured it down a rat hole.

Blazer locked the door and came forward as Gallegher stood up. The scientist missed his balance, lurched forward, and Blazer hesitated. Gallegher brought out the crazy egg-beater gun and snapped it up to eye level, squinting along its barrel at Blazer's face.

The thug went for something, either his gun or his sap. But the eerie contrivance Gallegher had leveled at him worried Blazer. His motion was arrested abruptly. He was wondering what menace confronted him. In another second he would act, one way or another – perhaps continuing that arrested smooth notion towards his belt.

Gallegher did not wait. Blazer's stare was on the gadget. With utter disregard for the Queensbury Rules, Gallegher kicked his opponent below the belt. As Blazer folded up, Gallegher followed his advantage by hurling himself headlong on the thug and bearing him down in a wild, octopuslike thrashing of lanky limbs. Blazer kept trying to reach his weapon, but that first foul blow had handicapped him.

Gallegher was still too drunk to co-ordinate properly. He compromised by crawling atop his enemy and beating the man repeatedly on the solar plexus. Such tactics proved effective. After a time, Gallegher was able to wrench the sap from Blazer's grasp and lay it firmly along the thug's temple.

That was that.

With a glance at the gadget, Gallegher arose, wondering what Blazer had thought it was. A death-ray projector, perhaps. Gallegher grinned faintly. He found the door key in his unconscious victim's pocket, let himself out of the attic, and warily descended a stairway. So far, so good.

A reputation for scientific achievements has its advantages. It had, at least, served the purpose of distracting Blazer's attention from the obvious.

What now?

The house was a three-storey, empty structure near the Battery. Gallegher escaped through a window. He did not pause till he was in an airtaxi, speeding uptown. There, breathing deeply, he flipped the wind filter and let the cool night breeze cool his perspiring cheeks. A full moon rode high in the black autumn sky. Below, through the earth-view transparent panel, he could see the brilliant ribbons of streets, with slashing bright diagonals marking the upper level speedways.

Smith. Fatty Smith. Connected with DU, somehow –

With an access of caution, he paid off the pilot and stepped out on a rooftop landing in the White Way district. There were televisor booths here, and Gallegher called his lab. The robot answered.

'Narcissus – '

'Joe,' the robot corrected. 'And you've been drinking some more. Why don't you sober up?'

'Shut up and listen. What's been happening?'

'Not much.'

'Those thugs. Did they come back?'

'No,' Narcissus said, 'but some officers came to arrest you. Remember that summons they served you with today? You should have appeared in court at 5 p.m.'

Summons. Oh, yeah. Dell Hopper – one thousand credits.

'Are they there now?'

'No. I said you'd taken a powder.'

'Why?' asked Gallegher.

'So they wouldn't hang around. Now you can come home whenever you like – if you take reasonable precautions.'

'Such as what?'

'That's your problem,' Narcissus said. 'Get a false beard. I've done my share.'

Gallegher said, 'All right, make a lot of black coffee. Any other calls?'

'One from Washington. A commander in the space police unit. He didn't give his name.'

'Space police! Are they after me, too? What did he want?'

'You,' the robot said. 'Goodbye. You interrupted a lovely song I was singing to myself.'

'Make that coffee,' Gallegher ordered as the image

76

faded. He stepped out of the booth and stood for a moment, considering, while he stared blankly at the towers of Manhattan rising around him, with their irregular patterns of lighted windows, square, oval, circular, crescent, or star-shaped.

A call from Washington.

Hopper cracking down.

Max Cuff and his thugs.

Fatty Smith.

Smith was the best bet. He tried the visor again, calling DU.

'Sorry, we have closed for the day.'

'This is important,' Gallegher insisted. 'I need some information. I've got to get in touch with a man –'

'I'm sorry.'

'S-m-i-t-h,' Gallegher spelled. 'Just look him up in the file or something, won't you? Or do you want me to cut my throat while you watch?' He fumbled in his pocket.

'If you will call tomorrow –'

'That'll be too late. Can't you just look it up for me? Please. Double please.'

'Sorry.'

'I'm a stockholder in DU,' Gallegher snarled. 'I warn you, my girl!'

'A . . . oh. Well, it's irregular, but – S-m-i-t-h? One moment. The first name is what?'

'I don't know. Give me all the Smiths.'

The girl disappeared and came back with a file box labelled SMI. 'Oh, dear,' she said, riffling through the cards. 'There must be several hundred Smiths.'

Gallegher groaned. 'I want a fat one,' he said wildly. 'There's no way of checking on that, I suppose.'

The secretary's lips tightened. 'Oh, a rib. I see. Good *night*!' She broke the connection.

Gallegher sat staring at the screen. Several hundred Smiths. Not so good. In fact, definitely bad.

Wait a minute. He had bought DU stock when it was on the skids. Why? He must have expected a rising market. But the stock had continued to fall, according to Arnie.

There might be a lead there.

He reached Arnie at the broker's home and was insistent. 'Break the date. This won't take you long. Just find out for me why DU's on the skids. Call me back at my lab. Or I'll break your neck. And make it fast! Get that dope, understand?'

Arnie said he would. Gallegher drank black coffee at a counter stand, went home warily by taxi, and let himself into his house. He double-locked the door behind him. Narcissus was dancing before the big mirror in the lab.

'Any calls?' Gallegher said.

'No. Nothing's happened. Look at this graceful *pas*.'

'Later. If anybody tries to get in, call me. I'll hide till you can get rid of 'em.' Gallegher squeezed his eyes shut. 'Is the coffee ready?'

'Black and strong. In the kitchen.'

The scientist went into the bathroom instead, stripped, cold-showered, and took a brief irradiation. Feeling less woozy, he returned to the lab with a gigantic cup full of steaming coffee. He perched on Bubbles and gulped the liquid.

'You look like Rodin's Thinker,' Narcissus remarked. 'I'll get you a robe. Your ungainly body offends my aesthetic feelings.'

Gallegher didn't hear. He donned the robe, since his sweating skin felt unpleasantly cool, but continued to drink the coffee and stare into space.

'Narcissus. More of this.'

Equation: a (or) b (or) c equals x. He had been trying to find the value of a, b, or c. Maybe that was the wrong way. He hadn't located J.W. at all. Smith remained a phantom. And Dell Hopper (one thousand credits) had been of no assistance.

It might be better to find the value of x. That blasted machine must have some purpose. Granted, it ate dirt. But matter cannot be destroyed; it can be changed into other forms.

Dirt went into the machine; nothing came out.

Nothing visible.

Free energy?'

That was invisible, but could be detected with instruments.

Voltmeter, ammeter – gold leaf –

Gallegher turned the machine on again briefly. Its singing was dangerously loud, but no one rang the door buzzer, and after a minute or two Gallegher snapped the switch back to OFF. He had learned nothing.

Arnie called. The broker had secured the information Gallegher wanted.

' 'Twasn't easy. I had to pull some wires. But I found out why DU stock's been dropping.'

'Thank Heaven for that! Spill it.'

'DU's a sort of exchange, you know. They farm out jobs. This one – it's a big office building to be constructed in downtown Manhattan. Only the contractor hasn't been able to start yet. There's a lot of dough tied up in the deal, and there's a whispering campaign that's hurt the DU stock.'

'Keep talking.'

Arnie went on. 'I got all the info I could, in case. There were two firms bidding on the job.'

'Who?'

'Ajax, and somebody named –'

'Not Smith?'

'That's it,' Arnie said. 'Thaddeus Smith. S-m-e-i-t-h, he spells it.'

There was a long pause. 'S-m-e-i-t-h,' Gallegher repeated at last. 'So that's why the girl at DU couldn't . . . eh? Oh, nothing. I ought to have guessed it.' Sure. When he'd asked Cuff whether Fatty spelled his name with an e or an i, the alderman had said both. Smeith. Ha!

'Smeith got the contract,' Arnie continued. 'He underbid Ajax. However, Ajax had political pull. They got some alderman to clamp down and apply an old statute that put the kibosh on Smeith. He can't do a thing.'

'Why not?'

'Because,' Arnie said, 'the law won't permit him to block Manhattan traffic. It's a question of air rights. Smeith's client – or DU's client, rather – bought the property lately, but air rights over it had been leased for a ninety-nine-year period to Transworld Strato. The stratoliners have their hangar just beyond that property, and you know they're not gyros. They need a straightaway course for a bit before they can angle up. Well, their right of way runs right over the property. Their lease is good. For ninety-nine years they've got the right to use the air over that land, above and over fifty feet above ground level.'

Gallegher squinted thoughtfully. 'How could Smeith expect to put up a building there, then?'

'The new owner possesses the property from fifty feet above soil down to the centre of the earth. Savvy? A big eighty-storey building – most of it underground. It's been done before, but not against political pull. If Smeith fails to fulfill his contract, the job goes to Ajax – and Ajax is hand-in-glove with that alderman.'

'Yeah. Max Cuff,' Gallegher said. 'I've met the lug. Still – what's this statute you mentioned?'

'An old one, pretty much obsolete, but still on the books. It's legal. I checked. You can't interfere with downtown traffic, or upset the stagger system of transport.'

'Well?'

'If you dig a hole for an eighty-storey building,' Arnie said, 'you get a lot of dirt and rock. How can you haul it away without upsetting traffic? I didn't try to figure out how many tons have to be removed.'

'I see,' Gallegher said softly.

'So there it is, on a platinum platter. Smeith took the contract. Now he's stymied. He can't get rid of the dirt he'll be excavating, and pretty soon Ajax will take over and wangle a permit to truck out the material.'

'How – if Smeith can't?'

'Remember the alderman? Well, a few weeks ago some of the streets downtown were blocked off, for repairs. Traffic was rerouted – right by that building site. It's been syphoned off there, and it's so crowded that dirt trucks would tangle up the whole business. Of course it's temporary' – Arnie laughed shortly – 'temporary until Smeith is forced out. Then the traffic will be rerouted again, and Ajax can wangle their permit.'

'Oh.' Gallegher looked over his shoulder at the machine. 'There may be a way –'

The door buzzer rang. Narcissus made a gesture of inquiry.

Gallegher said, 'Do me another favour, Arnie. I want to get Smeith down here to my lab, quick.'

'All right, vise him.'

'His visor's tapped. I don't dare. Can you hop over and bring him here, right away?'

Arnie sighed. 'I certainly earn my commission the hard way. But O.K.'

He faded. Gallegher listened to the door buzzer, frowned, and nodded to the robot. 'See who it is. I doubt if Cuff would try anything now, but – well, find out. I'll be in this closet.'

He stood in the dark, waiting, straining his ears, and wondering. Smeith – he had solved Smeith's problem. The machine ate dirt. The only effective way to get rid of earth without running the risk of a nitrogen explosion.

Eight hundred credits, on account, for a device or a method that would eliminate enough earth – safely – to provide space for an underground office building, a structure that had to be mostly subterranean because of prior-leased air rights.

Fair enough.

Only – *where did that dirt go?*

Narcissus returned and opened the closet door. 'It's a Commander John Wall. He vised from Washington earlier tonight. I told you, remember?'

'John Wall?'

J.W., fifteen hundred credits! The third client!

'Let him in,' Gallegher ordered breathlessly. 'Quick! Is he alone?'

'Yes.'

'Then step it up!'

Narcissus padded off, to return with a grey-haired, stocky figure in the uniform of the space police. Wall grinned briefly at Gallegher, and then his keen eyes shot towards the machine by the window.

'That it?'

Gallegher said, 'Hello, commander. I . . . I'm pretty sure that's it. But I want to discuss some details with you first.'

Wall frowned. 'Money? You can't hold up the government. Or am I misjudging you? Fifty thousand credits should hold you for a while.' His face cleared. 'You have fifteen hundred already; I'm prepared to write you a cheque as soon as you've completed a satisfactory demonstration.'

'Fifty thou –' Gallegher took a deep breath. 'No, it isn't that, of course. I merely want to make certain that I've filled the terms of our agreement. I want to be sure I've met every specification.' If he could only learn what Wall had requested! If he, too, had wanted a machine that ate dirt –

It was a farfetched hope, an impossible coincidence, but Gallegher had to find out. He waved the commander to a chair.

'But we discussed the problem in full detail –'

'A double-check,' Gallegher said smoothly. 'Narcissus, get the commander a drink.'

'Thanks, no.'

'Coffee?'

'I'd be obliged. Well, then – as I told you some weeks ago, we needed a spaceship control – a manual that would meet the requirements of elasticity and tensile strength.'

'Oh-oh,' Gallegher thought.

Wall leaned forward, his eyes brightening. 'A spaceship is necessarily big and complicated. Some manual controls are required. But they cannot move in a straight line; construction necessitates that such controls must turn sharp corners, follow an erratic and eccentric path from *here* to *here*.'

'Well –'

'Thus,' Wall said, 'you want to turn on a water faucet in a house two blocks away. And you want to do it while you're here, in your laboratory. How?'

'String. Wire. Rope.'

'Which could wind around corners as . . . say . . rigid rod could not. However, Mr Gallegher, let me repe my statement of two weeks ago. *That faucet is hard to turn.* And it must be turned often, hundreds of times a day when a ship is in free space. Our toughest wire cables have proved unsatisfactory. The stress and strain snap them. When a cable is *bent*, and when it is also *straight* — you see?'

Gallegher nodded. 'Sure. You can break wire by bending it back and forth often enough.'

'That is the problem we asked you to solve. You said it could be done. Now – have you done it? And how?'

A manual control that could turn corners and withstand repeated stresses. Gallegher eyed the machine. Nitrogen – a thought was moving in the back of his mind, but he could not quite capture it.

The buzzer rang. 'Smeith,' Gallegher thought, and nodded to Narcissus. The robot vanished.

He returned with four men at his heels. Two of them were uniformed officers. The others were, respectively, Smeith and Dell Hopper.

Hopper was smiling savagely. 'Hello, Gallegher,' he said. 'We've been waiting. We weren't fast enough when this man' – he nodded towards Commander Wall – 'came in, but we waited for a second chance.'

Smeith, his plump face puzzled, said, 'Mr Gallegher, what is this? I rang your buzzer, and then these men surrounded me – '

'It's O.K.,' Gallegher said. 'You're on top, at least. Look out that window.'

Smeith obeyed. He popped back in again, beaming.

'That hole – '

'Right. I didn't cart the dirt away, either. I'll give you a demonstration presently.'

'You will in jail,' Hopper said acidly. 'I warned you, Gallegher, that I'm not a man to play around with. I gave you a thousand credits to do a job for me, and you neither did the job nor returned the money.'

Commander Wall was staring, his coffee cup, forgotten, balanced in one hand. An officer moved forward and took Gallegher's arm.

'Wait a minute,' Wall began, but Smeith was quicker.

'I think I owe Mr Gallegher some credits,' he said, snatching out a wallet. 'I've not much more than a thousand on me, but you can take a cheque for the balance, I suppose. If this – gentleman – wants cash, there should be a thousand here.'

Gallegher gulped.

Smeith nodded at him encouragingly. 'You did *my* job for me, you know. I can begin construction – and excavation – tomorrow. Without bothering to get a trucking permit, either.'

Hopper's teeth showed. 'The devil with the money! I'm going to teach this man a lesson! My time is worth plenty, and he's completely upset my schedule. Options, scouts – I've gone ahead on the assumption that he could do what I paid him for, and now he blandly thinks he can wiggle out. Well, Mr Gallegher, you can't. You failed to observe that summons you were handed today, which makes you legally liable to certain penalties – and you're going to suffer them, Gammit!'

Smeith looked around. 'But – I'll stand good for Mr Gallegher. I'll reimburse –'

'No!' Hopper snapped.

'The man says no,' Gallegher murmured. 'It's just my heart's blood he wants. Malevolent little devil, isn't he?'

'You drunken idiot!' Hopper snarled. 'Take him to the jail, officers. Now!'

'Don't worry, Mr Gallegher,' Smeith encouraged. 'I'll have you out in no time. I can pull a few wires myself.'

Gallegher's jaw dropped. He breathed hoarsely, in an asthmatic fashion, as he stared at Smeith, who drew back.

'Wires,' Gallegher whispered. 'And a . . . a stereoscopic screen that can be viewed from any angle. You said – wires!'

'Take him away,' Hopper ordered brusquely.

Gallegher tried to wrench away from the officers holding him. 'Wait a minute! One minute! I've got the answer now. It *must* be the answer. Hopper, I've done what you wanted – and you, too, commander. Let me go.'

Hopper sneered and jerked his thumb towards the door.

Narcissus walked forward, cat-footed. 'Shall I break their heads, chief?' he inquired gently. 'I like blood. It's a primary colour.'

Commander Wall put down his coffee cup and rose, his voice sounding crisp and metallic. 'All right, officers. Let Mr Gallegher go.'

'Don't do it,' Hopper insisted. 'Who are you, anyway? A space captain!'

Wall's weathered cheeks darkened. He brought out a badge in a small leather case. 'Commander Wall,' he said. 'Administrative Space Commission. You' – he pointed to Narcissus – 'I'm deputising you as a government agent, *pro tem*. If these officers don't release Mr Gallegher in five seconds, go on and break their heads.'

But that was unnecessary. The Space Commission was *big*. It had the government behind it, and local officials were, by comparison, small potatoes. The officers hastily released Gallegher and tried to look as though they'd never touched him.

Hopper seemed ready to explode. 'By what right do you interfere with justice, Commander?' he demanded.

'Right of priority. The government needs a device Mr Gallegher has made for us. He deserves a hearing, at least.'

'He does *not*!'

Wall eyed Hopper coldly. 'I think he said, a few moments ago, that he had fulfilled your commission also.'

'With that?' The big shot pointed to the machine. 'Does that look like a stereoscopic screen?'

Gallegher said, 'Get me an ultraviolet, Narcissus. Fluorescent.' He went to the device, praying that his guess was right. But it had to be. There was no other possible answer. Extract nitrogen from dirt to rock, extract all gaseous content, and you have inert matter.

Gallegher touched the switch. The machine started to sing 'St James Infirmary.' Commander Wall looked startled and slightly less sympathetic. Hopper snorted. Smeith ran to the window and ecstatically watched the long tentacles eat dirt, swirling madly in the moonlit pit below.

'The lamp, Narcissus.'

It was already hooked up on an extension chord. Gallegher moved it slowly about the machine. Presently he had reached the grooved wheel at the extreme end, farthest from the window.

Something fluoresced.

It fluoresced blue – emerging from the little valve in the metal cylinder, winding about the grooved wheel, and piling in coils on the laboratory floor. Gallegher touched the switch; as the machine stopped, the valve snapped shut, cutting off the blue, cryptic thing that emerged from the cylinder. Gallegher picked up the coil. As he moved the light away, it vanished. He brought the lamp closer – it reappeared.

'Here you are, commander,' he said. 'Try it.'

Wall squinted at the fluorescence. 'Tensile strength?'

'Plenty,' Gallegher said. 'It has to be. Nonorganic, mineral content of solid earth, compacted and compressed into wire. Sure, it's got tensile strength. Only you couldn't support a ton weight with it.'

Wall nodded. 'Of course not. It would cut through steel like a thread through butter. Fine, Mr Gallegher. We'll have to make tests –'

'Go ahead. It'll stand up. You can run this wire around corners all you want, from one end of a spaceship to another, and it'll never snap under stress. It's too thin. It won't – it can't – be strained unevenly, because it's too thin. A wire cable couldn't do it. You needed flexibility that wouldn't cancel tensile strength. The only possible answer was a thin, tough wire.'

The commander grinned. That was enough.

'We'll have the routine tests,' he said. 'Need any money now, though? We'll advance anything you need, within reason – say up to ten thousand.'

Hopper pushed forward. 'I never ordered wire, Gallegher. So you haven't fulfilled my commission.'

Gallegher didn't answer. He was adjusting his lamp. The wire changed from blue to yellow, and then to red.

'This is your screen, wise guy,' Gallegher said. 'See the pretty colours?'

'Naturally I see them! I'm not blind. But – '

'Different colours, depending on how many angstroms I use. Thus. Red. Blue. Red again. Yellow. And when I turn off the lamp – '

The wire Wall still held became invisible.

Hopper closed his mouth with a snap. He leaned forward, cocking his head to one side.

Gallegher said, 'The wire's got the same refractive index as air. I made it that way, on purpose.' He had the grace to blush slightly. Oh, well – he could buy Gallegher Plus a drink later.

'On purpose?'

'You wanted a stereoscopic screen which could be viewed from any angle without optical distortion. And in colour – that goes without saying, these days. Well, here it is.'

Hopper breathed hard.

Gallegher beamed at him. 'Take a box frame and string each square with this wire. Make a mesh screen. Do that on all four sides. String enough wires inside of the box. You have, in effect, an invisible cube, made of wire. All right. Use ultraviolet to project your film or your television, and you have patterns of fluorescence, depending on the angstrom strength patterns. In other words – a picture. A coloured picture. A three-dimensional picture, because it's projected onto an invisible cube. And, finally, one that can be viewed from any angle without distortion, because it does more than give an optical illusion of stereoscopic vision – it's actually a three-dimensional picture. Catch?'

Hopper said feebly, 'Yes. I understand. You . . . why didn't you tell me this before?'

Gallegher changed the subject in haste. 'I'd like some police protection, Commander Wall. A crook named Max Cuff has been trying to get his hooks on this machine. His thugs kidnapped me this afternoon, and – '

'Interfering with government business, eh?' Wall said grimly. 'I know these jackpot politicians. Max Cuff won't trouble you any more – if I may use the visor?'

Smeith beamed at the prospect of Cuff getting it in the neck. Gallegher caught his eye. There was a pleasant, jovial gleam in it, and somehow, it reminded Gallegher to offer his guests drinks. Even the commander accepted this time, turning from his finished visor call to take the glass Narcissus handed him.

'Your laboratory will be under guard,' he told Gallegher. 'So you'll have no further trouble.'

He drank, stood up, and shook Gallegher's hand. 'I must make my report. Good luck, and many thanks. We'll call you tomorrow.'

He went out, after the two officers. Hopper, gulping his cocktail, said, 'I ought to apologise. But it's all water under the bridge, eh, old man?'

'Yeah,' Gallegher said. 'You owe me some money.'

'Trench will mail you the cheque. And . . . uh . . . and – ' His voice died away.

'Something?'

'N-nothing,' Hopper said, putting down his glass and turning green. 'A little fresh air . . . urp!'

The door slammed behind him. Gallegher and Smeith eyed each other curiously.

'Odd,' Smeith said.

'A visitation from heaven, maybe,' Gallegher surmised. 'The mills of the gods – '

'I see Hopper's gone,' Narcissus said, appearing with fresh drinks.

'Yeah. Why?'

'I thought he would. I gave him a Mickey Finn,' the robot explained. 'He never looked at me once. I'm not exactly vain, but a man so insensitive to beauty deserves a lesson. Now don't disturb me. I'm going into the kitchen and practice dancing, and you can get your own liquor out of the organ. You may come and watch if you like.'

Narcissus spun out of the lab, his innards racing. Gallegher sighed.

'That's the way it goes,' he said.

'What?'

'Oh, I dunno. Everything. I get, for example, orders for three entirely different things, and I get drunk and make a gadget that answers all three problems. My subconscious does things the easy way. Unfortunately, it's the hard way for me – after I sober up.'

'Then why sober up?' Smeith asked cogently. 'How does that liquor organ work?'

Gallegher demonstrated. 'I feel lousy,' he confided. 'What I need is either a week's sleep, or else – '

'What?'

'A drink. Here's how. You know – one item still worries me.'

'What, again?'

'The question of why that machine sings "St James Infirmary" when it's operating.'

'It's a good song,' Smith said.

'Sure, but my subconscious works logically. Crazy logic, I'll admit. Nevertheless – '

'Here's how,' Smeith said.

Gallegher relaxed. He was beginning to feel like himself again. A warm, rosy glow. There was money in the bank. The police had been called off. Max Cuff was, no doubt, suffering for his sins. And a heavy thumping announced that Narcissus was dancing in the kitchen.

It was past midnight when Gallegher choked on a drink and said, 'Now I remember!'

'Swmpmf,' Smeith said, startled. 'Whatzat?'

'I feel like singing.'

'So what?'

'Well, I feel like singing "St James Infirmary." '

'Go right ahead,' Smeith invited.

'But not alone,' Gallegher amplified. 'I *always* like to sing that when I get tight, but I figure it sounds best as duet. Only I was alone when I was working on that machine.'

'Ah?'

'I must have built in a recording play-back,' Gallegher said, lost in a vast wonder to the mad resources and curious deviations of Gallegher Plus. 'My goodness. A machine that performs four operations at once. It eats dirt, turns out a spaceship manual control, makes a stereoscopic nondistorting projection screen, and sings a duet with me. How strange it all seems.'

Smeith considered. 'You're a genius.'

'That, of course. Hm-m-m.' Gallegher got up, turned on the machine, and returned to perch atop Bubbles. Smeith, fascinated by the spectacle, went to hang on the window sill and watch the flashing tentacles eat dirt. Invisible wire spun out along the grooved wheel. The calm of the night was shattered by the more or less melodious tones of the 'St James Infirmary.'

Above the lugubrious voice of the machine rose a deeper bass, passionately exhorting someone unnamed to search the wild world over.

> 'But you'll never find
> Another sweet *ma-a-ahn* like me.'

Gallegher Plus was singing, too.

THE WORLD IS MINE

'Let me in!' shrilled the rabbity little creature outside the window. 'Let me in! The world is mine!'

Gallegher automatically rolled off his couch, reeling under the not unexpected gravity-pull of a colossal hangover, and gazed about in a bleary fashion. His laboratory, gloomy in grey morning light, swam into visibility around him. Two dynamos, decorated with tinsel, seemed to stare at him as though resentful of their festive garments. Why tinsel? Probably the result of those Tom-and-Jerries, Gallegher thought wanly. He must have decided that last night was Christmas Eve.

Brooding on the thought, he was recalled to himself by a repetition of the squeaky cry that had awakened him. Gallegher turned carefully, holding his head between steadying palms. A face, small, furry and fantastic, was regarding him steadfastly through the plexoglas of the nearest windows.

It was not the sort of face to see after a drinking bout. The ears were huge, round and furry, the eyes enormous, and a pink button of a nose shivered and twitched. Again the creature cried:

'Let me in! I gotta conquer the world!'

'What now?' Gallegher said under his breath, as he went to the door and opened it. The back yard was empty save for three remarkable animals that now stood in a row facing him, their furry white bodies fat and pushy as pillows. Three pink noses twitched. Three pairs of golden eyes watched Gallegher steadily. Three pairs of dumpy legs moved in unison as the creatures scuttled over the threshold, nearly upsetting Gallegher as they rushed past.

That was that. Gallegher went hurriedly to his liquor organ, mixed a quick one, and syphoned it down. He felt a little better – not much. The three guests were sitting or standing in a row, as usual, watching him unblinkingly.

Gallegher sat down on the couch. 'Who are you?' he demanded.

'We're Lybblas,' said the foremost.

'Ah.' Gallegher thought for a moment. 'What are Lybblas?'

'Us,' the Lybblas said.

It seemed to be a deadlock, broken when a shapeless bundle of blankets in one corner stirred and exposed a nut-brown, withered face, seamed with far too many wrinkles. A man emerged, thin, ancient and bright-eyed. 'Well, stupid,' he said, 'so you let 'em in, eh?'

Gallegher thought back. The old fellow, of course, was his grandfather, in Manhattan for a visit from his Maine farm. Last night – Hm-m-m. What had happened last night? Dimly he recalled Grandpa boasting about his capacity for liquor, and the inevitable result: a contest. Grandpa had won. But what else had happened?

He inquired.

'Don't you know?' Grandpa said.

'I never know,' Gallegher told him wearily. 'That's how I invent things. I get tight and work 'em out. Never know how, exactly. I invent by ear.'

'I know,' Grandpa nodded. 'That's just what you did. See that?' He pointed to a corner, where stood a tall, enigmatic machine Gallegher did not recognise. It buzzed quietly to itself.

'Oh? What is it?'

'You *made* it. Yourself. Last night.'

'I did, huh? Why?'

'How should I know?' Grandpa scowled. 'You started fiddling with gadgets and set the thing up. Then you said it was a time machine. Then you turned it on. Focused it into the back yard, for safety's sake. We went out to watch, and those three little guys popped out of empty air. We came back – in a hurry, I recall. Where's a drink?'

The Lybblas began to dance up and down impatiently. 'It was cold out there last night,' one of them said reproachfully. 'You should have let us in. The world is ours.'

Gallegher's long, horselike face grew longer. 'So. Well, if I built a time machine – though I don't remember a thing about it – you must have come out of some different time. Right?'

'Sure,' one of the Lybblas agreed. 'Five hundred years or so.'

'You're not – human? I mean – we're not going to evolve into you?'

'No,' said the fattest Lybbla complacently, 'it would take thousands of years for you to evolve into the dominant species. We're from Mars.'

'Mars – the future. Oh. You – talk English.'

'There are Earth people on Mars in our day. Why not? We read English, talk the lingo, know everything.'

Gallegher muttered under his breath. 'And you're the dominant species on Mars?'

'Well, not exactly,' a Lybbla hesitated. 'Not *all* Mars.'

'Not even half of Mars,' said another.

'Just Koordy Valley,' the third announced. 'But Koordy Valley is the centre of the universe. Very highly civilised. We have books. About Earth and so on. We're going to conquer Earth, by the way.'

'Are you?' Gallegher said blankly.

'Yes. We couldn't in our own time, you know, because Earth people wouldn't let us, but now it'll be easy. You'll all be our slaves,' the Lybbla said happily. He was about eleven inches tall.

'You got any weapons?' Grandpa asked.

'We don't need 'em. We're clever. We know everything. Our memories are capacious as anything. We can build disintegrator guns, heat rays, spaceships – '

'No, we can't,' another Lybbla countered. 'We haven't any fingers.' That was true. They had furry mittens, fairly useless, Gallegher thought.

'Well,' said the first Lybbla, 'we'll get Earth people to build us some weapons.'

Grandpa downed a shot of whisky and shuddered. 'Do these things happen all the time around here?' he wanted to know. 'I'd heard you were a big-shot scientist, but I figured scientists made atom-smashers and stuff like that. What good's a time machine?'

'It brought us,' a Lybbla said. 'Oh, happy day for Earth.'

'That,' Gallegher told him, 'is a matter of opinion. Before you get around to sending an ultimatum to Washington, would you care for a spot of refreshment? A saucer of milk or something?'

'We're not *animals*!' the fattest Lybbla said. 'We drink out of cups, we do.'

Gallegher brought three cups, heated some milk, and poured. After a brief hesitation, he put the cups on the floor. The tables were all far too high for the small creatures. The Lybblas, piping, 'Thank you,' politely, seized the cups between their hind feet and began to lap up the milk with long pink tongues.

'Good,' one said.

'Don't talk with your mouth full,' cautioned the fattest Lybbla, who seemed to be the leader.

Gallegher relaxed on the couch and looked at Grandpa. 'This time machine business –' he said. 'I can't remember a thing about it. We'll have to send the Lybblas back home. It'll take me a while to work out the method. Sometimes I think I drink too much.'

'Perish the thought,' Grandpa said. 'When I was your age, I didn't need a time machine to materialise little fellers a foot high. Corn likker did it,' he added, smacking withered lips. 'You work too hard, that's what it is.'

'Well –' Gallegher said helplessly. 'I can't help it. What was my idea in building the thing, anyhow?'

'Dunno. You kept talking about killing your own grandfather or something. Or foretelling the future. I couldn't make head nor tail of it myself.'

'Wait a minute. I remember – vaguely. The old time-travelling paradox. Killing your own grandfather –'

'I picked up an axe handle when you started in on that,' Grandpa said. 'Not quite ready to cash in my chips yet, young fellow.' He cackled. 'I can remember the gasoline age – but I'm still pretty spry.'

'What happened then?'

'The little guys came through the machine or whatever it

94

was. You said you hadn't adjusted it right, so you fixed it.'

'I wonder what I had in mind,' Gallegher pondered.

The Lybblas had finished their milk. 'We're through,' said the fat one. 'Now we'll conquer the world. Where'll we begin?'

Gallegher shrugged. 'I fear I can't advise you, gentlemen. I've never had the inclination myself. Wouldn't have the faintest idea how to go about it.'

'First we destroy the big cities,' said the smallest Lybbla excitedly, 'then we capture pretty girls and hold them for ransom or something. Then everybody's scared and we win.'

'How do you figure that out?' Gallegher asked.

'Its in the books. That's how it's always done. We know. We'll be tyrants and beat everybody. I want some more milk, please.'

'So do I,' said two other piping little voices.

Grinning, Gallegher served. 'You don't seem much surprised by finding yourselves here.'

'That's in the books, too.' *Lap-lap.*

'You mean – this?' Gallegher's eyebrows went up.

'Oh, no. But all about time-travelling. All the novels in our era are about science and things. We read lots. There isn't much else to do in the Valley,' the Lybbla ended, a bit sadly.

'Is that all you read?'

'No, we read everything. Technical books on science as well as novels. How disintegrators are made and so on. We'll tell you how to make weapons for us.'

'Thanks. That sort of literature is open to the public?'

'Sure. Why not?'

'I should think it would be dangerous.'

'So should I,' the fat Lybbla said thoughtfully, 'but it isn't, somehow.'

Gallegher pondered. 'Could you tell me how to make a heat ray, for example?'

'Yes,' was the excited reply, 'and then we'd destroy the big cities and capture –'

'I know. Pretty girls and hold them for ransom. Why?'

'We know what's what,' a Lybbla said shrewdly. 'We

read books, we do.' He spilled his cup, looked at the puddle of milk, and let his ears droop disconsolately.

The other two Lybblas hastily patted him on the back. 'Don't cry,' the biggest one urged.

'I gotta,' the Lybbla said. 'It's in the books.'

'You have it backwards. You *don't* cry over spilt milk.'

'Do. Will,' said the recalcitrant Lybbla, and began to weep.

Gallegher brought him more milk. 'About this heat ray,' he said. 'Just how –'

'Simple,' the fat Lybbla said, and explained.

It *was* simple. Grandpa didn't get it, of course, but he watched interestedly as Gallegher went to work. Within half an hour the job was completed. It was a heat ray, too. It burned a hole through a closet door.

'*Whew*!' Gallegher breathed, watching smoke rise from the charred wood. 'That's something!' He examined the small metal cylinder in his hand.

'It kills people, too,' the fat Lybbla murmured. 'Like the man in the back yard.'

'Yes, it – What? The man in –'

'The back yard. We sat on him for a while, but he got cold after a bit. There's a hole burned through his chest.'

'You did it,' Gallegher accused, gulping.

'No. He came out of time, too, I expect. There was a heat-ray hole in him.'

'Who . . . who was he?'

'Never saw him before in my life,' the fat Lybbla said, losing interest. 'I want more milk.' He leaped to the bench top and peered through the window at the towers of Manhattan's skyline. '*Wheeeee*! The world is ours!'

The doorbell sang. Gallegher, a little pale, said, 'Grandpa, see what it is. Send him away in any case. Probably a bill collector. They're used to being turned away. Oh, Lord! I've never committed a murder before –'

'I have,' Grandpa murmured, departing. He did not clarify the statement.

Gallegher went into the back yard, accompanied by the scuttling small figures of the Lybblas. The worst had happened. In the middle of the rose garden lay a dead body. It was the corpse of a man, bearded and ancient, quite bald, and wearing curious garments made, apparently, of flexible, tinted cellophane. Through his tunic and chest was the distinctive hole burned by a heat-ray projector.

'He looks familiar, somehow,' Gallegher decided. 'Dunno why. Was he dead when he came out of time?'

'Dead but warm,' one of the Lybblas said. 'That was nice.'

Gallegher repressed a shudder. Horrid little creatures. However, they must be harmless, or they wouldn't have been allowed access to dangerous information in their own time-era. Gallegher was far less troubled by the Lybblas than by the presence of the corpse. Grandpa's protesting voice came to his ears.

The Lybblas scurried under convenient bushes and disappeared as three men entered the back yard, escorting Grandpa. Gallegher, at sight of blue uniforms and brass buttons, dropped the heat-ray projector into a garden bed and surreptitiously kicked dirt over it. He assumed what he hoped was an ingratiating smile.

'Hello, boys. I was just going to notify Headquarters. Somebody dropped a dead man in my yard.'

Two of the newcomers were officers, Gallegher saw, burly, distrustful and keen-eyed. The third was a small, dapper man with grey-blond hair plastered close to his narrow skull, and a pencil-thin moustache. He looked rather like a fox.

He was wearing an Honorary Badge – which meant little or much, depending on the individual.

'Couldn't keep 'em out,' Grandpa said. 'You're in for it now, young fellow.'

'He's joking,' Gallegher told the officers. 'Honest, I was just going to –'

'Save it. What's your name?'

Gallegher said it was Gallegher.

'Uh-huh.' The officer knelt to examine the body. He blew out his breath sharply. '*Wh-ew*! What did you do to him?'

'Nothing. When I came out this morning, here he was.

97

Maybe he fell out of a window up there somewhere.' Gallegher pointed up vaguely to overshadowing skyscrapers.

'He didn't. Not a bone broken. Looks like you stabbed him with a red-hot poker,' the officer remarked. 'Who is he?'

'I don't know. Never saw him before. Who told you –'

'Never leave bodies in plain sight, Mr Gallegher. Somebody in a penthouse – like up there – might see it and 'vise Headquarters.'

'Oh. Oh, I see.'

'We'll find out who killed the guy,' the officer said sardonically. 'Don't worry about that. And we'll find out who he is. Unless you want to talk now and save yourself trouble.'

'Circumstantial evidence –'

'Save it.' The air was patted with a large palm. 'I'll 'vise the boys to come down with the coroner. Where's the 'visor?'

'Show him, Grandpa,' Gallegher said wearily. The dapper blond man took a step forward. His voice was crisp with authority.

'Groarty, take a look around the house while Banister's televising. I'll stay here with Mr Gallegher.'

'O.K., Mr Cantrell.' The officers departed with Grandpa.

Cantrell said, 'Excuse me,' and came forward swiftly. He dug slim fingers into the dirt at Gallegher's feet and brought up the heat-ray tube. Smiling slightly, Cantrell examined the projector.

Gallegher's heart nosedived. 'Wonder where that came from?' he gulped, in a frantic attempt at deception.

'You put it there,' Cantrell told him. 'I saw you do it. Luckily the officers didn't. I think I'll keep it.' He slipped the small tube into his pocket. 'Exhibit A. That's a damn peculiar wound in your corpse –'

'It's not my corpse!'

'It's in your yard. I'm interested in weapons, Mr Gallegher. What sort of gadget is this?'

'Uh – just a flashlight.'

Cantrell took it out and aimed it at Gallegher. 'I see. If I

98

press this button – '

'It's a heat ray,' Gallegher said quickly, ducking. 'For goodness sake, be careful!'

'Hm-m-m. You made it?'

'I . . . yes.'

'And you killed this man with it?'

'*No*!'

'I suggest,' Cantrell said, repocketing the tube, 'that you keep your mouth shut about this. Once the police get their hands on the weapon, your goose will be cooked. As it is, no known gun can make a wound like that. Proof will be difficult. For some reason, I believe you didn't kill the man, Mr Gallegher. I don't know why. Perhaps because of your reputation. You're known to be eccentric, but you're also known to be a pretty good inventor.'

'Thanks,' Gallegher said. 'But . . . the heat ray's mine.'

'Want me to mark it Exhibit A?'

'It's yours.'

'Fine,' Cantrell said, grinning. 'I'll see what I can do for you.'

He couldn't do much, as it proved. Almost anyone could wangle an Honorary Badge, but political pull didn't necessarily mean a police in. The machinery of the law, once started, couldn't easily be stopped. Luckily the rights of the individual were sacrosanct in this day and age, but that was chiefly because of the development of communication. A criminal simply couldn't make a getaway. They told Gallegher not to leave Manhattan, secure in the knowledge that if he tried, the televisor system would quickly lay him by the heels. It wasn't even necessary to set guards. Gallegher's three-dimensional photo was already on file at the transportation centres of Manhattan, so that if he tried to book passage on a stratoliner or a seasled, he could be recognised instantly and sent home with a scolding.

The baffled coroner had superintended the removal of the body to the morgue. The police and Cantrell had departed. Grandpa, the three Lybblas, and Gallegher sat in the laboratory and looked dazedly at one another.

'Time machine,' Gallegher said, pressing buttons on his

liquor organ. 'Bah! Why do I do these things?'

'They can't prove you're guilty,' Grandpa suggested.

'Trials cost money. If I don't get a good lawyer, I'm sunk.'

'Won't the court give you a lawyer?'

'Sure, but that isn't the way it works out. Jurisprudence has developed into something like a chess game these days. It takes a gang of experts to know all the angles. I could be convicted if I overlooked even one loophole. Attorneys have the balance of political power, Grandpa. So they've got their lobbies. Guilt and innocence don't mean as much as getting the best lawyers. And that takes money.'

'You won't need money,' the fattest Lybbla said. 'When we conquer the world, we'll set up our own monetary system!'

Gallegher ignored the creature. 'You got any dough, Grandpa?'

'Nope. Never needed much up in Maine.'

Gallegher cast desperate eyes around the laboratory. 'Maybe I can sell something. That heat-ray projector – but no. I'd be sunk if anybody knew I'd had the thing. I only hope Cantrell keeps it under cover. The time machine – ' He wandered over and stared at the cryptic object. 'Wish I could remember how it works. Or why.'

'You made it, didn't you?'

'My subconscious made it. My subconscious does the *damnedest* things. Wonder what that lever's for.' Gallegher investigated. Nothing happened. 'It's fearfully intricate. Since I don't know how it works, I can't very well raise money on it.'

'Last night,' Grandpa said thoughtfully, 'you were yelling about somebody named Hellwig who'd given you a commission.'

A light came into Gallegher's eyes, but died swiftly. 'I remember. A pompous big shot who's a complete nonentity. Terrific vanity complex. He wants to be famous. Said he'd pay me plenty if I could fix him up.'

'Well, why don't you?'

'How?' Gallegher demanded. 'I could invent something and let him pretend he'd made it, but nobody'd ever believe a pot-head like Rufus Hellwig could do more than add two and two. If that. Still – '

Gallegher tried the televisor. Presently a large, fat white face grew on the screen. Rufus Hellwig was an immensely fat, bald-headed man with a pug nose and the general air of a Mongolian idiot. By virtue of money, he had achieved power, but public recognition eluded him, to his intense distress. Nobody admired him. He was laughed at – simply because he had nothing but money. Some tycoons can carry this off well. Hellwig couldn't. He scowled at Gallegher now.

'Morning. Anything yet?'

'I'm working on something. But it's expensive. I need an advance.'

'Oh,' Hellwig said unpleasantly, 'you do, eh? I gave you an advance last week.'

'You could have,' Gallegher said. 'I don't remember it.'

'You were drunk.'

'Oh. Was I?'

'You were quoting Omar.'

'What part?'

'Something about spring vanishing with the rose.'

'Then I was drunk,' Gallegher said sadly. 'How much did I hook you for?'

Hellwig told him. The scientist shook his head.

'It just runs through my fingers like water. Oh, well. Give me more money.'

'You're crazy,' Hellwig growled. 'Show results first. Then you can write your own ticket.'

'Not in the gas chamber I can't,' Gallegher said, but the tycoon had broken the beam. Grandpa took a drink and sighed.

'What about this guy Cantrell? Maybe he can help.'

'I doubt it. He had me on the spot. Still has, in fact. I don't know anything about him.'

'Well, I'm going back to Maine,' Grandpa said.

Gallegher sighed. 'Running out on me?'

'Well, if you've got more liquor – '

'You can't leave, anyway. Accessory before the fact or

something of the sort. Sure you can't raise any money?'

Grandpa was sure. Gallegher looked at the time machine again and sighed unhappily. Damn his subconscious, anyway! That was the trouble with knowing science by ear, instead of the usual way. The fact that Gallegher was a genius didn't prevent him from getting into fantastic scrapes. Once before, he remembered, he'd invented a time machine of sorts, but it hadn't worked like this one. The thing sat sullenly in its corner, an incredibly complicated gadget of glistening metal, its focus of materialisation aimed somewhere in the back yard.

'I wonder what Cantrell wanted with that heat ray,' Gallegher mused.

The Lybblas had been investigating the laboratory with interested golden eyes and twitching pink noses. Now they came back to sit in a row before Gallegher.

'When we conquer the world, you won't have to worry,' they told the man.

'Thanks,' Gallegher said. 'That helps a lot. The immediate need, however, is dough, and lots of it. I must get me a lawyer.'

'Why?'

'So I won't be convicted for murder. It's hard to explain. You're not familiar with this time sector –' Gallegher's jaw dropped. 'Oh-oh. I got an idea.'

'What is it?'

'You told me how to make that heat ray. Well, if you can give me an angle on something else – something that'll bring in quick money –'

'Of course. We'll be glad to do that. But a mental hookup would help.'

'Never mind that. Start talking. Or let me ask questions. Yeah. What sort of gadgets do you have in your world?'

The doorbell sang. The visitor was a police detective, Mahoney, a tall, sardonic-looking chap with slick blue-black hair. The Lybblas, undesirous of attracting attention before they'd worked out a plan for world conquest, scuttled out of sight. Mahoney greeted the two men with a casual nod.

'Morning. We ran into a little snag at Headquarters. A mix-up – nothing important.'

'That's too bad,' Gallegher said. 'Have a drink?'

'No, thanks. I want to take your fingerprints. And your eyeprints, if you don't mind.'

'O.K. Go ahead.'

Mahoney called in a lab man who had accompanied him. Gallegher's fingertips were pressed against sensitised film, and a specially lensed camera snapped the pattern of rods, cones and blood vessels inside his eyes. Mahoney watched, scowling. Presently the lab man showed the result of his labours to the detective.

'That tears it,' Mahoney said.

'What?' Gallegher wanted to know.

'Nothing much. That corpse in your back yard – '

'Yeah?'

'His prints are the same as yours. And his eye-pattern, too. Even plastic surgery couldn't account for that. 'Who was that stiff, Gallegher?'

The scientist blinked. 'Jumping tomcats! My prints? It's crazy.'

'Crazy as the devil,' Mahoney agreed. 'Sure you don't know the answer?'

The lab man, at the window, let out a long whistle. 'Hey, Mahoney,' he called. 'Come over here a minute. Want to show you something.'

'It'll keep.'

'Not long, in this weather,' the lab man said. 'It's another corpse, out there in the garden.'

Gallegher exchanged horrified glances with Grandpa. He sat motionless even after the detective and his companion had tumultuously rushed out of the laboratory. Cries came from the back yard.

'Another one?' Grandpa said.

Gallegher nodded. 'Certainly looks like it. Come on. We'd better – '

'We'd better make a run for it!'

'No soap. Let's see what it is this time.'

It was, as Gallegher already knew, a body. It, too, had been killed by a narrow hole burned through the fabricloth vest and the torso beneath. A heat-ray blast, undoubtedly. The man himself gave Gallegher a poignant shock – with good reason. He was looking at his own corpse.

Not quite. The dead man looked about ten years older than Gallegher, the face was thinner, the dark hair sprinkled with grey. And the costume was of an extreme cut, unfamiliar and eccentric. But the likeness was unmistakable.

'Uh-huh,' Mahoney said, looking at Gallegher. 'Your twin brother, I suppose?'

'I'm as surprised as you are,' the scientist said feebly.

Mahoney clicked his teeth together. He took out a cigar and lit it with trembling fingers.

'Now look,' he said, 'I don't know what kind of funny business is going on here, but I don't like it. I got goose bumps. If this stiff's eyeprints and fingerprints tally with yours, I . . . won't . . . like . . . it. I'll hate it like hell. I don't want to feel that I'm going nuts. See?'

'It's impossible,' the lab man said.

Mahoney shepherded them into the house and televised Headquarters. 'Inspector? About that body that was brought in an hour ago – Gallegher, you know – '

'Found it?' the inspector asked.

Mahoney blinked. 'Huh? I mean the one with the funny fingerprints – '

'I know what you mean. Have you found it or haven't you?'

'But it's in the morgue!'

'It was,' the inspector said, 'up to about ten minutes ago. Then it was snatched. Right out of the morgue.'

Mahoney let that soak in briefly, while he licked his lips. 'Inspector,' he said presently, 'I've got another body for you. A different one, this time. I just found it in Gallegher's back yard. Same circumstances.'

'*What*?'

'Yeah. A hole burned through the chest. And it looks like Gallegher.'

'Looks like him – What about those prints I told you to check?'

'I did. The answer is yes.'

'It couldn't be.'

'Wait'll you see the new corpse,' Mahoney growled. 'Send the boys over, will you?'

'Right away. What sort of crazy business –'

The connection broke. Gallegher passed drinks and collapsed on the couch, manipulating the liquor organ. He felt giddy.

'One thing,' Grandpa said, 'you can't be tried for murdering that first body. If it's been stolen, there's no *corpus delicti*.'

'I'll be – That's right!' Gallegher sat up. 'Isn't that so, Mahoney?'

The detective hooded his eyes. 'Sure. Technically. Only don't forget what I just found outside. You can be gassed for his murder, once you're convicted.'

'Oh.' Gallegher lay back. 'That's right. But I didn't kill him.'

'That's your story.'

'O.K. I'm sticking to it. Wake me up when the fuss is over. I've got some thinking to do.' Gallegher slipped the syphon into his mouth, adjusted it to a slow trickle, and relaxed, absorbing cognac. He shut his eyes and pondered. The answer eluded him.

Abstractedly Gallegher realised that the room was filling, that the routine was gone over again. He answered questions with half his mind. In the end, the police left, bearing the second body. Gallegher's brain, stimulated by alcohol, was sharper now. His subconscious was taking over.

'I got it,' he told Grandpa. 'I hope. Let's see.' He went to the time machine and fiddled with levers. 'Oh-oh. I can't shut it off. It must have been set to a definite cycle pattern. I'm beginning to remember what happened last night.'

'About foretelling the future?' Grandpa asked.

'Uh-huh. Didn't we get in an argument about whether a man could foretell his own death?'

'Right.'

'Then that's the answer. I set the machine to foretell my own death. It follows the temporal line, catches up with my

105

own future *in articulo mortis*, and yanks my body back to this time sector. My future body, I mean.'

'You're crazy,' Grandpa suggested.

'No, that's the angle, all right,' Gallegher insisted. 'That first body was myself, at the age of seventy or eighty. I'm going to die then. I'll be killed, apparently, by a heat ray. In forty years from now or thereabouts,' he finished thoughtfully. 'Hm-m-m. Cantrell's got that ray projector –'

Grandpa made a face of distaste. 'What about the second corpse, then? You can't fit that in, I bet.'

'Sure I can. Parallel time developments. Variable futures. Probability lines. You've heard that theory.'

'Nope.'

'Well – it's the idea that there are an infinity of possible futures. If you change the present, you automatically switch into a different future. Like throwing a switch in a railroad yard. If you hadn't married Grandma, I wouldn't be here now. See?'

'Nope,' Grandpa said, taking another drink.

Gallegher went ahead, anyway. 'According to pattern *a*, I'm going to be killed by a heat ray when I'm seventy or so. That's one variable. Well, I brought back my dead body along the temporal line, and it appeared in the present. And, naturally, it altered the present. Originally, in pattern *a*, there was no place for the eighty-year-old dead body of Gallegher. It was introduced and changed the future. We automatically switched into another time track.'

'Pretty silly, eh?' Grandpa mumbled.

'Shut up, Grandpa. I'm working this out. The second track – pattern *b* – is in operation now. And in that track I'm going to be killed by a heat ray when I'm about forty-five. Since the time machine's set to bring back my body the minute it's killed, it did just that – materialised my forty-five-year-old corpse. At which the eighty-year-old corpse vanished.'

'Hah!'

'It had to. It was nonexistent in pattern *b*. When pattern *b* jelled, pattern *a* simply wasn't there any more. Likewise the first corpse.'

Grandpa's eyes lit up suddenly. 'I get it,' he said,

smacking his lips. 'Clever of you. You're going to plead insanity, eh?'

'Bah,' Gallegher snarled, and went to the time machine. He tried vainly to turn it off. It wouldn't turn off. It seemed to be fixed irrevocably in its business of materialising Gallegher's future probable corpses.

What would happen next? Temporal pattern b had taken over. But the b corpse wasn't intended to exist in this particular present. It was an x factor.

And b plus x would equal c. A new variable, and a new cadaver. Gallegher cast a harried glance into the back yard. As yet, it was empty. Thank God for small mercies.

At any rate, he thought, they couldn't convict him of murdering himself. Or could they? Would the law about suicide hold? Ridiculous. He hadn't committed suicide; he was still alive.

But if he was still alive, he couldn't be dead. Utterly confused, Gallegher fled to the couch, gulped strong drink, and longed for death. He foresaw a court battle of impossible contradictions and paradoxes – a battle of the century. Without the best lawyer on Earth, he'd be doomed.

A new thought came, and he laughed sardonically. Suppose he were to be convicted of murder and gassed? If he died in the present, his future corpse would instantly vanish – naturally. No *corpus delicti*. Inevitably – oh, very inevitably – he would be vindicated after he died.

The prospect failed to cheer him.

Reminded of the need for action, Gallegher yelled for the Lybblas. They had got into the cookie jar, but responded guiltily to his summons, brushing crumbs from their whiskers with furry paws. 'We want milk,' the fattest one said. 'The world is ours.'

'Yes,' said another, 'we'll destroy all the cities and then hold pretty girls for –'

'Leave it,' Gallegher told them tiredly. 'The world will wait. I can't. I've got to invent something in a hurry so I can get some money and hire a lawyer. I can't spend the rest of my life being indicted for my future corpses' murders.'

'You talk like a madman,' Grandpa said helpfully.

'Go away. Far away. I'm busy.'

Grandpa shrugged, donned a topcoat, and went out. Gallegher returned to his cross-questioning of the three Lybblas.

They were, he found, singularly unhelpful. It wasn't that they were recalcitrant; on the contrary, they were only too glad to oblige. But they had little idea of what Gallegher wanted. Moreover, their small minds were filled, to the exclusion of all else, with their own fond delusion. The world was theirs. It was difficult for them to realise that other problems existed.

Nevertheless, Gallegher persevered. Finally he got a clue to what he wanted, after the Lybblas had again referred to a mental hookup. Such devices, he learned, were fairly common in the world of the future. They had been invented by a man named Gallegher, long ago, the fat Lybbla said stupidly, not grasping the obvious implication.

Gallegher gulped. He *had* to make a mental hookup machine now, apparently, since that was in the cards. On the other hand, what if he didn't? The future would be changed again. How was it, he wondered, that the Lybblas hadn't vanished with the first corpse – when pattern *a* had switched to variable *b*?

Well, the question wasn't unanswerable. Whether or not Gallegher lived his life, the Lybblas, in their Martian valley, would be unaffected. When a musician strikes a false note, he may have to transpose for a few bars, but will drift back into the original key as soon as possible. Time, it seemed, trended towards the norm. Heigh-ho.

'What is this mental hookup business?' he demanded.

They told him. He pieced it out from their scatter-brained remarks, and discovered that the device was strange but practical. Gallegher said something about wild talents under his breath. It amounted to that.

With the mental hookup, a dolt could learn mathematics in a few moments. The application, of course, would require practice – mental dexterity must be developed. A stiff-fingered bricklayer could learn to be an expert pianist, but it would take time before his hands could be limbered up and made sufficiently responsive. However, the important point was that talents could be transferred from one brain to another.

It was a matter of induction, through charts of the electrical impulses emitted by the brain. The pattern varies. When a man is asleep, the curve levels out. When he is dancing, for example, his subconscious automatically guides his feet – if he's a sufficiently good dancer. That pattern is distinctive. Once recorded and recognised, it can be traced later – and the factors that go to make up a good dancer traced, as by a pantograph, on another brain.

Whew!

There was a lot more, involving memory centres and so forth, but Gallegher got the gist of it. He was impatient to begin work. It fitted a certain plan he had –

'Eventually you learn to recognise the chart lines at a glance,' one of the Lybblas told him. 'It – the device – is used a great deal in our time. People who don't want to study get the knowledge pumped into their minds from the brains of noted savants. There was an Earthman in the Valley once who wanted to be a famous singer, but he was tone-deaf. Couldn't carry a note. He used the mental hookup, and after six months he could sing anything.'

'Why six months?'

'His voice wasn't trained. That took time. But after he'd got in the groove he –'

'Make us a mental hookup,' the fat Lybbla suggested. 'Maybe we can use it to conquer Earth.'

'That,' Gallegher said, 'is exactly what I'm going to do. With a few reservations.'

Gallegher televised Rufus Hellwig, on the chance that he might induce the tycoon to part with some of his fortune, but without success. Hellwig was recalcitrant. 'Show me,' he said. 'Then I'll give you a blank cheque.'

'But I need the money now,' Gallegher insisted. 'I can't give you what you want if I'm gassed for murder.'

'Murder? Who'd you kill?' Hellwig wanted to know.

'I didn't kill anybody. I'm being framed –'

'So am I. But I'm not falling, this time. Show me results. I make you no more advances, Gallegher.'

'Look. Wouldn't you like to be able to sing like a Caruso? Dance like Nijinsky? Swim like Weissmuller? Make speeches like Secretary Parkinson? Make like Houdini?'

'Have you got a snootful!' Hellwig said ruminatively, and broke the beam. Gallegher glared at the screen. It looked as though he'd have to go to work, after all.

So he did. His trained, expert fingers flew, keeping pace with his keen brain. Liquor helped, liberating his demon subconscious. When in doubt, he questioned the Lybblas. Nevertheless the job took time.

He didn't have all the equipment he needed, and 'vised a supply company, managing to wangle sufficient credit to swing the deal on the cuff. He kept working. Once he was interrupted by a mild little man in a derby who brought a subpoena, and once Grandpa wandered in to borrow five credits. The circus was in town, and Grandpa, as an old big-top enthusiast, couldn't miss it.

'Want to come along?' he inquired. 'I might get in a crap game with some of the boys. Always got on well with circus people, somehow. Won five hundred once from a bearded lady. Nope? Well, good luck.'

He went away, and Gallegher returned to his mental hookup device. The Lybblas contentedly stole cookies and squabbled amicably about the division of the world after they'd conquered it. The machine grew slowly but inevitably.

As for the time machine itself, occasional attempts to turn it off proved only one thing: it had frozen into stasis. It seemed to be fixed in a certain definite pattern, from which it was impossible to budge it. It had been set to bring back Gallegher's variable corpses. Until it had fulfilled that task, it stubbornly refused to obey additional order. *'There was an old maid from Vancouver,'* Gallegher murmured absently. 'Let's see. I need a tight beam here – Yeah. *She jumped on his knee with a chortle of glee* – If I vary the receptor-sensibility on the electromagnetic current – Hm-m-m – *And nothing on earth could remove 'er.* Yeah, that does it.'

It was night. Gallegher hadn't been conscious of the

passing of hours. The Lybblas, bulging with filched cookies, had made no complaint, except occasional demands for more milk. Gallegher had drunk steadily as he worked, keeping his subconscious to the fore. He hadn't realised till now that he was hungry. Sighing, he looked at the completed mental hookup device, shook his head, and opened the door. The back yard lay empty before him.

Or –

No, it was empty. No more corpses just yet. Time-variable pattern b was still in operation. He stepped out and let the cool night air blow on his hot cheeks. The blazing towers of Manhattan made ramparts against the night around him. Above, the lights of air traffic flickered like devil fireflies.

There was a sodden thump near by. Gallegher whirled, startled. A body had fallen out of empty air and lay staring blankly up in the middle of his rose garden. His stomach cold, Gallegher investigated. The corpse was that of a middle-aged man, between fifty and sixty, with a silky dark moustache and eyeglasses. Unmistakably, though, it was Gallegher. A Gallegher aged and altered by time-variable c – c, now, not b any more – and with a hole burned through the breast by a heat-ray projector.

At that precise moment, Gallegher realised, corpse b must have vanished from the police morgue, like its predecessor.

Uh-huh. In time-pattern c, then, he wasn't to die till he was over fifty – but even then a heat ray would kill him. Depressing, Gallegher thought of Cantrell, who'd taken the ray projector, and shivered slightly. Matters were growing more and more confusing.

Well, presently the police would arrive. In the meantime, he was hungry. With a last shrinking glance at his own dead, aged face, Gallegher returned to the laboratory, picked up the Lybblas on the way, and herded them into the kitchen, where he fixed a makeshift supper. There were steaks, luckily, and the Lybblas gobbled their portions like pigs, talking excitedly about their fantastic plans. They'd decided to make Gallegher their Grand Vizier.

'Is he wicked?' the fat one demanded.

'I don't know. Is he?'

'He's gotta be wicked. In the novels the Grand Vizier's *always* wicked. *Whee*!' The fat Lybbla choked on a bit of steak. 'Ug . . . uggle . . . *ulp*! The world is ours!'

Deluded little creatures, Gallegher mused. Incurable romanticists. Their optimism was, to say the least, remarkable.

His own troubles engrossed him as he slid the plates into the Burner – 'It Burns Them Clean' – and fortified himself with a beer. The mental hookup device should work. He knew of no reason why it shouldn't. His genius subconscious had really built the thing –

Hell, it had to work. Otherwise the Lybblas wouldn't have mentioned that the gadget had been invented by Gallegher, long in their past. But he couldn't very well use Hellwig as a guinea pig.

A rattle at the door made Gallegher snap his fingers in triumph. Grandpa, of course! That was the answer.

Grandpa appeared, beaming. 'Had fun. Circuses are always fun. Here's a couple of hundred for you, stupid. Got to playing stud poker with the tattooed man and the guy who dives off a ladder into a tank. Nice fellows. I'm seeing 'em tomorrow.'

'Thanks,' Gallegher said. The two hundred was pennyante stuff, but he didn' want to antagonise the old goat now. He managed to lure Grandpa into the laboratory and explain that he wanted to make an experiment.

'Experiment away,' said Grandpa, who had found the liquor organ.

'I've made some charts of my own mental patterns and located my bump of mathematics. It amounts to that. The atomic structure of pure learning, maybe – It's a bit vague. But I can transfer the contents of my mind to yours, and I can do it selectively. I can give you my talent for mathematics –'

'Thanks,' Grandpa said. 'Sure you won't be needing it?'

'I'll still have it. It's the matrix, that's all.'

'Mattress?'

'Matrix. Pattern. I'll just duplicate that pattern in your brain. See?'

'Sure,' Grandpa said, and allowed himself to be led to a chair where a wired helmet was fitted over his head. Gallegher donned another helmet and began to fiddle with the device. It made noises and flashed lights. Presently a low buzzing rose to a crescendo scream, and then stopped. That was all.

Gallegher removed both helmets. 'How do you feel?' he asked.

'Fit as a fiddle.'

'No different?'

'I want a drink.'

'I didn't give you my drinking ability, because you already had your own. Unless I doubled it – ' Gallegher paled. 'If I gave you my thirst, too, you couldn't stand it. You'd die.'

Muttering something about blasted foolishness, Grandpa replenished his dry palate. Gallegher followed him and stared perplexedly at the old fellow.

'I couldn't have made a mistake. The charts – What's the value of *pi*?' he snapped suddenly.

'A dime is plenty,' Grandpa said. 'For a big slice.'

Gallegher cursed. The machine must have worked. It *had* to work, for a number of reasons, chief of which was the question of logic. Perhaps –

'Let's try it again. I'll be the subject this time.'

'O.K.,' Grandpa said contentedly.

'Only – hm-m-m. You haven't got any talents. Nothing unusual. I couldn't be sure whether it worked or not. If you'd only been a concert pianist or a singer,' Gallegher moaned.

'Hah!'

'Wait a minute. I've an idea. I've got connection at a teleview studio – maybe I can wangle something.' Gallegher used the 'visor. It took some time, but presently he managed to induce Senor Ramon Firez, the Argentine tenor, to hop an air taxi and come down to the laboratory in a hurry.

'Firez!' Gallegher gloated. 'That'll prove it, one way or

the other. One of the greatest voices in the hemisphere! If I suddenly find myself singing like a lark, I'll know I can use the gadget on Hellwig.'

Firez, it seemed, was night-clubbing but at the studio's request he shelved his nocturnal activities for the nonce and appeared within ten minutes, a burly, handsome man with a wide, mobile mouth. He grinned at Gallegher.

'You say there is trouble, that I can help with my great voice, and so I am at your service. A recording, is it?'

'Something of the sort.'

'To win a bet, perhaps?'

'You can call it that,' Gallegher said, easing Firez into a chair. 'I want to record the mental patterns of your voice.'

'Ah-h, that is something new! Explain, please!'

The scientist obediently launched into a completely meaningless jargon that served the purpose of keeping Senor Firez pacified while he made the necessary charts. That didn't take long. The significant curves and patterns showed unmistakably. The graph that represented Firez's singing ability – his great talent.

Grandpa watched sceptically while Gallegher made adjustments, fitted the helmets into place, and turned on the device. Again lights flashed and wires hummed. And stopped.

'It is a success? May I see – '

'It takes awhile to develop the prints,' Gallegher lied unscrupulously. He didn't want to burst into song while Firez was still present. 'I'll bring the results out to your apartment as soon as they're done.'

'Ah-h, good. *Muy bueno.*' White teeth flashed. 'I am always happy to be of service, *amigo*!'

Firez went away. Gallegher sat down and looked at the wall, waiting. Nothing happened. He had a slight headache, that was all.

'Through fiddling?' Grandpa demanded.

'Yeah. *Do-re-mi-fa-s* – '

'What?'

'Shut up. *I Pagliacci* – '

'You're crazy as a bedbug.'

114

'*I love a parade!*' howled the frantic Gallegher, his voice cracking. 'Oh, hell! *Seated one day at the organ* – '

'*She'll be coming 'round the mountain,*' Grandpa chimed in chummily. '*She'll be coming 'round the mountain* – '

'*I was weary and ill at ease* – '

'*She'll be coming 'round the mountain* – '

'*And my fingers wandered idly* –'

'*WHEN SHE COMES!*' Grandpa blatted, always the life of the party. 'Used to carry a tune pretty well in my young days. Let's get together now. Know "Frankie and Johnnie"?'

Gallegher repressed an impulse to burst into tears. With a cold glance at Grandpa, he went into the kitchen and opened a bulb of beer. The cool catnip taste refreshed him, but failed to raise his spirits. He couldn't sing. Not in the manner of Firez, anyhow. Now would six months of training his larynx work any appreciable change, he knew. The device simply had failed to work. Mental hookup, nuts.

Grandpa's voice called shrilly.

'Hey! I found something in the back yard!'

'I don't need three guesses,' Gallegher said moodily, and went to work on the beer.

Three hours later – at ten p.m. – the police arrived. The reason for the delay was simply explained: the body in the morgue had vanished, but its disappearance hadn't been detected for some time. Then there had been a thorough search, yielding, of course, not the slightest result. Mahoney appeared, with his cohorts, and Gallegher waved them into the yard. 'You'll find it there,' he sighed.

Mahoney glared at him. 'More funny business, eh?' he snapped.

'None of my doing.'

The troupe poured out of the lab, leaving a slim, blond man eyeing Gallegher thoughtfully.

'How goes it?' Cantrell inquired.

'Uh – O.K.'

'You got any more of those – gadgets – hidden around here?'

'The heat-ray projectors? No.'

'Then how do you keep killing people that way?' Cantrell asked plaintively. 'I don't get it.'

'He explained it to me,' Grandpa said, 'but I didn't understand what he was talking about. Not then. I do now, of course. It's simply a matter of variable temporal lines. Planck's uncertainty principle enters into it, and Heisenberg, obviously. Laws of thermodynamics show clearly that a universe tends to return to the norm, which is our known rate of entropy, and variations from that norm must necessarily be compensated for by corresponding warps in the temporal-spatial structure of the universal cosmos-equation.'

There was silence.

Gallegher went to the wall and drew a glass of water, which he poured slowly over his head. 'You understand that, do you?' he asked.

'Sure,' Grandpa said. 'Why not? The mental hookup gave me your mathematical talent – which included vocabulary, I suppose.'

'You been holding out on me?'

'Hell, no. It takes awhile for the brain to readjust to the new values. That's a safety valve, I guess. The sudden influx of a completely novel set of thought-patterns would disrupt the mind completely. It sinks in – three hours or so it takes. It's been that long or more, hasn't it?'

'Yeah,' Gallegher said. 'Yeah.' He caught sight of the watching Cantrell and managed a smile. 'A little joke Grandpa and I have between ourselves. Nothing to it.'

'Hm-m-m,' Cantrell said, his eyes hooded. 'That so?'

'Yeah. Sure. That's all.'

A body was carried in from the back yard and through the laboratory. Cantrell winked, patted his pocket significantly, and drew Gallegher into a corner.

'If I showed anybody that heat ray of yours, you'd be sunk, Gallegher. Don't forget that.'

'I'm not. What the devil do you want, anyhow?'

'Oh – I dunno. A weapon like this might come in plenty handy. One never knows. Lots of holdups these days. I feel safer with this thing in my pocket.'

He drew back as Mahoney came in, chewing his lips. The detective was profoundly disturbed.

'That guy in the back yard – '

'Yeah?'

'He looks like you, a bit. Only older.'

'How about the fingerprints, Mahoney?' Cantrell asked.

The detective growled something under his breath. 'You know the answer. Impossible, as usual. Eyeprints check, too. Now listen, Gallegher, I'm going to ask you some questions and I want straight answers. Don't forget you're under suspicion of murder.'

'Whom did I murder?' Gallegher asked. 'The two guys who vanished from the morgue? There's no *corpus delicti*. Under the new Codex, eyewitnesses and photographs aren't enough to prove murder.'

'You know why that was put into effect,' Mahoney said. 'Three-dimensional broadcast images that people thought were real corpses – there was a stink about that five years ago. But those stiffs in your back yard aren't three-dis. They're real.'

'Are?'

'Two were. One is. You're still on the spot. Well?'

Gallegher said, 'I don't – ' He stopped, his throat working. Abruptly, he stood up, eyes closed.

'*Drink to me only with thine eyes, and I will pledge with mine,*' Gallegher sang, in a blasting tenor that, though untrained, rang true and resonant. '*Or leave a kiss within the cup –*'

'Hey!' Mahoney snapped, springing up. 'Lay off. Hear me?'

' *– and I'll not ask for wine! The thirst that from the soul doth rise –*'

'Stop it!' the detective shouted. 'We're not here to listen to you sing!'

Nevertheless, he listened. So did the others. Gallegher, caught in the grip of Senor Firez's wild talent, sang on and on, his unaccustomed throat gradually relaxing and pouring out the notes like the beak of a nightingale. Gallegher – sang!

They couldn't stop him. They fled, with threats. They

117

would return later – with a strait jacket.

Grandpa also seemed caught in the throes of some strange affliction. Words poured out of him, strange semantic terms, mathematics translated into word-symbols, ranging from Euclid to Einstein and beyond. Grandpa, it seemed, had certainly acquired Gallegher's wild talent for math.

It came to an end, as all things, good or bad, inevitably do. Gallegher croaked hoarsely from a dry throat and, after a few feeble gasps, relapsed into silence. He collapsed on the couch, eyeing Grandpa, who was crumpled in a chair, wide-eyed. The three Lybblas had come out of hiding and stood in a row, each with a cookie clasped in furry paws.

'The world is mine,' the fattest one said.

Events marched. Mahoney 'vised to say he was getting out a special injunction, and that Gallegher would be clapped into jail as soon as the machinery could be swung into action. Tomorrow, that meant.

Gallegher 'vised an attorney – the best one on the Eastern seaboard. Yes, Persson could quash the injunction, and certainly win the case, or – well, anyhow, Gallegher would have nothing to worry about if he retained the lawyer. The fee was payable partially in advance.

'How much? . . . *Uh*!'

'Call me,' Persson said, 'when you wish me to take charge. You may mail your cheque tonight.'

'All right,' Gallegher said, and hurriedly 'vised Rufus Hellwig. The tycoon, luckily, was in.

Gallegher explained. Hellwig was incredulous. He agreed, however, to be at the laboratory early the next morning for a test. He couldn't make it before then. Nor could he advance any money till matters had been proved beyond a doubt.

'Make me an excellent concert pianist,' he said, 'and I'll be convinced.'

After that, Gallegher 'vised the teleview studio again, and managed to get in touch with Joey Mackenzie, the blonde, beautiful pianist who had taken New York by storm recently and had instantly been signed by the telecompany. She said she'd be over in the morning. Gallegher had to talk her into it, but he dropped enough hints to rouse the girl's interest to fever pitch. She seemed to class science with black magic, and was fascinated by both.

She'd be there.

And another body appeared in the back yard, which meant probability-line d was taking over. No doubt the third corpse, at the same time, had vanished from the morgue. Gallegher almost felt sorry for Mahoney.

The wild talents settled down. Apparently the irresistible outburst came only at the beginning, some three hours or more after the initial treatment. After that, the ability could be turned on or off at will. Gallegher was no longer impelled to burst into song, but he found he could sing, and sing well, when he wished. Likewise Grandpa had a fine sense of mathematics when he chose to use it.

Finally, at five o'clock in the morning, Mahoney arrived with two officers, arrested Gallegher, and carried him off to jail.

He was incommunicado for three days.

Persson, the attorney, came on the evening of the third day armed with writs of *habeas corpus* and foul language. He sprang Gallegher, somehow – perhaps on his reputation. Later, in the air taxi, he threw up his hands and howled complaints.

'What kind of a case is this? Political pressure, legal tangles – it's crazy! Corpses appearing in your back yard – seven of them already – and vanishing from the morgue. What's behind it, Gallegher?'

'I'm not sure. You . . . uh . . . you're acting as my attorney?'

'Obviously.' The taxi skimmed precariously past a skyscraper.

'The cheque – ' Gallegher hazarded.

'Your grandfather gave it to me. Oh, he gave me a message, too. He said he'd treated Rufus Hellwig along the lines you'd suggested, and collected the fee. I can't feel that I've earned any part of my retainer, yet, though. Letting you stay in jail for three days! But I was up against powerful political pull. Had to pull plenty of wires myself.'

So that was it. Grandpa, of course, had acquired Gallegher's mathematical talent, and knew all about the mental hookup and how it worked. He'd treated Hellwig – successfully, it seemed. At least, they were in the chips now. But would that be enough?

Gallegher explained as much as he dared. Persson shook his head.

'The time machine's behind it, you say? Well, you've got to turn it off somehow. Stop those corpses from coming through.'

'I can't even smash it,' Gallegher confessed. 'I tried, but it's in a state of stasis. Completely out of this temporal-spatial sector. I don't know how long that'll last. It's set to bring back my own corpse – and it'll keep doing that.'

'So. All right. I'll do my best. Anyway, you're a free man now. But I can't guarantee anything unless you eliminate those incessant corpses of yours, Mr Gallegher. I get out here. See you tomorrow. At my office, at noon? Good.'

Gallegher shook hands and directed the cabman to his own place. An unpleasant surprise awaited him. It was Cantrell who opened the door.

The man's narrow, pale face twitched into a smile. 'Evening,' he said pleasantly, stepping back. 'Come in, Gallegher.'

'I am in. What are you doing here?'

'Visiting. Visiting your grandfather.'

Gallegher glanced around the laboratory. 'Where is he?'

'I dunno. See for yourself.'

Sensing danger of some kind, the scientist began to search. He found Grandpa eating pretzels in the kitchen, and feeding the Lybblas. The old man evaded his gaze.

'O.K.,' Gallegher said, 'let's have it.'

' 'Twasn't my fault. Cantrell said he'd turn over the heat ray to the police if I didn't do what he wanted. I knew that'd be your finish –'

'*What's been happening*?'

'Now take it easy. I got it all worked out. It can't do any harm –'

'What? *What*?'

'Cantrell's been making me use the machine on him,'

Grandpa confessed. 'He peeked through the window when I treated Hellwig and figured out the answer. He threatened to get you convicted unless I gave him some extra talents.'

'Whose?'

'Oh – Gulliver, Morleyson, Kottman. Denys, St Malory –'

'That's enough,' Gallegher said weakly. 'The greatest technicians of the age, that's all! And their knowledge in Cantrell's brain! How did he wangle 'em into it?'

'Fast talking. He didn't let on what he wanted. Made up some cock-and-bull story – He got your mathematical talent, too. Through me.'

'That's just fine,' Gallegher said, looking grim. 'What the devil is he up to?'

'He wants to conquer the world,' the fattest Lybbla said sadly. 'Oh, don't let him do it. We want to conquer the world.'

'Not quite that,' Grandpa said, 'but bad enough. He's got the same knowledge we have now – enough to build another mental hookup. And he's taking the stratoliner to Europe in an hour.'

'This means trouble,' Gallegher siad.

'Yeah, I know. I'm commencing to feel Cantrell's just a mite unscrupulous. He's the one responsible for your being kept in jail the last few days.'

Cantrell opened the door and looked in. 'There's a new corpse in the garden. It just appeared. We won't bother about it now, though. I'll be leaving shortly. Any word from Van Decker?'

'Van Decker!' Gallegher gulped. 'You haven't got him –'

The man with the world's highest I.Q.!

'Not yet,' Cantrell smiled. 'I tried to get in touch with him for days, and he 'vised me only this morning. I was afraid I'd miss him. But he said he'd be over tonight.' Cantrell glanced at his watch. 'Hope he's on time. Stratoliners won't wait.'

'Just a minute,' Gallegher said, moving forward. 'I'd like to know your plans, Cantrell.'

'He's going to conquer the world!' one of the Lybblas piped.

Cantrell sent an amused look downward. 'It's not too fantastic, at that,' he admitted. 'I'm completely amoral, luckily, so I can take full advantage of this opportunity. The talents of the world's greatest minds – they'll come in handy. I'll be a success in almost anything. I mean anything,' he added, winking.

'Dictator complex,' Grandpa scowled.

'Not yet,' Cantrell told him. 'Some day, maybe. Give me time. I'm pretty much of a superman already, you know.'

Gallegher said, 'You can't –'

'No? Don't forget I've got that heat ray of yours.'

'Yeah,' the scientist said, 'and those corpses in the back yard – my own corpses – were all killed with a heat ray. You're the only guy who had one, so far. Apparently you're ticketed to kill me, eventually.'

'Eventually's better than now, isn't it?' Cantrell asked softly.

Gallegher didn't answer. The other man went on.

'I've skimmed the cream from the best minds on the East coast, and now I'll do the same thing to Europe. Anything can happen.'

One of the Lybblas began to cry bitterly, seeing his plan of world conquest shattered.

The doorbell sang. Grandpa, at Cantrell's nod, went out, to return with a squat, beak-nosed man wearing a bushy red beard. 'Ha!' he bellowed. 'I am here! Not late I trust? Good.'

'Dr. van Decker?'

'Who else?' the redbeard shouted. 'Now hurry, hurry, hurry. I am a busy man. This experiment of yours; as you explained it on the 'visor, it will not work, but I am willing to try. Projecting one's astral is foolishness.'

Grandpa nudged Gallegher. 'Cantrell told him that was the idea,' he muttered.

'Yeah? Listen, we can't –'

'Take it easy,' Grandpa said, and one eye closed in a significant wink. 'I got your talents now, son. I thought of the answer. See if you can. I used your math. *Sh-h-h!*'

122

There was no time for more. Cantrell shepherded them all into the laboratory. Gallegher, scowling and biting his lip, pondered the problem. He couldn't let Cantrell get away with this. But, on the other hand, Grandpa had said it was all right – that everything was under control.

The Lybblas, of course, had disappeared, probably in search of cookies. Cantrell, eyeing his watch, urged Van Decker into a chair. He kept one hand significantly on his pocket, and from time to time looked towards Gallegher. The ray gun was still around; its outline was visible beneath the flexocloth of Cantrell's coat.

'Show you how easy I can do it,' Grandpa cackled, tottering on spindly legs towards the mental hookup device and throwing switches.

'Careful, Grandpa,' Cantrell warned, his voice tight.

Van Decker stared. 'Something is wrong?'

'No, no,' Grandpa said. 'Mr Cantrell is afraid I will make a mistake. But no. This helmet –'

He fitted it on Van Decker's head. A stylus scratched wavering lines on graphs. Deftly Grandpa sheafed them together, fell over his own feet and collapsed, the cards flying far and wide. Before Cantrell could move the old man was up again, muttering oaths as he collected the charts.

He laid them on a table. Gallegher moved forward, peering over Cantrell's shoulder. *Whew*! This was the real thing, all right. Van Decker's I.Q. was tremendous. His wild talents were – well, wildly remarkable.

Cantrell – who also knew the details of the mental hookup now, since he had absorbed Gallegher's mathematical ability via Grandpa – nodded with satisfaction. He fitted a helmet on his own head and moved towards the device. With a cursory glance at Van Decker to see that all was well, he threw the switches. Lights blazed; the humming rose to a scream. And died.

Cantrell removed the helmet. As he reached into his pocket, Grandpa lifted a casual hand and showed a small, gleaming pistol.

'Don't do it,' Grandpa said.

Cantrell's eyes narrowed. 'Drop that gun.'

123

'Nope. I figured you'd want to kill us and smash the machine, so you'd stay unique. It won't work. This gun's got a hair trigger. You can burn a hole in me, Cantrell, but you'll be dead while you're doing it.'

Cantrell considered. 'Well?'

'Get out. I don't want to be burned down, any more than you want a bullet in your stomach. Live and let live. Beat it.'

Cantrell laughed softly. 'Fair enough, Grandpa. You've earned it. Don't forget, I still know how to build the machine. And – I've skimmed the cream. You can do the same thing, but not any better than I can.'

'So it's even,' Grandpa said.

'Yes, it's even. We'll meet again. Don't forget what killed those corpses in your yard, Gallegher,' Cantrell said, and backed out of the door, smiling tightly.

Gallegher came to life with a jump. 'We've got to 'vise the police!' he snapped. 'Cantrell's too dangerous now to let loose.'

'Take it easy,' Grandpa cautioned, waving the gun. 'I told you it was all fixed up. You don't want to be convicted for murder, do you? If Cantrell's arrested – and we couldn't make a charge stick, anyway – the police would find the heat-ray projector. This way's better.'

'What way?' Gallegher demanded.

'O.K., Mickey,' Grandpa said, grinning at Dr Simon van Decker, who took off his red beard and wig and started to laugh triumphantly.

Gallegher's jaw dropped. 'A ringer!' he gulped.

'Sure. I 'vised Mickey privately a few days ago. Told him what I wanted. He dressed up, 'vised Cantrell, and pretended to be Van Decker. Made an appointment for tonight.'

'But the charts. They showed a genius I.Q. – '

'I switched charts when I dropped 'em on the floor,' Grandpa confessed. 'I'd made up some fakes in advance.'

Gallegher scowled. 'That doesn't alter the situation, though. Cantrell's still loose, and with too damn much knowledge.'

'Hold your horses, young fellow,' Grandpa said. 'Wait'll

I explain.'

He explained.

About three hours later the telecast news came through: a man named Roland Cantrell had fallen to his death from the Atlantic stratoliner.

Gallegher, however, knew the exact moment of Cantrell's death. For the corpse in the back yard had vanished at that time.

Because, with the heat-ray projector destroyed, Gallegher's future no longer could involve his death through a heat beam. Unless he made another, which he would take care not to do.

The time machine came out of its stasis and returned to normal. Gallegher guessed why. It had been set to fulfil a definite pattern – involving the death of Gallegher according to a certain set of variables. Within the limits of those variables, it was frozen. It could not stop operating till it had exhausted all the possibilities. As long as any of Gallegher's probable futures held heat-ray death – corpses would appear.

Now the future was altered drastically. No longer did it involve a, b, c, et cetera. The heat ray – the prime factor of the parameter – was destroyed in the present. So Gallegher's probable futures now involved a-1, b-1, c-1, et cetera.

And the machine wasn't set for such radical variations. It had fulfilled the task for which it had been set. Now it awaited new orders.

But Gallegher studied it thoroughly before using it again.

He had plenty of time. Without a single *corpus delicti*, Persson had no difficulty in getting the case quashed, though the unfortunate Mahoney nearly went mad trying to figure out what had happened. As for the Lybblas –

Gallegher absently passed around the cookies, wondering how he could get rid of the small, stupid creatures without hurting their feelings. 'You don't want to stay here all your lives, do you?' he inquired.

'Well, no,' one of them replied, brushing crumbs from

his whiskers with a furry paw. 'But we gotta conquer the Earth,' he pointed out plaintively.

'Mm-m-m,' Gallegher said. And went out to make a purchase, returning later with some apparatus he surreptitiously attached to the televisor.

Shortly thereafter, the regular telecast was broken off for what purported to be a news flash. By a curious coincidence, the three Lybblas were watching the 'visor at the time. The scene on the screen faded into a close-up of the newscaster, whose face was almost entirely concealed by the sheaf of papers he held. From the eyebrows up – the only part visible – he looked much like Gallegher, but the Lybblas were too intrigued to notice.

'Flash!' said the 'visor excitedly. 'Important bulletin! For some time the world has known of the presence of three distinguished visitors from Mars. They have –'

The Lybblas exchanged startled glances. One of them started to pipe a question and was hastily shushed. They listened again.

'They had been planning to conquer the Earth, it has been learned, and we are pleased to report that the world's entire population has gone over to the side of the Lybblas. A bloodless revolution has taken place. The Lybblas are unanimously acclaimed as our sole rulers –'

'*Whee!*' cried a small voice.

' – and the new form of government is already being set up. There will be a different fiscal system, and coins bearing the heads of the Lybblas are being minted. It is expected that the three rulers will shortly return to Mars to explain the situation to their friends there.'

The newscaster's partially exposed face vanished from the screen, and the regular telecast resumed. After a while Gallegher appeared, smiling secretively. He was greeted with shrill shouts from the Lybblas.

'We gotta go home now. It was a bloodless –'

'Revolution! The world is ours!'

Their optimism was surpassed only by their credulity. Gallegher allowed himself to be convinced that the Lybblas must go back to Mars.

'O.K.,' Gallegher agreed. 'The machine's all ready. One last cookie all around, and then off you go.'

He shook each fuzzy paw, bowed politely, and the three Lybblas, ears bobbing, piping excitedly among themselves, were shot back to Mars, five hundred years in the future. They were anxious to return to their friends and relate their adventures. They did – but nobody ever believed them.

There were no repercussions from Cantrell's death, though Gallegher, Grandpa and Mickey waited rather worriedly for several days before they felt able to relax. After that, Grandpa and Gallegher went on a terrific binge and felt far better.

Mickey couldn't join them. Regretfully, he returned to the circus lot, where, twice a day, he capitalised on his peculiar talents by diving from the top of a thirty-foot ladder into a tub filled with water . . .

EX MACHINA

I got the idea out of a bottle labelled "Drink Me",' Gallegher said wanly. 'I'm no technician, except when I'm drunk. I don't know the difference between an electron and an electrode, except that one's invisible. At least I do know, sometimes, but they get mixed up. My trouble is semantics.'

'Your trouble is you're a lush,' said the transparent robot, crossing its legs with a faint crash. Gallegher winced.

'Not at all. I get along fine when I'm drinking. It's only during my periods of sobriety that I get confused. I have a technological hangover. The aqueous humor in my eyeballs is coming out by osmosis. Does that make sense?'

'No,' said the robot, whose name was Joe. 'You're crying, that's all. Did you turn me on just to have an audience? I'm busy at the moment.'

'Busy with what?'

'I'm analysing philosophy, *per se*. Hideous as you humans are, you sometimes get bright ideas. The clear, intellectual logic of pure philosophy is a revelation to me.'

Gallegher said something about a hard, gemlike flame. He still wept sporadically, which reminded him of the bottle labelled 'DRINK ME,' which reminded him of the liquor organ beside the couch. Gallegher stiffly moved his long body across the laboratory, detouring around three bulky objects which might have been the dynamos, Monstro and Bubbles, except for the fact that there were three of them. This realisation flickered only dimly through Gallegher's mind. Since one of the dynamos was looking at him, he hurriedly averted his gaze, sank down on the couch, and maniupulated several buttons. When no liquor flowed through the tube into his parched mouth, he removed the mouthpiece, blinked at it hopelessly, and ordered Joe to bring beer.

The glass was brimming as he raised it to his lips. But it was empty before he drank.

'That's very strange,' Gallegher said. 'I feel like Tantalus.'

'Somebody's drinking your beer,' Joe explained. 'Now do leave me alone. I've an idea I'll be able to appreciate my baroque beauty even more after I've mastered the essentials of philosophy.'

'No doubt,' Gallegher said. 'Come away from that mirror. Who's drinking my beer? A little green man?'

'A little brown animal,' Joe explained cryptically, and turned to the mirror again, leaving Gallegher to glare at him hatefully. There were times when Mr Galloway Gallegher yearned to bind Joe securely under a steady drip of hydrocholoric. Instead, he tried another beer, with equal ill luck.

In a sudden fury, Gallegher rose and procured soda water. The little brown animal had even less taste for such fluids than Gallegher himself; at any rate, the water didn't mysteriously vanish. Less thirsty but more confused than ever, Gallegher circled the third dynamo with the bright blue eyes and morosely examined the equipment littering his workbench. There were bottles filled with ambiguous liquids, obviously nonalcoholic, but the labels meant little or nothing. Gallegher's subconscious self, liberated by liquor last night, had marked them for easy reference. Since Gallegher Plus, though a top-flight technician, saw the world through thoroughly distorted lenses, the labels were not helpful. One said 'RABBITS ONLY.' Another inquired 'WHY NOT?' A third said 'CHRISTMAS NIGHT.'

There was also a complicated affair of wheels, gears, tubes, sprockets and light tubes plugged into an electric outlet.

'*Cogito, ergo sum*,' Joe murmured softly. 'When there's no one around on the quad. No. Hm-m-m.'

'What about this little brown animal?' Gallegher wanted to know. 'Is it real or merely a figment?'

'What is reality?' Joe inquired, thus confusing the issue

still further. 'I haven't resolved that yet to my own satisfaction.'

'Your satisfaction!' Gallegher said. 'I wake up with a tenth-power hangover and can't get a drink. You tell me fairy stories about little brown animals stealing my liquor. Then you quote mouldy philosophical concepts at me. If I pick up that crowbar over there, you'll neither be *nor* think in very short order.'

Joe gave ground gracefully. 'It's a small creature that moves remarkably fast. So fast it can't be seen.'

'How come you see it?'

'I don't. I varish it,' said Joe, who had more than the five senses normal to humans.

'Where is it now?'

'It went out a while ago.'

'Well – ' Gallegher sought inconclusively for words. 'Something must have happened last night.'

'Naturally,' Joe agreed. 'But you turned me off after the ugly man with the ears came in.'

'I remember that. You were beating your plastic gums . . . *what* man?'

'The ugly one. You told your grandfather to take a walk, too, but you couldn't pry him loose from his bottle.'

'Grandpa. Uh. Oh. Where's he?'

'Maybe he went back to Maine,' Joe suggested. 'He kept threatening to do that.'

'He never leaves till he's drunk out the cellar,' Gallegher said. He tuned in the audio system and called every room in the house. There was no response. Presently Gallegher got up and made a search. There was no trace of Grandpa.

He came back to the laboratory, trying to ignore the third dynamo with the big blue eyes, and hopelessly studied the workbench again. Joe, posturing before the mirror, said he thought he believed in the basic philosophy of intellectualism. Still, he added, since obviously Gallegher's intellect was in abeyance, it might pay to hook up the projector and find out what had happened last night.

This made sense. Some time before, realising that Gallegher sober never remembered the adventures of Gallegher tight, he had installed a visio-audio gadget in the laboratory, cleverly adjusted to turn itself on whenever circumstances warranted it. How the thing worked Gallegher wasn't quite sure any more, except that it could run off miraculous blood-alcohol tests on its creator and start recording when the percentage was sufficiently high. At the moment the machine was shrouded in a blanket. Gallegher whipped this off, wheeled over a screen, and watched and listened to what had happened last night.

Joe stood in a corner, turned off, probably cogitating. Grandpa, a wizened little man with a brown face like a bad-tempered nutcracker, sat on a stool cuddling a bottle. Gallegher was removing the liquor-organ mouthpiece from between his lips, having just taken on enough of a load to start the recorder working.

A slim, middle-aged man with large ears and an eager expression jittered on the edge of his relaxer, watching Gallegher.

'Claptrap,' Grandpa said in a squeaky voice. 'When I was a kid we went out and killed grizzlies with our hands. None of these new-fangled ideas – '

'Grandpa,' Gallegher said, 'shut up. You're not that old. And you're a liar anyway.'

'Reminds me of the time I was out in the woods and a grizzly came at me. I didn't have a gun. Well, I'll tell you. I just reached down his mouth – '

'Your bottle's empty,' Gallegher said cleverly, and there was a pause while Grandpa, startled, investigated. It wasn't.

'You were highly recommended,' said the eager man. 'I do hope you can help me. My partner and I are about at the end of our rope.'

Gallegher looked at him dazedly. 'You have a partner? Who's he? For that matter, who are you?'

Dead silence fell while the eager man fought with his bafflement. Grandpa lowered his bottle and said: 'It wasn't empty, but it is now. Where's another?'

The eager man blinked. 'Mr Gallegher,' he said faintly. 'I don't understand. We've been discussing – '

Gallegher said, 'I know. I'm sorry. It's just that I'm

no good on technical problems unless I'm . . . ah . . . stimulated. Then I'm a genius. But I'm awfully absent-minded. I'm sure I can solve your problem, but the fact is I've forgotten what it is. I suggest you start from the beginning. Who are you and have you given me any money yet?'

'I'm Jonas Harding,' the eager man said. 'I've got fifty thousand credits in my pocket, but we haven't come to any terms yet.'

'Then give me the dough and we'll come to terms,' Gallegher said with ill-concealed greed. 'I need money.'

'You certainly do,' Grandpa put in, searching for a bottle. 'You're so overdrawn at the bank that they lock the doors when they see you coming. I want a drink.'

'Try the organ,' Gallegher suggested. 'Now then, Mr Harding – '

'I want a bottle. I don't trust that dohinkus of yours.'

Harding, for all his eagerness, could not quite conceal a growing scepticism. 'As for the credits,' he said, 'I think perhaps we'd better talk a little first. You were very highly recommended, but perhaps this is one of your off days.'

'Not at all. Still – '

'Why should I give you the money before we come to terms?' Harding pointed out. 'Especially since you've forgotten who I am and what I wanted.'

Gallegher sighed and gave up. 'All right. Tell me what you are and who you want. I mean – '

'I'll go back home,' Grandpa threatened. 'Where's a bottle?'

Harding said desperately, 'Look, Mr Gallegher, there's a limit. I come in here and that robot of yours insults me. Your grandfather insists I have a drink with him. I'm nearly poisoned – '

'I was weaned on corn likker,' Grandpa muttered. 'Young whippersnappers can't take it.'

'Then let's get down to business,' Gallegher said brightly. 'I'm beginning to feel good. I'll just relax here on the couch and you can tell me everything.' He relaxed and sucked idly at the organ's mouthpiece, which trickled a gin buck. Grandpa cursed.

'Now,' Gallegher said, 'the whole thing, from the beginning.'

Harding gave a little sigh. 'Well – I'm half partner in Adrenals, Incorporated. We run a service. A luxury service, keyed to this day and age. As I told you –'

'I've forgotten it all,' Gallegher murmured. 'You should have made a carbon copy. What is it you do? I've got a mad picture of you building tiny prefabricated houses on top of kidneys, but I know I must be wrong.'

'You are,' Harding said shortly. 'Here's your carbon copy. We're in the adrenal-rousing business. Today man lives a quiet, safe life –'

'Ha!' Gallegher interjected bitterly.

' – what with safety controls and devices, medical advances, and the general structure of social living. Now the adrenal glands serve a vital functional purpose, necessary to the health of a normal man.' Harding had apparently launched into a familiar sales talk. 'Ages ago we lived in caves, and when a sabre-tooth burst out of the jungle, our adrenals, or suprarenals, went into instant action, flooding our systems with adrenalin. There was an immediate explosion of action, either towards fight or flight, and such periodic flooding of the blood stream gave tone to the whole system. Not to mention the psychological advantages. Man is an aggressive animal. He's losing that instinct, but it can be roused by artificial stimulation of the adrenals.'

'A drink?' Grandpa said hopefully, though he understood practically nothing of Harding's explanation.

Harding's face became shrewder. He leaned forward confidentially.

'Glamour,' he said. 'That's the answer. We offer adventure. Safe, thrilling, dramatic, exciting, glamorous adventure to the jaded modern man or woman. Not the vicarious, unsatisfactory excitement of television; the real article. Adrenals, Incorporated, will give you adventure plus, and at the same time improve your health physically and mentally. You must have seen our ads: "Are you in a rut? Are you jaded? Take a Hunt – and return refreshed, happy, and healthy, ready to lick the world!'

'A Hunt?'

'That's our most popular service,' Harding said, relapsing into more businesslike tones. 'It's not new, really. A long time ago travel bureaus were advertising thrilling tiger hunts in Mexico –'

'Ain't no tigers in Mexico,' Grandpa said. 'I been there. I warn you, if you don't find me a bottle, I'm going right back to Maine.'

But Gallegher was concentrating on the problem. 'I don't see why you need me, then. I can't supply tigers for you.'

'The Mexican tiger was really a member of the cat family. Puma, I think. We've got special reservations all over the world – expensive to set up and maintain – and there we have our Hunts, with every detail carefully planned in advance. The danger must be minimised – in fact, eliminated. But there must be an illusion of danger or there's no thrill for the customer. We've tried conditioning animals so they'll stop short of hurting anyone, but . . . ah . . . that isn't too successful. We lost several customers, I'm sorry to say. This is an enormous investment, and we've got to recoup. But we've found we can't use tigers or, in fact, any of the large carnivora. It simply isn't safe. Yet there must be that illusion of danger! The trouble is, we're degenerating into a trapshooting club. And there's no personal danger involved in trapshooting.'

Grandpa said: 'Want some fun, eh? Come on up to Maine with me and I'll show you some real hunting. We still got bear back in the mountains.'

Gallegher said: 'I'm beginning to see. But that personal angle – I wonder! What is the definition of danger, anyhow?'

'Danger's when something's trying to git you,' Grandpa pointed out.

'The unknown – the strange – is dangerous too, simply because we don't understand it. That's why ghost stories have always been popular. A roar in the dark is more frightening than a tiger in the daylight.'

Harding nodded. 'I see your point. But there's another

factor. The game mustn't be made too easy. It's a cinch to outwit a rabbit. And, naturally, we have to supply our customers with the most modern weapons.'

'Why?'

'Safety precautions. The trouble is, with those weapons and scanners and scent-analysers, any fool can track down and kill an animal. There's no thrill involved unless the animal's a man-eating tiger, and that's a little too thrilling for our underwriters!'

'So what do you want?'

'I'm not sure,' Harding said slowly. 'A new animal, perhaps. One that fulfills the requirements of Adrenals, Incorporated. But I'm not sure what the answer is, or I wouldn't be asking you.'

Gallegher said: 'You don't make new animals out of thin air.'

'Where do you get them?'

'I wonder. Other planets? Other time-sectors? Other probability-worlds? I got hold of some funny animals once – Lybblas – by turning on a future time-era on Mars, but they wouldn't have filled the bill.'

'Other planets, then?'

Gallegher got up and strolled to his workbench. He began to piece together stray cogs and tubes. 'I'm getting a thought. The latent factors inherent in the human brain – My latent factors are rousing to life. Let me see. Perhaps –'

Under his hands a gadget grew. Gallegher remained preoccupied. Presently he cursed, tossed the device aside, and settled back to the liquor-organ. Grandpa had already tried it, but choked on his first sip of a gin buck. He threatened to go back home and take Harding with him and show him some real hunting.

Gallegher pushed the old gentleman off the couch. 'Now look, Mr Harding,' he said. 'I'll have this for you tomorrow. I've got some thinking to do –'

'Drinking, you mean,' Harding said, taking out a bundle of credits. 'I've heard a lot about you, Mr Gallegher. You never work except under pressure. You've got to have a deadline, or you won't do a thing. Well – do you see this?

Fifty thousand credits.' He glanced at his wrist watch. 'I'm giving you one hour. If you don't solve my problem by then, the deal's off.'

Gallegher started up from the couch as though he had been bitten. 'That's ridiculous. An hour isn't time enough – '

Harding said obdurately: 'I'm a methodical man. I know enough about you to realise that you're not. I can find other specialists and technicians, you know. One hour! Or I go out that door and take these fifty thousand credits with me!'

Gallegher eyed the money greedily. He took a quick drink, cursed quietly, and went back to his gadget. This time he kept working on it.

After a while a light shot up from the worktable and hit Gallegher in the eye. He staggered back, yelping.

'Are you all right?' Harding asked, jumping up.

'Sure,' Gallegher growled, cutting a switch. 'I think I'm getting it. That light . . . ouch. I've sunburned my eye-balls.' He blinked back tears. Then he went over to the liquor-organ.

After a hearty swig, he nodded at Harding. 'I'm getting on the trail of what you want. I don't know how long it'll take, though.' He winced. 'Grandpa. Did you change the setting on this thing?'

'I dunno. I pushed some buttons.'

'I thought so. This isn't a gin buck. Wheeooo!'

'Got a wallop, has it?' Grandpa said, getting interested and coming over to try the liquor-organ again.

'Not at all,' Gallegher said, walking on his knees towards the audio-sonic recorder. 'What's this? A spy, huh? We know how to deal with spies in this house, you dirty traitor.' So saying, he rose to his feet, seized a blanket, and threw it over the projector.

At that point the screen, naturally enough, was blank.

'I cleverly outwit myself every time,' Gallegher remarked, rising to switch off the projector. 'I go to the trouble of building that recorder and then blindfold it just when matters get interesting. I know less than I did before, because there are more unknown factors now.'

'Men can know the nature of things,' Joe murmured.

'An important concept,' Gallegher admitted. 'The Greeks found it out quite a while ago, though. Pretty soon, if you keep on thinking hard, you'll come up with the bright discovery that two and two are four.'

'Be quiet, you ugly man,' Joe said. 'I'm getting into abstractions now. Answer the door and leave me alone.'

'The door? Why? The bell isn't singing.'

'It will,' Joe pointed out. 'There it goes.'

'Visitors at this time of the morning,' Gallegher sighed. 'Maybe it's Grandpa, though.' He pushed a button, studied the doorplate screen, and failed to recognise the lantern-jawed, bushy-browed face. 'All right,' he said. 'Come in. Follow the guide-line.' Then he turned to the liquor-organ thirstily before remembering his current Tantalus proclivities.

The lantern-jawed man came into the room. Gallegher said: 'Hurry up. I'm being followed by a little brown animal that drinks all my liquor. I've several other troubles, too, but the little brown animal's the worst. If I don't get a drink, I'll die. So tell me what you want and leave me alone to work out my problems. I don't owe you money, do I?'

'That depends,' said the newcomer, with a strong Scots accent. 'My name is Murdoch Mackenzie, and I assume you're Mr Gallegher. You look untrustworthy. Where is my partner and the fifty thousand credits he had with him?'

Gallegher pondered. 'Your partner, eh? I wonder if you mean Jonas Harding?'

'That's the lad. My partner in Adrenals, Incorporated?'

'I haven't seen him –'

With his usual felicity, Joe remarked, 'The ugly man with the big ears. How hideous he was.'

'Vurra true,' Mackenzie nodded. 'I note you're using the past tense, or rather that great clanking machine of yours is. Have you perhaps murdered my partner and disposed of his body with one of your scientific gadgets?'

'Now look –' Gallegher said. 'What's the idea? Have I got the mark of Cain on my forehead or something? Why should you jump to a conclusion like that? You're crazy.'

Mackenzie rubbed his long jaw and studied Gallegher

137

from under his bushy grey brows. 'It would be no great loss, I know,' he admitted. 'Jonas is little help in the business. Too methodical. But he had fifty thousand credits on his person when he came here last night. There is also the question of the body. The insurance is perfectly enormous. Between ourselves, Mr Gallegher, I would not hold it against you if you had murdered my unfortunate partner and pocketed the fifty thousand. In fact, I would be willing to consider letting you escape with . . . say . . . ten thousand, provided you gave me the rest. But not unless you provided me with legal evidence of Jonas's death, so my underwriters would be satisfied.'

'Logic,' Joe said admiringly. 'Beautiful logic. It's amazing that such logic should come from such an opaque horror.'

'I would look far more horrible, my friend, if I had a transparent skin like you,' Mackenzie said, 'if the anatomy charts are accurate. But we were discussing the matter of my partner's body.'

Gallegher said wildly: 'This is fantastic. You're probably laying yourself open to compounding a felony or something.'

'Then you admit the charge.'

'Of course not! You're entirely too sure of yourself, Mr Mackenzie. I'll bet you killed Harding yourself and you're trying to frame me for it. How do you know he's dead?'

'Now that calls for some explanation, I admit,' Mackenzie said. 'Jonas was a methodical man. Vurra. I have never known him to miss an appointment for any reason whatsoever. He had appointments last night, and more this morning. One with me. Moreover, he had fifty thousand credits on him when he came here to see you last night.'

'How do you know he got here?'

'I brought him, in my aircab. I let him out at your door. I saw him go in.'

'Well, you didn't see him go out, but he did,' Gallegher said.

Mackenzie, quite unruffled, went on checking points on his bony fingers.

'This morning I checked your record, Mr Gallegher, and it is not a good one. Unstable, to say the least. You have been mixed up in some shady deals, and you have been accused of crimes in the past. Nothing was ever proved, but you're a sly one, I suspect. The police would agree.'

'They can't prove a thing. Harding's probably home in bed.'

'He is not. Fifty thousand credits is a lot of money. My partner's insurance amounts to much more than that. The business will be tied up sadly if Jonas remains vanished, and there will be litigation. Litigation costs money.'

'I didn't kill your partner!' Gallegher cried.

'Ah,' Mackenzie smiled. 'Still, if I can prove that you did, it will come to the same thing, and be reasonably profitable for me. You see your position, Mr Gallegher. Why not admit it, tell me what you did with the body, and escape with five thousand credits.'

'You said ten thousand a while ago.'

'You're daft,' Mackenzie said firmly. 'I said nothing of the sort. At least, you canna prove that I did.'

Gallegher said: 'Well, suppose we have a drink and talk it over.' A new idea had struck him.

'An excellent suggestion.'

Gallegher found two glasses and manipulated the liquor-organ. He offered one drink to Mackenzie, but the man shook his head and reached for the other glass. 'Poison, perhaps,' he said cryptically. 'You have an untrustworthy face.'

Gallegher ignored that. He was hoping that with two drinks available, the mysterious little brown animal would show its limitations. He tried to gulp the whisky fast, but only a tantalizing drop burned on his tongue. The glass was empty. He lowered it and stared at Mackenzie.

'A cheap trick,' Mackenzie said, putting his own glass down on the workbench. 'I did not ask for your whisky, you know. How did you make it disappear like that?'

Furious with disappointment, Gallegher snarled: 'I'm a wizard. I've sold my soul to the devil. For two cents I'd make you disappear too.'

Mackenzie shrugged. 'I am not worried. If you could, you'd have done it before this. As for wizardry, I am far from sceptical, after seeing that monster squatting over there.' He indicated the third dynamo that wasn't a dynamo.

'What? You mean you see it, too?'

'I see more than you think, Mr Gallegher,' Mackenzie said darkly. 'In fact, I am going to the police now.'

'Wait a minute. You can't gain anything by that –'

'I can gain nothing by talking to you. Since you remain obdurate, I will try the police. If they can prove that Jonas is dead, I will at least collect his insurance.'

Gallegher said: 'Now wait a minute. Your partner did come here. He wanted me to solve a problem for him.'

'Ah. And have you solved it?'

'N-no. At least –'

'Then I can get no profit from you,' Mackenzie said firmly, and turned to the door. 'You will hear from me vurra soon.'

He departed. Gallegher sank down miserably on the couch and brooded. Presently he lifted his eyes to stare at the third dynamo.

It was not, then, a hallucination, as he had at first suspected. Nor was it a dynamo. It was a squat, shapeless object like a truncated pyramid that had begun to melt down, and two large blue eyes were watching him. Eyes, or agates, or painted metal. He couldn't be sure. It was about three feet high and three feet in diameter at the base.

'Joe,' Gallegher said, 'why didn't you tell me about that thing?'

'I thought you saw it,' Joe explained.

'I did, but – what is it?'

'I haven't the slightest idea.'

'Where could it have come from?'

'Your subconscious alone knows what you were up to last night,' Joe said. 'Perhaps Grandpa and Jonas Harding know, but they're not around, apparently.'

Gallegher went to the teleview and put in a call to Maine.

'Grandpa may have gone back home. It isn't likely he'd have taken Harding with him, but we can't miss any bets. I'll check on that. One thing, my eyes have stopped watering. What *was* that gadget I made last night?' He passed to the workbench and studied the cryptic assemblage. 'I wonder why I put a shoehorn in that circuit?'

'If you'd keep a supply of materials available here, Gallegher Plus wouldn't have to depend on makeshifts,' Joe said severely.

'Uh. I could get drunk and let my subconscious take over again . . . no, I can't. Joe, I can't drink any more! I'm bound hand and foot to the water wagon!'

'I wonder if Dalton had the right idea after all?'

Gallegher snarled: 'Do you have to extrude your eyes that way? I need help!'

'You won't get it from me,' Joe said. 'The problem's extremely simple, if you'd put your mind to it.'

'Simple, is it? Then suppose you tell me the answer!'

'I want to be sure of a certain philosophical concept first.'

'Take all the time you want. When I'm rotting in jail, you can spend your leisure hours pondering abstracts. *Get me a beer*! No, never mind. I couldn't drink it anyway. What does this little brown animal look like?'

'Oh, use your head,' Joe said.

Gallegher growled, 'I could use it for an anchor, the way it feels. You know all the answers. Why not tell me instead of babbling?'

'Men can know the nature of things,' Joe said. 'Today is the logical development of yesterday. Obviously you've solved the problem Adrenals, Incorporated, gave you.'

'What? Oh. I see. Harding wanted a new animal or something.'

'Well?'

'I've got two of 'em,' Gallegher said. 'That little brown invisible dipsomaniac and that blue-eyed critter sitting on the floor. Oh-*ho*! Where did I pick them up? Another dimension?'

'How should I know? You've got 'em.'

'I'll say I have,' Gallegher agreed. 'Maybe I made a

machine that scooped them off another world – and maybe Grandpa and Harding are on that world now! A sort of exchange of prisoners. I don't know. Harding wanted non-dangerous beasts elusive enough to give hunters a thrill – but where's the element of danger?' He gulped. 'Conceivably the pure alienage of the critters provides that illusion. Anyway, I'm shivering.'

'Flooding of the blood stream with adrenalin gives tone to the whole system,' Joe said smugly.

'So I captured or got hold of those beasts somehow, apparently, to solve Harding's problem . . . mm-m.' Gallegher went to stand in front of the shapeless blue-eyed creature. 'Hey, you,' he said.

There was no response. The mild blue eyes continued to regard nothing. Gallegher poked a finger tentatively at one of them.

Nothing at all happened. The eye was immovable and hard as glass. Gallegher tried the thing's bluish, sleek skin. It felt like metal. Repressing his mild panic, he tried to lift the beast from the floor, but failed completely. It was either enormously heavy or it had sucking-discs on its bottom.

'Eyes,' Gallegher said. 'No other sensory organs, apparently. That isn't what Harding wanted.'

'I think it clever of the turtle,' Joe suggested.

'Turtle? Oh. Like the armadillo. That's right. It's a problem, isn't it? How can you kill or capture a . . . a beast like this? Its exoderm feels plenty hard, it's immovable – that's it, Joe. Quarry doesn't have to depend on flight or fight. The turtle doesn't. And a barracuda could go nuts trying to eat turtle. This would be perfect quarry for the lazy intellectual who wants a thrill. But what about adrenalin?'

Joe said nothing. Gallegher pondered, and presently seized upon some reagents and apparatus. He tried a diamond drill. He tried acids. He tried every way he could think of to rouse the blue-eyed beast. After an hour his furious curses were interrupted by a remark from the robot.

'Well, what about adrenalin?' Joe inquired ironically.

'Shut up!' Gallegher yelped. 'That thing just sits there

looking at me! Adren . . . what?'

'Anger as well as fear stimulates the suprarenals, you know. I suppose any human would become infuriated by continued passive resistance.'

'That's right,' said the sweating Gallegher, giving the creature a final kick. He turned to the couch. 'Increase the nuisance quotient enough and you can substitute anger for fear. But what about that little brown animal? I'm not mad at it.'

'Have a drink,' Joe suggested.

'All right, I am mad at the cleptomaniacal so-and-so! You said it moved so fast I can't see it. How can I catch it?'

'There are undoubtedly methods.'

'It's as elusive as the other critter is invulnerable. Could I immobilise it by getting it drunk?'

'Metabolism.'

'Burns up its fuel too fast to get drunk? Probably. But it must need a lot of food.'

'Have you looked in the kitchen lately?' Joe asked.

Visions of a depleted larder filling his mind, Gallegher rose. He paused beside the blue-eyed object.

'This one hasn't got any metabolism to speak of. But it has to eat, I suppose. Still, eat what? Air? It's possible.'

The doorbell sang. Gallegher moaned. 'What now?' and admitted the guest. A man with a ruddy face and a belligerent expression came in, told Gallegher he was under tentative arrest, and called in the rest of his crew, who immediately began searching the house.

'Mackenzie sent you, I suppose?' Gallegher said.

'That's right. My name's Johnson. Department of Violence, Unproved. Do you want to call counsel?'

'Yes,' said Gallegher, jumping at the opportunity. He used the visor to get an attorney he knew, and began outlining his troubles. But the lawyer interrupted him.

'Sorry. I'm not taking any jobs on spec. You know my rates.'

'Who said anything about spec?'

'Your last cheque bounced yesterday. It's cash on the line this time, or no deal.'

'I . . . now wait! I've just finished a commissioned job that's paying off big. I can have the money for you –'

'When I see the colour of your credits, I'll be your lawyer,' the unsympathetic voice said, and the screen blanked. The detective, Johnson, tapped Gallegher on the shoulder.

'So you're overdrawn at the bank, eh? Needed money?'

'That's no secret. Besides, I'm not broke now, exactly. I finished a –'

'A job. Yeah, I heard that, too. So you're suddenly rich. How much did this job pay you? It wouldn't be fifty thousand credits, would it?'

Gallegher drew a deep breath. 'I'm not saying a word,' he said, and retreated to the couch, trying to ignore the Department men who were searching the lab. He needed a lawyer. He needed one bad. But he couldn't get one without money. Suppose he saw Mackenzie –

The visor put him in touch with the man. Mackenzie seemed cheerful.

'Hello,' he said. 'I see the police have arrived.'

Gallegher said, 'Listen, that job your partner gave me – I've solved your problem. I've got what you want.'

'Jonas's body, you mean?' Mackenzie seemed pleased.

'No! The animals you wanted! The perfect quarry!'

'Oh. Well. Why didn't you say so sooner?'

'Get over here and call off the police!' Gallegher insisted. 'I tell you, I've got your ideal Hunt animals for you!'

'I dinna ken if I can call off the bloodhounds,' Mackenzie said, 'but I'll be over directly. I will not pay vurra much, you understand?'

'Bah!' Gallegher snarled, and broke the connection. The visor buzzed at him. He touched the receiver, and a woman's face came in.

She said: 'Mr Gallegher, with reference to your call of inquiry regarding your grandfather, we report that investigation shows that he has not returned to our Maine sector. That is all.'

She vanished. Johnson said: 'What's this? Your grandfather? Where's he at?'

'I ate him,' Gallegher said, twitching. 'Why don't you leave me alone?'

Johnson made a note. 'Your grandfather. I'll just check up a bit. Incidentally, what's that thing over there?' He pointed to the blue-eyed beast.

'I've been studying a curious case of degenerative osteomyelitis affecting a baroque cephalopod!'

'Oh, I see. Thanks. Fred, see about this guy's grandfather. What are you gaping at?'

Fred said: 'That screen. It's set up for projection.'

Johnson moved to the audio-sonic recorder. 'Better impound it. Probably not important, but – ' He touched a switch. The screen stayed blank, but Gallegher's voice said: *We know how to deal with spies in this house, you dirty traitor.'*

Johnson moved the switch again. He glanced at Gallegher, his ruddy face impassive, and in silence began to rewind the wire tape. Gallegher said: 'Joe, get me a dull knife. I want to cut my throat, and I don't want to make it too easy for myself. I'm getting used to doing things the hard way.'

But Joe, pondering philosophy, refused to answer.

Johnson began to run off the recording. He took out a picture and compared it with what showed on the screen.

'That's Harding, all right,' he said. 'Thanks for keeping this for us, Mr Gallegher.'

'Don't mention it,' Gallegher said. 'I'll even show the hangman how to tie the knot around my neck.'

'Ha-ha. Taking notes, Fred? Right.'

The reel unrolled relentlessly. But, Gallegher tried to make himself believe, there was nothing really incriminating recorded.

He was disillusioned after the screen went blank, at the point when he had thrown a blanket over the recorder last night. Johnson held up his hand for silence. The screen still showed nothing, but after a moment or two voices were clearly audible.

'You have thirty-seven minutes to go, Mr Gallegher.'

'Just stay where you are. I'll have this in a minute. Besides, I want to get my hands on your fifty thousand credits.'

'*But –*'

'*Relax. I'm getting it. In a very short time your worries will be over.*'

'Did I say that?' Gallegher thought wildly. 'What a fool I am! Why didn't I turn off the radio when I covered up the lens?'

Grandpa's voice said: '*Trying to kill me by inches, eh, you young whippersnapper!*'

'All the old so-and-so wanted was another bottle,' Gallegher moaned to himself. 'But try to make those flatfeet believe that! Still – ' He brightened. 'Maybe I can find out what really happened to Grandpa and Harding. If I shot them off to another world, there might be some clue – '

'*Watch closely now*,' Gallegher's voice said from last night. '*I'll explain as I proceed. Oh-oh. Wait a minute. I'm going to patent this later, so I don't want any spies. I can trust you two not to talk, but that recorder's still turned on to audio. Tomorrow, if I played it back, I'd be saying to myself, "Gallegher, you talk too much. There's only one way to keep a secret safe." Off it goes!*'

Someone screamed. The shriek was cut off midway. The projector stopped humming. There was utter silence.

The door opened to admit Murdoch Mackenzie. He was rubbing his hands.

'I came right down,' he said briskly. 'So you've solved our problem, eh, Mr Gallegher? Perhaps we can do business then. After all, there's no real evidence that you killed Jonas – and I'll be willing to drop the charges, *if* you've got what Adrenals, Incorporated, wants.'

'Pass me those handcuffs, Fred,' Johnson requested.

Gallegher protested, 'You can't do this to me!'

'A fallacious theorem,' Joe said, 'which, I note, is now being disproved by the empirical method. How illogical, all you ugly people are.

The social trend always lags behind the technological one. And while technology tended, in these days, towards simplification, the social pattern was immensely complicated, since it was partly an outgrowth of historical pre-

146

cedent and partly a result of a scientific advance of the era. Take jurisprudence. Cockburn and Blackwood and a score of others had established certain general and specific rules – say, regarding patents – but those rules could be made thoroughly impractical by a single gadget. The Integrators could solve problems no human brain could manage, so, as a governor, it was necessary to build various controls into those semimechanical colloids. Moreover, an electronic duplicator could infringe not only on patents but on property rights, and attorneys prepared voluminous briefs on such questions as whether 'rarity rights' are real property, whether a gadget made on a duplicator is a 'representation' or a copy, and whether mass-duplication of chinchillas is unfair competition to a chinchilla breeder who depended on old-fashioned biological principles. All of which added up to the fact that the world, slightly punch-drunk with technology, was trying desperately to walk a straight line. Eventually the confusion would settle down.

It hadn't settled down yet.

So legal machinery was a construction far more complicated than an Integrator. Precedent warred with abstract theory as lawyer warred with lawyer. It was all perfectly clear to the technicians, but they were much too impractical to be consulted; they were apt to remark wickedly, 'So my gadget unstabilises property rights? Well – why have property rights, then?'

And you can't do that!

Not to a world that had found security, of a sort, for thousands of years in rigid precedents of social intercourse. The ancient dyke of formal culture was beginning to leak in innumerable spots, and, had you noticed, you might have seen hundreds of thousands of frantic, small figures rushing from danger-spot to danger-spot, valorously plugging the leaks with their fingers, arms, or heads. Some day it would be discovered that there was no encroaching ocean beyond that dyke, but that day hadn't yet come.

In a way, that was lucky for Gallegher. Public officials were chary about sticking their necks out. A simple suit for false arrest might lead to fantastic ramifications and big trouble. The hard-headed Murdoch Mackenzie took advantage of this situation to 'vise his own personal attorney and toss a monkey wrench in the legal wheels. The attorney spoke to Johnson.

There was no corpse. The audio-sonic recording was not sufficient. Moreover, there were vital questions involving *habeas corpus* and search warrants. Johnson called Headquarters Jurisprudence and the argument raged over the heads of Gallegher and the imperturbable Mackenzie. It ended with Johnson leaving, with his crew – and the incriminating record – and threatening to return as soon as a judge could issue the appropriate writs and papers. Meanwhile, he said, there would be officers on guard outside the house. With a malignant glare for MacKenzie, he stamped out.

'And now to business,' said Mackenzie, rubbing his hands. 'Between ourselves' – he leaned forward confidentially – 'I'm just as glad to get rid of that partner of mine. Whether or no you killed him, I hope he stays vanished. Now I can run the business my way, for a change.'

'It's all right about that,' Gallegher said, 'but what about me? I'll be in custody again as soon as Johnson can wangle it.'

'But not convicted,' Mackenzie pointed out. 'A clever lawyer can fix you up. There was a similar case in which the defendant got off with a defence of *non esse* – his attorney went into metaphysics and proved that the murdered man had never existed. Quite specious, but so far the murderer's gone free.'

Gallegher said: 'I've searched the house, and Johnson's men did, too. There's simply no trace of Jonas Harding or my grandfather. And I'll tell you frankly, Mr Mackenzie, I haven't the slightest idea what happened to them.'

Mackenzie gestured airily. 'We must be methodical. You mentioned you had solved a certain problem for Adrenals, Incorporated. Now, I'll admit, that interested me.'

Silently Gallegher pointed to the blue-eyed dynamo. Mackenzie studied the object thoughtfully

'Well?' he said.

'That's it. The perfect quarry.'

Mackenzie walked over to the thing, rapped its hide, and looked deeply into the mild azure eyes. 'How fast can it run?' he asked shrewdly.

Gallegher said: 'It doesn't have to run. You see, it's invulnerable.'

'Ha. Hum. Perhaps if you'd explain a wee bit more –'

But Mackenzie did not seem pleased with the explanation. 'No,' he said, 'I don't see it. There would be no thrill to hunting a critter like that. You forget out customers demand excitement – adrenal stimulation.'

'They'll get it. Anger has the same effect as rage – ' Gallegher went into detail.

But Mackenzie shook his head. 'Both fear and anger give you excess energy you've got to use up. You can't, against a passive quarry. You'll just cause neuroses. We try to get rid of neuroses, not create them.'

Gallegher, growing desperate, suddenly remembered the little brown beast and began to discuss that. Once Mackenzie interrupted with a demand to see the creature. Gallegher slid around that one fast.

'Ha,' Mackenzie said finally. 'It isna canny. How can you hunt something that's invisible?'

'Oh – ultraviolet. Scent-analysers. It's a test for ingenuity – '

'Our customers are not ingenious. They don't want to be. They want a change and a vacation from routine, hard work – or easy work, as the case may be – they want a rest. They don't want to beat their brains working out methods to catch a thing that moves faster than a pixie, nor do they want to chase a critter that's out of sight before it even gets there. You are a vurra clever man, Mr Gallegher, but it begins to look as though Jonas's insurance is my best bet after all.'

'Now wait – '

Mackenzie pursed his lips. 'I'll admit the beasties *may* – I say may – have some possibilities. But what good is quarry that can't be caught? Perhaps if you'd work out a way to capture these other-worldly animals of yours, we might do business. At present, I willna buy a pig in a poke.'

'I'll find a way,' Gallegher promised wildly. 'But I can't do it in jail.'

'Ah. I am a little irritated with you, Mr Gallegher. You tricked me into believing you had solved our problem. Which you havena done – yet. Consider the thought of jail. Your adrenalin may stimulate your brain into working out a way to trap these animals of yours. Though, even so, I can make no rash promises –'

Murdock Mackenzie grinned at Gallegher and went out, closing the door softly behind him. Gallegher began to dine off his finger nails.

'Men can know the nature of things,' Joe said, with an air of solid conviction.

At that point matters were complicated even further by the appearance, on the televisor screen, of a grey-haired man who announced that one of Gallegher's cheques had just bounced. Three hundred and fifty credits, the man said, and how about it?

Gallegher looked dazedly at the identification card on the screen. 'You're with United Cultures? What's that?'

The grey-haired man said silkily, 'Biological and medical supplies and laboratories, Mr Gallegher.'

'What did I order from you?'

'We have a receipt for six hundred pounds of Vitaplasm, first grade. We made delivery within an hour.'

'And when –'

The grey-haired man went into more detail. Finally Gallegher made a few lying promises and turned from the blanking screen. He looked wildly around the lab.

'Six hundred pounds of artificial protoplasm,' he murmured. 'Ordered by Gallegher Plus. He's got delusions of economic grandeur.'

'It was delivered,' Joe said. 'You signed the receipt, the night Grandpa and Jonas Harding disappeared.'

'But what could I do with the stuff? It's used for plastic surgery and for humano-prosthesis. Artificial limbs and stuff. It's cultured cellular tissue, this Vitaplasm. Did I use it to *make* some animals? That's biologically impossible. I think. How could I have moulded Vitaplasm into a little brown animal that's invisible? What about the brain and the neural structure? Joe, six hundred pounds of Vitaplasm has simply disappeared. Where has it gone?

But Joe was silent.

Hours later Gallegher was furiously busy. 'The trick is,' he explained to Joe, 'to find out all I can about those critters. Then maybe I can tell where they came from and how I got 'em. Then perhaps I can discover where Grandpa and Harding went. Then –'

'Why not sit down and think about it?'

'That's the difference between us. You've got no instinct of self-preservation. You could sit down and think while a chain reaction took place in your toes and worked up, but not me. I'm too young to die. I keep thinking of Reading Gaol. I need a drink. If I could only get high, my demon subconscious could work out the whole problem for me. Is that little brown animal around?'

'No,' Joe said.

'Then maybe I can steal a drink.' Gallegher exploded, after an abortive attempt that ended in utter failure: 'Nobody can move *that* fast.'

'Accelerated metabolism. It must have smelled the alcohol. Or perhaps it has additional senses. Even I can scarcely varish it.'

'If I mixed kerosene with the whisky, maybe the dipsomaniacal little monster wouldn't like it. Still, neither would I. Ah, well. Back to the mill,' Gallegher said, as he tried reagent after reagent on the blue-eyed dynamo, without any effect at all.

'Men can know the nature of things,' Joe said irritatingly.

'Shut up. I wonder if I could electroplate this creature? That would immobilise it, all right. But it's immobilised already. How does it eat?'

'Logically, I'd say osmosis.'

'Very likely. Osmosis of what?'

Joe clicked irritatedly. 'There are dozens of ways you could solve your problem. Instrumentalism. Empiricism. Vitalism. Work from *a posteriori* to *a priori*. It's perfectly obvious to me that you've solved the problem Adrenals, Incorporated, set you.'

'I have?'

151

'Certainly.'

'How?'

'Very simple. Men can know the nature of things.'

'Will you stop repeating that outmoded basic and try to be useful? You're wrong, anyway. Men can know the nature of things by experiment and reason combined!'

Joe said: 'Ridiculous. Philosophical incompetence. If you can't prove your point by logic, you've failed. Anybody who has to depend on experiment is beneath contempt.'

'Why should I sit here arguing philosophical concepts with a robot?' Gallegher demanded of no one in particular. 'How would you like me to demonstrate the fact that ideation is dependent on your having a radioatomic brain that isn't scattered all over the floor?'

'Kill me, then,' Joe said. 'It's your loss and the world's. Earth will be a poorer place when I die. But coercion means nothing to me. I have no instinct of self-preservation.'

'Now look,' Gallegher said, trying a new tack, 'if you know the answer, why not tell me? Demonstrate that wonderful logic of yours. Convince me without having to depend on experiment. Use pure reason.'

'Why should I want to convince you? *I'm* convinced. And I'm so beautiful and perfect that I can achieve no higher glory than to admire me.'

'Narcissus,' Gallegher snarled. 'You're a combination of Narcissus and Nietzsche's Superman.'

'Men can know the nature of things,' Joe said.

The next development was a subpoena for the transparent robot. The legal machinery was beginning to move, an immensely complicated gadget that worked on a logic as apparently twisted as Joe's own. Gallegher himself, it seemed, was temporarily inviolate, through some odd interpretation of jurisprudence. But the State's principle was that the sum of the parts was equal to the whole. Joe was classified as one of the parts, the total of which equalled Gallegher. Thus the robot found itself in court, listening to a polemic with impassive scorn.

Gallegher, flanked by Murdoch Mackenzie and a corps of attorneys, was with Joe. This was an informal hearing. Gallegher didn't pay much attention; he was concentrating on finding a way to put the bite on the recalcitrant robot, who knew all the answers but wouldn't talk. He had been studying the philosophers, with an eye towards meeting Joe on his own ground, but so far had succeeded only in acquiring a headache and an almost unendurable longing for a drink. Even out of his laboratory, though, he remained Tantalus. The invisible little brown animal followed him around and stole his liquor.

One of Mackenzie's lawyers jumped up. 'I object,' he said. There was a brief wrangle as to whether Joe should be classified as a witness or as Exhibit A. If the latter, the subpoena had been falsely served. The Justice pondered.

'As I see it,' he declared, 'the question is one of determinism versus voluntarism. If this . . . ah . . . robot has free will – '

'Ha!' Gallegher said, and was shushed by an attorney. He subsided rebelliously.

' – then it, or he, is a witness. But, on the other hand, there is the possiblity that the robot, in acts of apparent choice, is the mechanical expression of heredity and past environment. For heredity read . . . ah . . . initial mechanical basics.'

'Whether or not the robot is a rational being, Mr Justice, is beside the point,' the prosecutor put in.

'I do not agree. Law is based on *res* – '

Joe said: 'Mr Justice, may I speak?'

'Your ability to do so rather automatically gives you permission,' the Justice said, studying the robot in a baffled way. 'Go ahead.'

Joe had seemingly found the connection between law, logic, and philosophy. He said happily: 'I've figured it all out. A thinking robot is a rational being. I am a thinking robot – therefore I am a rational being.'

'What a fool,' Gallegher groaned, longing for the sane logics of electronics and chemistry. 'The old Socratic syllogism. Even I could point out the flaw in that!'

'Quiet,' Mackenzie whispered. 'All the lawyers really depend on is tying up the case in such knots nobody can figure it out. Your robot is perhaps not such a fool as you think.'

An argument started as to whether thinking robots really were rational beings. Gallegher brooded. He couldn't see the point, really. Nor did it become clear until, from the maze of contradictions, there emerged the tentative decision that Joe was a rational being. This seemed to please the prosecutor immensely.

'Mr Justice,' he announced, 'we have learned that Mr Galloway Gallegher two nights ago inactivated the robot before us now. Is this not true, Mr Gallegher?'

But Mackenzie's hand kept Gallegher in his seat. One of the defending attorneys rose to meet the question.

'We admit nothing,' he said. 'However, if you wish to pose a theoretical question, we will answer it.'

The query was posed theoretically.

'Then the theoretical answer is "yes," Mr Prosecutor. A robot of this type can be turned on and off at will.'

'Can the robot turn itself off?'

'Yes.'

'But this did not occur? Mr Gallegher inactivated the robot at the time Mr Jonas Harding was with him in his laboratory two nights ago?'

'Theoretically, that is true. There was a temporary inactivation.'

'Then,' said the prosecutor, 'we wish to question the robot, who has been classed as a rational being.'

'The decision was tentative,' a defence attorney objected.

'Accepted. Mr Justice –'

'All right,' said the Justice, who was still staring at Joe, 'you may ask your questions.'

'Ah . . . ah – ' The prosecutor, facing the robot, hesitated.

'Call me Joe,' Joe said.

'Thank you. Ah . . . is this true? Did Mr Gallegher inactivate you at the time and place stated?'

'Yes.'

'Then,' the prosecutor said triumphantly, 'I wish to bring a charge of assault and battery against Mr Gallegher. Since this robot has been tentatively classed as a rational being, any activity causing him, or it, to lose consciousness or the power of mobility is *contra bonos mores*, and may be classed as mayhem.'

Mackenzie's attorneys were ruffled. Gallegher said: 'What does that mean?'

A lawyer whispered: 'They can hold you, and hold that robot as a witness.' He stood up. 'Mr Justice. Our statements were in reply to purely theoretical questions.'

The prosecutor said. 'But the robot's statmement answered a nontheoretical question.'

'The robot was not on oath.'

'Easily remedied,' said the prosecutor, while Gallegher saw his last hopes slipping rapidly away. He thought hard, while matters proceeded.

'Do you solemnly swear to tell the truth the whole truth and nothing but the truth so help you God?'

Gallegher leaped to his feet. 'Mr Justice. I object.'

'Indeed. To what?'

'To the validity of that oath.'

Mackenzie said: 'Ah-*ha*!'

The Justice was thoughtful. 'Will you please elucidate, Mr Gallegher? Why should the oath not be administered to this robot?'

'Such an oath is applicable to man only.'

'And?'

'It presupposes the existence of the soul. At least it implies theism, a personal religion. Can a robot take an oath?'

The Justice eyed Joe. 'It's a point, certainly. Ah . . . Joe. Do you believe in a personal deity?'

'I do.'

The prosecutor beamed. 'Then we can proceed.'

'Wait a minute,' Murdoch Mackenzie said, rising. 'May I ask a question, Mr Justice?'

'Go ahead.'

Mackenzie stared at the robot. 'Well, now. Will you tell me, please, what this personal deity of yours is like?'

'Certainly,' Joe said. 'Just like me.'

After a while it degenerated into a theological argument. Gallegher left the attorneys debating the apparently vital point of how many angels could dance on the head of a pin, and went home temporarily scot-free, with Joe. Until such points as the robot's religious basics were settled, nothing could be done. All the way, in the aircab, Mackenzie insisted on pointing out the merits of Calvinism to Joe.

At the door Mackenzie made a mild threat. 'I did not intend to give you so much rope, you understand. But you will work all the harder with the threat of prison hanging over your head. I don't know how long I can keep you a free man. If you can work out an answer quickly – '

'What sort of answer?'

'I am easily satisfied. Jonas's body, now – '

'Bah!' Gallegher said, and went into his laboratory and sat down morosely. He syphoned himself a drink before he remembered the little brown animal. Then he lay back, staring from the blue-eyed dynamo to Joe and back again.

Finally he said: 'There's an old Chinese idea that the man who first stops arguing and starts swinging with his fists admits his intellectual defeat.'

Joe said: 'Naturally. Reason is sufficient; if you need experiment to prove your point, you're a lousy philosopher and logician.'

Gallegher fell back on casuistry. 'First step, animal. Fist-swinging. Second step, human. Pure logic. But what about the third step?'

'What third step?'

'Men can know the nature of things – but you're not a man. Your personal deity isn't an anthropomorphic one. Three steps; animal, man, and what we'll call for convenience superman, though *man* doesn't necessarily enter into it. We've always attributed godlike traits to the theoretical superbeing. Suppose, just for the sake of having a label, we call this third-stage entity Joe.'

'Why not?' Joe said.

'Then the two basic concepts of logic don't apply. Men can know the nature of things by pure reason, and also by experiment *and* reason. But such second-stage concepts are as elementary to Joe as Plato's ideas were to Bacon.' Gallegher crossed his fingers behind his back. 'The question is, then, what's the third-stage operation for Joe?'

'Godlike?' the robot said.

'You've got special senses, you know. You can varish, whatever that is. Do you need ordinary logical methods? Suppose – '

'Yes,' Joe said, 'I can varish, all right. I can skren, too. Hm-m-m.'

Gallegher abruptly rose from the couch. 'What a fool I am. "DRINK ME." That's the answer. Joe, shut up. Go off in a corner and varish.'

'I'm skrenning,' Joe said.

'Then skren. I've finally got an idea. When I woke up yesterday, I was thinking about a bottle labelled "DRINK ME." When Alice took a drink, she changed size, didn't she?' Where's the reference book? I wish I knew more about technology. Vasoconstrictor . . . hemostatic . . . here it is – demonstrates the metabolic regulation mechanisms of the vegetative nervous system. Metabolism. I wonder now – '

Gallegher rushed to the workbench and examined the bottles. 'Vitalism. Life is the basic reality, of which everything else is a form of manifestation. Now. I had a problem to solve for Adrenals, Incorporated. Jonas Harding and Grandpa were here. Harding gave me an hour to fill the bill. The problem . . . a dangerous and harmless animal. Paradox. That isn't it. Harding's clients wanted thrills and safety at the same time. I've got no lab animals on tap at the moment . . . *Joe*!'

'Well?'

'Watch,' Gallegher said. He poured a drink and watched the liquid vanish before he tasted it. 'Now. What happened?'

'The little brown animal drank it.'

'Is that little brown animal, by any chance – Grandpa?'

'That's right,' Joe said.

Gallegher blistered the robot's transparent hide with sulphurous oaths. 'Why didn't you tell me? You – '

'I answered your question,' the robot said smugly. 'Grandpa's brown, isn't he? And he's an animal.'

'But – little! I thought it was a critter about as big as a rabbit.'

'The only standard of comparison is the majority of the species. That's the yardstick. Compared to the average height of humans, Grandpa *is* little. A little brown animal.'

'So it's Grandpa, is it?' Gallegher said, returning to the workbench. 'And he's simply speeded up. Accelerated metabolism. Adrenalin. Hm-m-m. Now I know what to look for, maybe –'

He fell to. But it was sundown before Gallegher emptied a small vial into a glass, syphoned whisky into it, and watched the mixture disappear.

A flickering began. Something flashed from corner to corner of the room. Gradually it became visible as a streaking brownness that resolved itself, finally, into Grandpa. He stood before Gallegher, jittering like mad as the last traces of the accelerative formula wore off.

'Hello, Grandpa,' Gallegher said placatingly.

Grandpa's nutcracker face wore an expression of malevolent fury. For the first time in his life, the old gentleman was drunk. Gallegher stared in utter amazement.

'I'm going back to Maine,' Grandpa cried, and fell over backwards.

'Never seen such a lot of slow pokes in my life,' Grandpa said, devouring a steak. 'My, I'm hungry. Next time I let you stick a needle in me I'll know better. How many months have I been like this?'

'Two days,' Gallegher said, carefully mixing up a formula. 'It was a metabolic accelerator, Grandpa. You just lived faster, that's all.'

'All! Bah. Couldn't eat nothing. Food was solid as a rock. Only thing I could get down my gullet was liquor.'

'Oh?'

'Hard chewing. Even with my store teeth. Whisky tasted red-hot. As for a steak like this, I couldn't of managed it.'

'You were living faster.' Gallegher glanced at the robot, who was still quietly skrenning in a corner. 'Let me see. The antithesis of an accelerator is a decelerator – Grandpa, where's Jonas Harding?'

'In there,' Grandpa said, pointing to the blue-eyed dynamo and thus confirming Gallegher's suspicion.

'Vitaplasm. So that was it. That's why I had a lot of Vitaplasm sent over a couple of nights ago. Hm-m-m.' Gallegher examined the sleek, impermeable surface of the apparent dynamo. After a while he tried a hypodermic syringe. He couldn't penetrate the hard shell.

Instead, using a new mixture he had concocted from the bottles on his workbench, he dripped a drop of the liquid on the substance. Presently it softened. At that spot Gallegher made an injection, and was delighted to see a colour-change spread out from the locus till the entire mass was pallid and plastic.

'Vitaplasm,' he exulted. 'Ordinary artificial protoplasm cells, that's all. No wonder it looked hard. I'd given it a decelerative treatment. An approach to molecular stasis. Anything metabolising that slowly would seem hard as iron.' He wadded up great bunches of the surrogate and dumped it into a convenient vat. Something began to form around the blue eyes – the shape of a cranium, broad shoulders, a torso –

Freed from the disguising mass of Vitaplasm, Jonas Harding was revealed crouching on the floor, silent as a statue.

His heart wasn't beating. He didn't breathe. The decelerator held him in an unbreakable grip of passivity.

Not quite unbreakable. Gallegher, about to apply the hypodermic, paused and looked from Joe to Grandpa. 'Now why did I do that?' he demanded.

Then he answered his own question.

'The time limit. Harding gave me an hour to solve his problem. Time's relative – especially when your metabolism is slowed down. I must have given Harding a shot of the decelerator so he wouldn't realise how much time had passed. Let's see.' Gallegher applied a drop to Harding's impermeable skin and watched the spot soften and change hue. 'Uh-huh. With Harding frozen like that, I could take weeks to work on the problem, and when he woke up, he'd figure only a short time had passed. But why did I use the Vitaplasm on him?'

Grandpa downed a beer. 'When you're drunk, you're apt to do anything,' he said, reaching for another steak.

'True, true. But Gallegher Plus is logical. A strange, eerie kind of logic, but logic, nevertheless. Let me see. I shot the decelerator into Harding, and then – there he was. Rigid and stiff. I couldn't leave him kicking around the lab, could I? If anybody came in, they'd think I had a corpse on my hands!'

'You mean he ain't dead?' Grandpa demanded.

'Of course not. Merely decelerated. I know! I camouflaged Harding's body. I sent out for Vitaplasm, moulded the stuff around his body, and then applied the decelerator to the Vitaplasm. It works on living cellular substance – slows it down. And slowed down to that extent, it's impermeable and immovable!'

'You're crazy,' Grandpa said.

'I'm short-sighted,' Gallegher admitted. 'At least, Gallegher Plus is. Imagine leaving Harding's eyes visible, so I'd be reminded the guy was under that pile when I woke up from my binge! What did I construct that recorder for, anyhow? The logic Gallegher Plus uses is far more fantastic than Joe's.'

'Don't bother me,' Joe said. 'I'm still skrenning.'

Gallegher put the hypodermic needle into the soft spot on Harding's arm. He injected the accelerator, and within a moment or two Jonas Harding stirred, blinked his blue eyes, and got up from the floor. 'Ouch!' he said, rubbing his arm. 'Did you stick me with something?'

'An accident,' Gallegher said, watching the man warily. 'Uh . . . this problem of yours –'

Harding found a chair and sat down, yawning. 'Solved it?'

'You gave me an hour.'

'Oh. Yes, of course.' Harding looked at his watch. 'It's stopped. Well, what about it?'

'Just how long a time do you think has elapsed since you came into this laboratory?'

'Half an hour?' Harding hazarded.

'Two months,' Grandpa snapped.

'You're both right,' Gallegher said. 'I'd have another answer, but I'd be right, too.'

Harding obviously thought that Gallegher was still drunk. He stayed doggedly on the subject.

'What about that specialised animal we need? You still have half an hour –'

'I don't need it,' Gallegher said, a great white light dawning in his mind. 'I've got your answer for you. But it isn't quite what you think it is.' He relaxed on the couch and considered the liquor organ. Now he could drink again, he found he preferred to prolong the anticipation.

'I came upon no wine so wonderful as thirst,' he remarked.

'Claptrap,' Grandpa said.

Gallegher said: 'The clients of Adrenals, Incorporated, want to hunt animals. They want a thrill, so they need dangerous animals. They have to be safe, so they can't have dangerous animals. It seems paradoxical, but it isn't. The answer doesn't lie in the animal. It's in the hunter.'

Harding blinked. 'Come again?'

'Tigers. Ferocious man-eating tigers. Lions. Jaguars. Water buffalo. The most vicious, carnivorous animals you can get. That's part of the answer.'

'Listen – ' Harding said. 'Maybe you've got the wrong idea. The tigers aren't our customers. We don't supply clients to the animals, it's the other way round.'

'I must make a few more tests,' Gallegher said, 'but the basic principle's right here in my hand. An accelerator. A latent metabolic accelerator with a strong concentration of adrenalin as the catalyst. Like this – '

He sketched a vivid verbal picture.

Armed with a rifle, the client wandered through the artificial jungle, seeking quarry. He had already paid his fee to Adrenals, Incorporated, and got his intravenous shot of the latent accelerator. That substance permeated his blood stream, doing nothing as yet, waiting for the catalyst.

The tiger launched itself from the underbrush. It shot towards the client like catapulted murder, fangs bared. As the claws neared the man's back, the suprarenals shot adrenalin into the blood stream in strong concentration.

That was the catalyst. The latent accelerative factor became active.

The client speeded up – tremendously.

He stepped away from the tiger, which was apparently frozen in mid-air, and did what seemed best to him before the effect of the accelerator wore off. When it did, he returned to normal – and by that time he could be in the supply station of Adrenals, Incorporated, getting another intravenous shot – unless he'd decided to bag his tiger the easy way.

It was as simple as that.

'Ten thousand credits,' Gallegher said, happily counting them. 'The balance due as soon as I work out the catalytic angle. Which is a cinch. Any forth-rate chemist could do it. What intrigues me is the forthcoming interview between Harding and Murdoch Mackenzie. When they compare the time element, it's going to be funny.'

'I want a drink,' Grandpa said. 'Where's a bottle?'

'Even in court, I think I could prove I only took an hour or less to solve the problem. It was Harding's hour, of course, but time *is* relative. Entropy – metabolism – what a legal battle *that* would be! Still, it won't happen. I know the formula for the accelerator and Harding doesn't. He'll pay the other forty thousand – and Mackenzie won't have any kicks. After all, I'm giving Adrenals, Incorporated the success factor they needed.'

'Well, I'm still going back to Maine,' Grandpa contended. 'Least you can do is give me a bottle.'

'Go out and buy one,' Gallegher said, tossing the old gentleman several credits. 'Buy several. I often wonder what the vintners buy –'

'Eh?'

' – one-half so precious as the stuff they sell. No, I'm not tight. But I'm going to be.' Gallegher clutched the liquor-organ's mouthpiece in a loving grip and began to play alcoholic arpeggios on the keyboard. Grandpa, with a parting sneer at such new-fangled contraptions, took his departure.

Silence fell over the laboratory. Bubbles and Monstro, the two dynamos, sat quiescent. Neither of them had bright blue eyes. Gallegher experimented with cocktails and felt a warm, pleasant glow seep through his soul.

Joe came out of his corner and stood before the mirror, admiring his gears.

'Finished skrenning?' Gallegher asked sardonically.

'Yes.'

'Rational being, forsooth. You and your philosophy. Well, my fine robot, it turned out I didn't need your help after all. Pose away.'

'How ungrateful you are,' Joe said, 'after I've given you the benefit of my superlogic.'

'Your . . . what? You've slipped a gear. What super-logic?'

'The third stage, of course. What we were talking about a while back. That's why I was skrenning. I hope you didn't think all your problems were solved by your feeble brain, in that opaque cranium of yours.'

Gallegher sat up. 'What are you talking about? Third-stage logic? You didn't – '

'I don't think I can describe it to you. It's more abstruse than the noumenon of Kant, which can't be perceived except by thought. You've got to be able to skren to understand it, but – well, it's the third stage. It's . . . let's see . . . demonstrating the nature of things by making things happen by themselves.'

'Experiment?'

'No. By skrenning, I reduce all things from the material plane to the realm of pure thought, and figure out the logical concepts and solutions.'

'But . . . wait. Things have been *happening*! I figured out about Grandpa and Harding and worked out the accelerator – '

'You think you did,' Joe said. 'I simply skrenned. Which is a purely superintellectual process. After I'd done that, things couldn't help happening. But I hope you don't think they happened by themselves.'

Gallegher said: 'What's skrenning?'

'You'll never know.'

'But . . . you're contending you're the First Cause . . . no, it's voluntarism . . . third-stage logic? No – ' Gallegher fell back on the couch, staring. 'Who do you think you are?

Deus ex machina?'

Joe glanced down at the conglomeration of gears in his torso.

'What else?' he asked smugly.

TIME LOCKER

Gallegher played by ear, which would have been all right had he been a musician – but he was a scientist. A drunken and erratic one, but good. He'd wanted to be an experimental technician, and would have been excellent at it, for he had a streak of genius at times. Unfortunately, there had been no funds for such specialised education, and now Gallegher, by profession an integrator machine supervisor, maintained his laboratory purely as a hobby. It was the damnedest-looking lab in six States. Gallegher had once spent months building what he called a liquor organ, which occupied most of the space. He could recline on a comfortably padded couch and, by manipulating buttons, syphon drinks of marvellous quantity, quality, and variety down his scarified throat. Since he had made the liquor organ during a protracted period of drunkenness, he never remembered the basic principles of its construction. In a way, that was a pity.

There was a little of everything in the lab, much of it incongruous. Rheostats had little skirts on them, like ballet dancers, and vacuously grinning faces of clay. A generator was conspicuously labelled, 'Monstro,' and a much smaller one rejoiced in the name of 'Bubbles.' Inside a glass retort was a china rabbit, and Gallegher alone knew how it had got there. Just inside the door was a hideous iron dog, originally intended for Victorian lawns or perhaps for Hell, and its hollowed ears served as sockets for test tubes.

'But how do you do it?' Vanning asked.

Gallegher, his lank form reclining under the liquor organ, syphoned a shot of double Martini into his mouth. 'Huh?'

'You heard me. I could get you a swell job if you'd use that screwball brain of yours. Or even learn to put up a front.'

'Tried it,' Gallegher mumbled. 'No use. I can't work when I concentrate, except at mechanical stuff. I think my subconscious must have a high I.Q.'

Vanning, a chunky little man with a scarred, swarthy face, kicked his heels against Monstro. Sometimes Gallegher annoyed him. The man never realised his own potentialities, or how much they might mean to Horace Vanning, Commerce Analyst. The 'commerce,' of course, was extra-legal, but the complicated trade relationships of the day left loopholes a clever man could slip through. The fact of the matter was, Vanning acted in an advisory capacity to crooks. It paid well. A sound knowledge of jurisprudence was rare in these days; the statutes were in such a tangle that it took years of research before one could even enter a law school. But Vanning had a staff of trained experts, a colossal library of transcripts, decisions, and legal data, and, for a suitable fee, he could have told Dr Crippen how to get off scot-free.

The shadier side of his business was handled in strict privacy, without assistants. The matter of the neuro-gun, for example –

Gallegher had made that remarkable weapon, quite without realising its function. He had hashed it together one evening, piecing out the job with court plaster when his welder went on the fritz. And he'd given it to Vanning, on request. Vanning didn't keep it long. But already he had earned thousands of credits by lending the gun to potential murderers. As a result, the police department had a violent headache.

A man in the know would come to Vanning and say, 'I heard you can beat a murder rap. Suppose I wanted to –'

'Hold on! I can't condone anything like that.'

'Huh? But –'

'Theoretically, I suppose a perfect murder might be possible. Suppose a new sort of gun had been invented, and suppose – just for the sake of an example – it was in a locker at the Newark Stratoship Field.'

'Huh?'

'I'm just theorising. Locker Number 79, combination thirty-blue-eight. These little details always help one to

166

visualise a theory, don't they?'

'You mean –'

'Of course if our murderer picked up this imaginary gun and used it, he'd be smart enough to have a postal box ready, addressed to . . . say . . . Locker 40, Brooklyn Port. He could slip the weapon into the box, seal it, and get rid of the evidence at the nearest mail conveyer. But that's all theorising. Sorry I can't help you. The fee for an interview is three thousand credits. The receptionist will take your cheque.'

Later, conviction would be impossible. Ruling 875-M, Illinois Precinct, case of State vs Dupson, set the precedent. Cause of death must be determined. Element of accident must be considered. As Chief Justice Duckett had ruled during the trial of Sanderson vs Sanderson, which involved the death of the accused's mother-in-law –

Surely the prosecuting attorney, with his staff of toxicological experts, mut realise that –

And in short, your honour, I must respectfully request that the case be dismissed for lack of evidence and proof of *casus mortis* –

Gallegher never even found out that his neuro-gun was a dangerous weapon. But Vanning haunted the sloppy laboratory, avidly watching the results of his friend's scientific doodling. More than once he had acquired handy little devices in just this fashion. The trouble was, Gallegher wouldn't *work*!

He took another sip of Martini, shook his head, and unfolded his lanky limbs. Blinking, he ambled over to a cluttered workbench and began toying with lengths of wire.

'Making something?'

'Dunno. Just fiddling. That's the way it goes. I put things together, and sometimes they work. Trouble is, I never know exactly what they're going to do. *Tsk*!' Gallegher dropped the wires and returned to his couch. 'Hell with it.'

He was, Vanning reflected, an odd duck. Gallegher was essentially amoral, thoroughly out of place in this too-complicated world. He seemed to watch, with a certain wry amusement, from a vantage point of his own, rather disinterested for the most part. And he made things –

But always and only for his own amusement. Vanning sighed and glanced around the laboratory, his orderly soul shocked by the mess. Automatically he picked up a rumpled smock from the floor, and looked for a hook. Of course there was none. Gallegher, running short of conductive metal, had long since ripped them out and used them in some gadget or other.

The so-called scientist was creating a zombie, his eyes half closed. Vanning went over to a metal locker in one corner and opened the door. There were no hooks, but he folded the smock neatly and laid it on the floor of the locker.

Then he went back to his perch on Monstro.

'Have a drink?' Gallegher asked.

Vanning shook his head. 'Thanks, no. I've got a case coming up tomorrow.'

'There's always thiamin. Filthy stuff. I work better when I've got pneumatic cushions around my brain.'

'Well, I don't.'

'It is purely a matter of skill,' Gallegher hummed, 'to which each may attain if he will . . . What are you gaping at?'

'That – locker,' Vanning said, frowning in a baffled way. 'What the – ' He got up. The metal door hadn't been securely latched and had swung open. Of the smock Vanning had placed within the metal compartment there was no trace.

'It's the paint,' Gallegher explained sleepily. 'Or the treatment. I bombarded it with gamma rays. But it isn't good for anything.'

Vanning went over and swung a fluorescent into a more convenient position. The locker wasn't empty, as he had at first imagined. The smock was no longer there, but instead there was a tiny blob of – something, pale-green and roughly spherical.

'It melts things?' Vanning asked, staring.

'Uh-uh. Pull it out. You'll see.'

Vanning felt hesitant about putting his hand inside the locker. Instead, he found a long pair of test-tube clamps and teased the blob out. It was –

Vanning hastily looked away. His eyes hurt. The green blob was changing in colour, shape and size. A crawling, nongeometrical blur of motion rippled over it. Suddenly the clamps were remarkably heavy.

No wonder. They were gripping the original smock.

'It does that, you know,' Gallegher said absently. 'Must be a reason, too. I put things in the locker and they get small. Take 'em out, and they get big again. I suppose I could sell it to a stage magician.' His voice sounded doubtful.

Vanning sat down, fingering the smock and staring at the metal locker. It was a cube, approximately 3 x 3 x 5, lined with what seemed to be greyish paint, sprayed on. Outside, it was shiny black.

'How'd you do it?'

'Huh? I dunno. Just fiddling around.' Gallegher sipped his zombie. 'Maybe it's a matter of dimensional extension. My treatment may have altered the spatio-temporal relationships inside the locker. I wonder what that means?' he murmured in a vague aside. 'Words frighten me sometimes.'

Vanning was thinking about tesseracts. 'You mean it's bigger inside than it is outside?'

'A paradox, a paradox, a most delightful paradox. *You* tell *me*. I suppose the inside of the locker isn't in this space-time continuum at all. Here, shove that bench in it. You'll see.' Gallegher made no move to rise; he waved towards the article of furniture in question.

'You're crazy. That bench is bigger than the locker.'

'So it is. Shove it in a bit at a time. That corner first. Go ahead.'

Vanning wrestled with the bench. Despite his shortness, he was stockily muscular.

'Lay the locker on its back. It'll be easier.'

'I . . . *uh*! . . . O.K. Now what?'

'Edge the bench down into it.'

Vanning squinted at his companion, shrugged, and tried to obey. Of course the bench wouldn't go into the locker. One corner did, that was all. Then, naturally, the bench stopped, balancing precariously at an angle.

'Well?'

'Wait.'

The bench moved. It settled slowly downward. As Vanning's jaw dropped, the bench seemed to crawl into the locker, with the gentle motion of a not-too-heavy object sinking through water. It wasn't sucked down. It melted down. The portion still outside the locker was unchanged. But that, too, settled, and was gone.

Vanning craned forward. A blur of movement hurt his eyes. Inside the locker was – something. It shifted its contours, shrank, and became a spiky sort of scalene pyramid, deep purple in hue.

It seemed to be less than four inches across at its widest point.

'I don't believe it,' Vanning said.

Gallegher grinned. 'As the Duke of Wellington remarked to the subaltern, it was a demned small bottle, sir.'

'Now wait a minute. How the devil could I put an eight-foot bench inside of a five-foot locker?'

'Because of Newton,' Gallegher said. 'Gravity. Go fill a test tube with water and I'll show you.'

'Wait a minute . . . O.K. Now what?'

'Got it brim-full? Good. You'll find some sugar cubes in that drawer labelled "Fuses." Lay a cube on top of the test tube, one corner down so it touches the water.'

Vanning racked the tube and obeyed. 'Well?'

'What do you see?'

'Nothing. The sugar's getting wet. And melting.'

'So there you are,' Gallegher said expansively. Vanning gave him a brooding look and turned back to the tube. The cube of sugar was slowly dissolving and melting down.

Presently it was gone.

'Air and water are different physical conditions. In air a sugar cube can exist as a sugar cube. In water it exists in solution. The corner of it extending into water is subject to aqueous conditions. So it alters physically, though not chemically. Gravity does the rest.'

'Make it clearer.'

'The analogy's clear enough, no? The water represents the

particular condition existing inside that locker. The sugar cube represents the workbench. Now! The sugar soaked up the water and gradually dissolved it, so gravity could pull the cube down into the tube as it melted. See?'

'I think so. The bench soaked up the . . . the x condition inside the locker, eh? A condition that shrank the bench –'

'*In partis*, not *in toto*. A little at a time. You can shove a human body into a small container of sulphuric acid, bit by bit.'

'Oh,' Vanning said, regarding the cabinet askance. 'Can you get the bench out again?'

'Do it yourself. Just reach in and pull it out.'

'*Reach* in? I don't want my hand to melt!'

'It won't. The action isn't instantaneous. You saw that yourself. It takes a few minutes for the change to take place. You can reach into the locker without any ill effects, if you don't leave your hand exposed to the conditions for more than a minute or so. I'll show you.' Gallegher languidly arose, looked around, and picked up an empty demijohn. He dropped this into the locker.

The change wasn't immediate. It occurred slowly, the demijohn altering its shape and size till it was a distorted cube the apparent size of a cube of sugar. Gallegher reached down and brought it up again, placing the cube on the floor.

It grew. It was a demijohn again.

'Now the bench. Look out.'

Gallegher rescued the little pyramid. Presently it became the original workbench.

'You see? I'll bet a storage company would like this. You could probably pack all the furniture in Brooklyn in here, but there'd be trouble in getting what you wanted out again. The physical change, you know –'

'Keep a chart,' Vanning suggested absently. 'Draw a picture of how the thing looks inside the locker, and note down what it was.'

'The legal brain,' Gallegher said. 'I want a drink.' He returned to his couch and clutched the syphon in a grip of death.

'I'll give you six credits for the thing,' Vanning offered.

'Sold. It takes up too much room anyway. Wish I could put it inside itself.' The scientist chuckled immoderately. 'That's very funny.'

'Is it?' Vanning said. 'Well, here you are.' He took credit coupons from his wallet. 'Where'll I put the dough?'

'Stuff it into Monstro. He's my bank . . . Thanks.'

'Yeah. Say, elucidate this sugar business a bit, will you? It isn't just gravity that affects the cube so it slips into a test tube. Doesn't the water soak up into the sugar – '

'You're right at that. Osmosis. No, I'm wrong. Osmosis has something to do with eggs. Or is that ovulation? Conduction, convection – absorption! Wish I'd studied physics: then I'd know the right words. Just a mad genius, that's me. I shall take the daughter of the Vine to spouse,' Gallegher finished incoherently and sucked at the syphon.

'Absorption,' Vanning scowled. 'Only not water, being soaked up by the sugar. The . . . the *conditions* existing inside the locker, being soaked up by your workbench – in that particular case.'

'Like a sponge or a blotter.'

'The bench?'

'Me,' Gallegher said succinctly, and relapsed into a happy silence, broken by occasional gurgles as he poured liquor down his scarified gullet. Vanning sighed and turned to the locker. He carefully closed and latched the door before lifting the metal cabinet in his muscular arms.

'Going? G'night. Fare thee well, fare thee well – '

'Night.'

'*Fare* –thee – well!' Gallegher ended, in a melancholy outburst of tunefulness, as he turned over preparatory to going to sleep.

Vanning sighed again and let himself out into the coolness of the night. Stars blazed in the sky, except towards the south, where the aurora of Lower Manhattan dimmed them. The glowing white towers of skyscrapers rose in a jagged pattern. A sky-ad announced the virtues of Vambulin – 'It Peps You Up.'

His speeder was at the curb. Vanning edged the locker into the trunk compartment and drove towards the Hudson

Floatway. He was thinking about Poe.

The Purloined Letter, which had been hidden in plain sight, but re-folded and re-addressed, so that its superficial appearance was changed. Holy Hecate! What a perfect safe the locker would make! No thief could crack it, for the obvious reason that it wouldn't be locked. No thief would *want* to clean it out. Vanning could fill the locker with credit coupons and instantly they'd become unrecognisable. It was the ideal cache.

How the devil did it work?

There was little use in asking Gallegher. He played by ear. A primrose by the river's rim a simple primrose was to him – not *Primula vulgaris*. Syllogisms were unknown to him. He reached the conclusion without the aid of either major or minor premises.

Vanning pondered. Two objects cannot occupy the same space at the same time. *Ergo*, there was a different sort of space in the locker –

But Vanning was jumping at conclusions. There was another answer – the right one. He hadn't guessed it yet.

Instead, he tooled the speeder downtown to the office building where he maintained a floor, and brought the locker upstairs in the freight lift. He didn't put it in his private office; that would have been too obvious. He placed the metal cabinet in one of the storerooms, sliding a file cabinet in front of it for partial concealment. It wouldn't do to have the clerks using this particular locker.

Vanning stepped back and considered. Perhaps –

A bell rang softly. Preoccupied, Vanning didn't hear it at first. When he did, he went back to his own office and pressed the acknowledgement button on the Winchell. The grey, harsh, bearded face of Counsel Hatton appeared, filling the screen.

'Hello,' Vanning said.

Hatton nodded. 'I've been trying to reach you at your home. Thought I'd try the office – '

'I didn't expect you to call now. The trial's tomorrow. It's a bit late for discussion, isn't it?'

'Dugan & Sons wanted me to speak to you. I advised against it.'

173

'Oh?'

Hatton's thick grey brows drew together. 'I'm prosecuting, you know. There's plenty of evidence against MacIlson.'

'So you say. But peculation's a difficult charge to prove.'

'Did you get an injunction against scop?'

'Naturally,' Vanning said. 'You're not using truth serum on my client!'

'That'll prejudice the jury.'

'Not on medical grounds. Scop affects MacIlson harmfully. I've got a covering prognosis.'

'Harmfully is right!' Hatton's voice was sharp. 'Your client embezzled those bonds, and I can prove it.'

'Twenty-five thousand in credits, it comes to, eh? That's a lot for Dugan & Sons to lose. What about that hypothetical case I posed? Suppose twenty thousand were recovered –'

'Is this a private beam? No recordings?'

'Naturally. Here's the cut-off.' Vanning held up a metal-tipped cord. 'This strictly *sub rosa*.'

'Good,' Counsel Hatton said. 'Then I can call you a lousy shyster.'

'*Tch*!'

'Your gag's too old. It's moth-eaten. MacIlson swiped five grand in bonds, negotiable into credits. The auditors start checking up. MacIlson comes to you. You tell him to take twenty grand more, and offer to return that twenty if Dugan & Sons refuse to prosecute. MacIlson splits with you on the five thousand, and on the plat standard, that ain't hay.'

'I don't admit to anything like that.'

'Naturally you don't, not even on a closed beam. But it's tacit. However, the gag's moth-eaten, and my clients won't play ball with you. They're going to prosecute.'

'You called me up just to tell me that?'

'No, I want to settle the jury question. Will you agree to let 'em use scop on the panel?'

'O.K.,' Vanning said. He wasn't depending on a fixed jury tomorrow. His battle would be based on legal technicalities. With scop-tested talesmen, the odds would be even. And such an arrangement would save days or weeks of argument and challenge.

'Good,' Hatton grunted. 'You're going to get your pants licked off.'

Vanning replied with a mild obscenity and broke the connection. Reminded of the pending court fight, he forced the matter of the fourth-dimensional locker out of his mind and left the office. Later –

Later would be time enough to investigate the possibilities of the remarkable cabinet more thoroughly. Just now, he didn't want his brain cluttered with nonessentials. He went to his apartment, had the servant mix him a short highball, and dropped into bed.

And, the next day, Vanning won his case. He based it on complicated technicalities and obscure legal precedents. The crux of the matter was that the bonds had not been converted into government credits. Abstruse economic charts proved that point for Vanning. Conversion of even five thousand credits would have caused a fluctuation in the graph line, and no such break existed. Vanning's experts went into monstrous detail.

In order to prove guilt, it would have been necessary to show, either actually or by inference, that the bonds had been in existence since last December 20th, the date of their most recent check-and-recording. The case of Donovan vs Jones stood as a precedent.

Hatton jumped to his feet. 'Jones later confessed to his defalcation, your honour!'

'Which does not affect the original decision,' Vanning said smoothly. 'Retroaction is not admissible here. The verdict was not proven.'

'Counsel for the defence will continue.'

Counsel for the defence continued, building up a beautifully intricate edifice of casuistic logic.

Hattan writhed. 'Your honour! I –'

'If my learned opponent can produce one bond – just one of the bonds in question – I will concede the case.'

The presiding judge looked sardonic. 'Indeed! If such a piece of evidence could be produced, the defendant would be jailed as fast as I could pronounce sentence. You know that very well, Mr Vanning. Proceed.'

'Very well. My contention, then, is that the bonds never existed. They were the result of a clerical error in notation.'

'A clerical error in a Pederson Calculator?'

'Such errors have occurred, as I shall prove. If I may call my next witness –'

Unchallenged, the witness, a math technician, explained how a Pederson Calculator can go haywire. He cited cases.

Hatton caught him up on one point. 'I protest this proof. Rhodesia, as everyone knows, is the location of a certain important experimental industry. Witness has refrained from stating the nature of the work performed in this particular Rhodesian factory. Is it not a fact that the Henderson United Company deals largely in radioactive ores?'

'Witness will answer.'

'I can't. My records don't include that information.'

'A significant omission,' Hatton snapped. 'Radioactivity damages the intricate mechanism of a Pederson Calculator. There is no radium nor radium by-product in the offices of Dugan & Sons.'

Vanning stood up. 'May I ask if those offices have been fumigated lately?'

'They have. It is legally required.'

'A type of chlorine gas was used?'

'Yes.'

'I wish to call my next witness.'

The next witness, a physicist and official in the Ultra Radium Institute, exlplained that gamma radiations affect chlorine strongly, causing ionization. Living organisms could assimilate by-products of radium and transmit them in turn. Certain clients of Dugan & Sons had been in contact with radioactivity –

'This is ridiculous, your honour! Pure theorisation –'

Vanning looked hurt. 'I cite the case of Dangerfield vs Austro Products, California, 1963. Ruling states that the uncertainty factor is prime admissible evidence. My point is simply that the Pederson Calculator which recorded the bonds could have been in error. If this be true, there were no bonds, and my client is guiltless.'

'Counsel will continue,' said the judge, wishing he were Jeffrey so he could send the whole damned bunch to the scaffold. Jurisprudence should be founded on justice, and not be a three-dimensional chess game. But, of course, it was the natural development of the complicated political and economic factors of modern civilisation. It was already evident that Vanning would win the case.

And he did. The jury was directed to find for the defendant. On a last, desperate hope, Hatton raised a point of order and demanded scop, but his petition was denied. Vanning winked at his opponent and closed his brief case.

That was that.

Vanning returned to his office. At four-thirty that afternoon trouble started to break. The secretary announced a Mr MacIlson, and was pushed aside by a thin, dark, middle-aged man lugging a gigantic suedette suitcase.

'Vanning! I've got to see you –'

The attorney's eyes hooded. He rose from behind his desk, dismissing the secretary with a jerk of his head. As the door closed, Vanning said brusquely, 'What are you doing here? I told you to stay away from me. What's in that bag?'

'The bonds,' MacIlson explained, his voice unsteady. 'Something's gone wrong –'

'You crazy fool! Bringing the bonds here –' With a leap Vanning was at the door, locking it. 'Don't you realise that if Hatton gets his hands on that paper, you'll be yanked back to jail? And I'll be disbarred! Get 'em out of here.'

'Listen a minute, will you? I took the bonds to Finance Unity, as you told me, but . . . but there was an officer there, waiting for me. I saw him just in time. If he'd caught me –'

Vanning took a deep breath. 'You were supposed to leave the bonds in that subway locker for two months.'

MacIlson pulled a news sheet from his pocket. 'But the government's declared a freeze on ore stocks and bonds. It'll go into effect in a week. I couldn't wait – the money would have been tied up indefinitely.'

'Let's see that paper.' Vanning examined it and cursed

softly. 'Where'd you get this?'

'Bought it from a boy outside the jail. I wanted to check the current ore quotations.'

'Uh-huh. I see. Did it occur to you that this sheet might be faked?'

MacIlson's jaw dropped. 'Fake?'

'Exactly. Hatton figured I might spring you, and had this paper ready. You bit. You led the police right to the evidence, and a swell spot you've put me in.'

'B-but – '

Vanning grimaced. 'Why do you suppose you saw that cop at Finance Unity? They could have nabbed you any time. But they wanted to scare you into heading for my office, so they could catch both of us on the same hook. Prison for you, disbarment for me. Oh, hell!'

MacIlson licked his lips. 'Can't I get out a back door?'

'Through the cordon that's undoubtedly waiting? Orbs! Don't be more of a sap than you can help.'

'Can't you – hide the stuff?'

'Where? They'll ransack this office with X rays. No, I'll just – ' Vanning stopped. 'Oh. Hide it, you said. *Hide it –* '

He whirled to the dictograph. 'Miss Horton? I'm in conference. Don't disturb me for anything. If anybody hands you a search warrant, insist on verifying it through headquarters. Got me? O.K.'

Hope had returned to MacIlson's face. 'Is it all right?'

'Oh, shut up!' Vanning snapped. 'Wait here for me. Be back directly.' He headed for a side door and vanished. In a surprisingly short time he returned, awkwardly lugging a metal cabinet.

'Help me . . . *uh*! . . . here. In this corner. Now get out.'

'But – '

'Flash,' Vanning ordered. 'Everything's under control. Don't talk. You'll be arrested, but they can't hold you without evidence. Come back as soon as you're sprung.' He urged MacIlson to the door, unlocked it, and thrust the man through. After that, he returned to the cabinet, swung open the door, and peered in. Empty. Sure.

The suedette suitcase –

Vanning worked it into the locker, breathing hard. It took a little time, since the valise was larger than the metal cabinet. But at last he relaxed, watching the brown case shrink and alter its outline till it was tiny and distorted, the shape of an elongated egg, the colour of a copper cent piece.

'*Whew*!' Vanning said.

Then he leaned closer, staring. Inside the locker, something was moving. A grotesque little creature less than four inches tall was visible. It was a shocking object, all cubes and angles, a bright green in tint, and it was obviously alive.

Someone knocked on the door.

The tiny – thing – was busy with the copper-coloured egg. Like an ant, it was lifting the egg and trying to pull it away. Vanning gasped and reached into the locker. The fourth-dimensional creature dodged. It wasn't quick enough. Vanning's hand descended, and he felt wriggling movement against his palm.

He squeezed.

The movement stopped. He let go of the dead thing and pulled his hand back swiftly.

The door shook under the impact of fists.

Vanning closed the locker and called, 'Just a minute.'

'Break it down,' somebody ordered.

But that wasn't necessary. Vanning put a painful smile on his face and turned the key. Counsel Hatton came in, accompanied by bulky policemen. 'We've got MacIlson,' he said.

'Oh? Why?'

For answer Hatton jerked his hand. The officers began to search the room, Vanning shrugged.

'You've jumped the gun,' he said. 'Breaking and entering – '

'We've got a warrant.'

'Charge?'

'The bonds, of course.' Hatton's voice was weary. 'I don't know where you've hid that suitcase, but we'll find it.'

'What suitcase?' Vanning wanted to know.

'The one MacIlson had when he came in. The one he

179

didn't have when he went out.'

'The game,' Vanning said sadly, 'is up. You win.'

'Eh?'

'If I tell you what I did with the suitcase, will you put in a good word for me?'

'Why . . . yeah. Where – '

'I ate it,' Vanning said, and retired to the couch, where he settled himself for a nap. Hatton gave him a long, hating look. The officers tore in –

They passed by the locker, after a casual glance inside. The X rays revealed nothing, in walls, floor, ceiling, or articles of furniture. The other offices were searched, too. Vanning applauded the painstaking job.

In the end, Hatton gave up. There was nothing else he could do.

'I'll clap suit on you tomorrow,' Vanning promised. 'Same time I get a habeas corpus on MacIlson.'

'Step to hell,' Hatton growled.

' 'Bye now.'

Vanning waited till his unwanted guests had departed. Then, chuckling quietly, he went to the locker and opened it.

The copper-coloured egg that represented the suedette suitcase had vanished. Vanning groped inside the locker, finding nothing.

The significance of this didn't strike Vanning at first. He swung the cabinet around so that it faced the window. He looked again, with identical results.

The locker was empty.

Twenty-five thousand credits in negotiable ore bonds had disappeared.

Vanning started to sweat. He picked up the metal box and shook it. That didn't help. He carried it across the room and set it up in another corner, returning to search the floor with painstaking accuracy. *Holy* –

Hatton?

No. Vanning hadn't let the locker out of his sight from the time the police had entered till they left. An officer had swung open the cabinet's door, looked inside, and closed it again. After that the door had remained shut, till just now.

The bonds were gone.

So was the abnormal little creature Vanning had crushed. All of which meant – what?

Vanning approached the locker and closed it, clicking the latch into position. Then he reopened it, not really expecting that the copper-coloured egg would reappear.

He was right. It didn't.

Vanning staggered to the 'visor and called Gallegher.

'Whatzit? Huh? Oh. What do you want?' The scientist's gaunt face appeared on the screen, rather the worse for wear. 'I got a hangover. Can't use thiamin, either. I'm allergic to it. How'd your case come out?'

'Listen,' Gallegher said urgently. 'I put something inside that damn locker of yours and now it's gone.'

'The locker? That's funny.'

'No! The thing I put in it. A . . . a suitcase.'

Gallegher shook his head thoughtfully. 'You never know, do you? I remember once I made a – '

'The hell with that. I want that suitcase back!'

'An heirloom?' Gallegher suggested.

'No, there's money in it.'

'Wasn't that a little foolish of you? There hasn't been a bank failure since 1999. Never suspected you were a miser, Vanning. Like to have the stuff around, so you can run it through your birdlike fingers, eh?'

'You're drunk.'

'I'm *trying*,' Gallegher corrected. 'But I've built up an awful resistance over a period of years. It takes time. Your call's already set me back two and a half drinks. I must put an extension on the syphon, so I can teletalk and guzzle at the same time.'

Vanning almost chattered incoherently into the mike. 'My suitcase! What happened to it? I want it back.'

'Well, I haven't got it.'

'Can't you find out where it is?'

'Dunno. Tell me the details. I'll see what I can figure out.'

Vanning complied, revising his story as caution prompted.

'O.K.' Gallegher said at last, rather unwillingly. 'I hate working out theories, but just as a favour . . . My diagnosis will cost you fifty credits.'

'What? Now listen – '

'Fifty credits,' Gallegher repeated unflinchingly. 'Or no prognosis.'

'How do I know you can get it back for me?'

'Chances are I can't. Still, maybe . . . I'll have to go over to Mechanistra and use some of their machines. They charge a good bit, too. But I'll need forty-brain-power calculators – '

'O.K., O.K.!' Vanning growled. 'Hop to it. I want that suitcase back.'

'What interests me is that little bug you squashed. In fact, that's the only reason I'm tackling your problem. Life in the fourth dimension – ' Gallegher trailed off, murmuring. His face faded from the screen. After a while Vanning broke the connection.

He re-examined the locker, finding nothing new. Yet the suedette suitcase had vanished from it, into thin air. Oh, hell!

Brooding over his sorrows, Vanning shrugged into a top coat and dined vinously at the Manhattan Roof. He felt very sorry for himself.

The next day he felt even sorrier. A call to Gallegher had given the blank signal, so Vanning had to mark time. About noon MacIlson dropped in. His nerves were shot.

'You took your time in springing me,' he started immediately. 'Well, what now? Have you got a drink anywhere around?'

'You don't need a drink,' Vanning grunted. 'You've got a skinful already, by the look of you. Run down to Florida and wait till this blows over.'

'I'm sick of waiting. I'm going to South America. I want some credits.'

'Wait'll I arrange to cash the bonds.'

'I'll take the bonds. A fair half, as we agreed.'

Vanning's eyes narrowed. 'And walk out into the hands of the police. Sure.'

MacIlson looked uncomfortable. 'I'll admit I made a boner. But this time – no, I'll play smart now.'

'You'll wait, you mean.'

'There's a friend of mine on the roof parking lot, in a helicopter. I'll go up and slip him the bonds, and then I'll just walk out. The police won't find anything on me.'

'I said no,' Vanning repeated. 'It's too dangerous.'

'It's dangerous as things are. If they locate the bonds –'

'They won't.'

'Where'd you hide 'em?'

'That's my business.'

MacIlson glowered nervously. 'Maybe. But they're in this building. You couldn't have finagled 'em out yesterday before the cops came. No use playing your luck too far. Did they use X rays?'

'Yeah.'

'Well, I heard Counsel Hatton's got a batch of experts going over the blueprints on this building. He'll find your safe. I'm getting out of here before he does.'

Vanning patted the air. 'You're hysterical. I've taken care of you, haven't I? Even though you almost screwed the whole thing up.'

'Sure,' MacIlson said, pulling at his lip. 'But I –' He chewed a fingernail. 'Oh, damn! I'm sitting on the edge of a volcano with termites under me. I can't stay here and wait till they find the bonds. They can't extradite me from South America – where I'm going, anyway.'

'You're going to wait,' Vanning said firmly. 'That's your best chance.'

There was suddenly a gun in MacIlson's hand. 'You're going to give me half the bonds. Right now. I don't trust you a little bit. You figure you can stall me along – hell, get those bonds!'

'No,' Vanning said.

'I'm not kidding.'

'I know you aren't. I can't get the bonds.'

'Eh? Why not?'

'Ever heard of a time lock?' Vanning asked, his eyes watchful. 'You're right; I put the suitcase in a concealed safe. But I can't open that safe till a certain number of hours have passed.'

'Mm-m.' MacIlson pondered. 'When – '

'Tomorrow.'

'All right. You'll have the bonds for me then?'

'If you want them. But you'd better change your mind. It'd be safer.'

For answer MacIlson grinned over his shoulder as he went out. Vanning sat motionless for a long time. He was, frankly, scared.

The trouble was, MacIlson was a manic-depressive type. He'd kill. Right now, he was cracking under the strain, and imagining himself a desperate fugitive. Well – precautions would be advisable.

Vanning called Gallegher again, but got no answer. He left a message on the recorder and thoughtfully looked into the locker again. It was empty, depressingly so.

That evening Gallegher let Vanning into his laboratory. The scientist looked both tired and drunk. He waved comprehensively towards a table, covered with scraps of paper.

'What a headache you gave me! If I'd known the principles behind that gadget, I'd have been afraid to tackle it. Sit down. Have a drink. Got the fifty credits?'

Silently Vanning handed over the coupons. Gallegher shoved them into Monstro. 'Fine. Now – ' He settled himself on the couch. 'Now we start. The fifty credit question.'

'Can I get the suitcase back?'

'No,' Gallegher said flatly. 'At least, I don't see how it can be worked. It's in another spatio-temporal sector.'

'Just what does that mean?'

'It means the locker works something like a telescope, only the thing isn't merely visual. The locker's a window, I figure. You can reach through it as well as look through it. It's an opening into Now plus x.'

Vanning scowled. 'So far you haven't said anything.'

'So far all I've got is theory, and that's all I'm likely to get. Look. I was wrong originally. The things that went into the locker didn't appear in another space, because there would have been a spatial constant. I mean, they wouldn't have got smaller. Size is size. Moving a one-inch cube from here to Mars wouldn't make it any larger or smaller.'

'What about a different density in the surrounding

medium? Wouldn't that crush an object?'

'Sure, and it'd stay squashed. It wouldn't return to its former size and shape when it was taken out of the locker again. X plus y never equal xy. But x times y –'

'So?'

'That's a pun,' Gallegher broke off to explain. 'The things we put in the locker went into time. Their time-rate remained constant, but not the spatial relationships. Two things can't occupy the same place at the same time. *Ergo*, your suitcase went into a different time. Now plus x. And what x represents I don't know, though I suspect a few million years.'

Vanning looked dazed. 'The suitcase is a million years in the future?'

'Dunno how far, but – I'd say plenty. I haven't enough factors to finish the equation. I reasoned by induction, mostly, and the results are screwy as hell. Einstein would have loved it. My theorem shows that the universe is expanding and contracting at the same time.'

'What's that got to do –'

'Motion is relative,' Gallegher continued inexorably. 'That's a basic principle. Well, the universe *is* expanding, spreading out like a gas, but its component parts are shrinking at the same time. The *parts* don't actually grow, you know – not the suns and atoms. They just run away from the central point. Galloping off in all directions . . . where was I? Oh. Actually, the universe, taken as a unit, is shrinking.'

'So it's shrinking. Where's my suitcase?'

'I told you. In the future. Deductive reasoning showed that. It's beautifully simple and logical. And it's quite impossible of proof, too. A hundred, a thousand, a million years ago the Earth – the universe – was larger than it is now. And it continues to contract. Sometime in the future the Earth will be just half as small as it is now. Only we won't notice it because the universe will be proportionately smaller.'

Gallegher went on dreamily. 'We put a workbench into the locker, so it emerged sometime in the future. The locker's an open window into a different time, as I told you.

Well, the bench was affected by the conditions of that period. It shrank, after we gave it a few seconds to soak up the entropy or something. Do I mean entropy? Allah knows. Oh, well.'

'It turned into a pyramid.'

'Maybe there's geometric distortion, too. Or it might be a visual illusion. Perhaps we can't get the exact focus. I doubt if things will really look different in the future – except that they'll be smaller – but we're using a window into the fourth dimension. We're taking a pleat in time. It must be like looking through a prism. The alteration in size is real, but the shape and colour are altered to our eyes by the fourth-dimensional prism.'

'The whole point, then, is that my suitcase is in the future. Eh? But why did it disappear from the locker?'

'What about that little creature you squashed? Maybe he had pals. They wouldn't be visible till they came into the very narrow focus of the whatchmacallit, but – figure it out. Sometime in the future, in a hundred or a thousand or a million years, a suitcase suddenly appears out of thin air. One of our descendants investigates. You kill him. His pals come along and carry the suitcase away, out of range of the locker. In space it may be anywhere, and the time factor's an unknown quantity. Now plus x. It's a time locker. Well?'

'Hell!' Vanning exploded. 'So that's all you can tell me? I'm supposed to chalk it up to profit and loss?'

'Uh-huh. Unless you want to crawl into the locker yourself after your suitcase. God knows where you'd come out, though. The composition of the air probably would have changed in a few thousand years. There might be other alterations, too.'

'I'm not that crazy.'

So there he was. The bonds were gone, beyond hope of redemption. Vanning could resign himself to that loss, once he knew the securities wouldn't fall into the hands of the police. But MacIlson was another matter, especially after a bullet spattered against the glassolex window of Vanning's office.

An interview with MacIlson had proved unsatisfactory. The defaulter was convinced that Vanning was trying to bilk him. He was removed forcibly, yelling threats. He'd go to the police – he'd confess –

Let him. There was no proof. The hell with him. But, for safety's sake, Vanning clapped an injunction on his quondam client.

It didn't land. MacIlson clipped the official on the jaw and fled. Now, Vanning suspected, he lurked in dark corners, armed, and anxious to commit homicide. Obviously a manic-depressive type.

Vanning took a certain malicious pleasure in demanding a couple of plain-clothes men to act as his guards. Legally, he was within his rights, since his life had been threatened. Until MacIlson was under sufficient restriction, Vanning would be protected. And he made sure that his guards were two of the best shots on the Manhattan force.

He also found out that they had been told to keep their eyes peeled for the missing bonds and the suedette suitcase. Vanning televised Counsel Hatton and grinned at the screen.

'Any luck yet?'

'What do you mean?'

'My watchdogs. Your spies. They won't find the bonds, Hatton. Better call 'em off. Why make the poor devils do two jobs at once?'

'One job would be enough. Finding the evidence. If MacIlson drilled you, I wouldn't be too unhappy.'

'Well, I'll see you in court,' Vanning said. 'You're prosecuting Watson, aren't you?'

'Yes. Are you waiving scop?'

'On the jurors? Sure. I've got this case in the bag.'

'That's what you think,' Hatton said, and broke the beam.

Chuckling, Vanning donned his topcoat, collected the guards, and headed for court. There was no sign of MacIlson –

Vanning won the case, as he had expected. He returned to his offices, collected a few unimportant messages from the switchboard girl, and walked towards his private suite. As he opened the door, he saw the suedette suitcase on the carpet in one corner.

He stopped, hand frozen on the latch. Behind him he could hear the heavy footsteps of the guards. Over his shoulder Vanning said, 'Wait a minute,' and dodged into the office, slamming and locking the door behind him. He caught the tail end of a surprised question.

The suitcase. There it was, unequivocally. And, quite as unequivocally, the two plain-clothes men, after a very brief conference, were hammering on the door, trying to break it down.

Vanning turned green. He took a hesitant step forward, and then saw the locker, in the corner to which he had moved it. The time locker –

That was it. If he shoved the suitcase inside the locker, it would become unrecognisable. Even if it vanished again, that wouldn't matter. What mattered was the vital importance of getting rid – immediately! – of incriminating evidence.

The door rocked on its hinges. Vanning scuttled towards the suitcase and picked it up. From the corner of his eye he saw movement.

In the air above him, a hand had appeared. It was the hand of a giant, with an immaculate cuff fading into emptiness. Its huge fingers were reaching down –

Vanning screamed and sprang away. He was too slow. The hand descended, and Vanning wriggled impotently against the palm.

The hand contracted into a fist. When it opened, what was left of Vanning dropped squashily to the carpet, which it stained.

The hand withdrew into nothingness. The door fell in and the plain-clothes men stumbled over it as they entered.

It didn't take long for Hatton and his cohorts to arrive. Still, there was little for them to do except clean up the mess. The suedette bag, containing twenty-five thousand credits in negotiable bonds, was carried off to a safer place. Vanning's body was scraped up and removed to the morgue. Photographers flashed pictures, fingerprint experts insufflated their white powder, X ray men worked busily. It was all done with swift efficiency, so that within an hour the office was empty and the door sealed.

Thus there were no spectators to witness the advent of a gigantic hand that appeared from nothingness, groped around as though searching for something, and presently vanished once more –

The only person who could have thrown light on the matter was Gallegher, and his remarks were directed to Monstro, in the solitude of his laboratory. All he said was:

'So that's why that workbench materialised for a few minutes here yesterday. Hm-m-m. Now plus x – and x equals about a week. Still, why not? It's all relative. But – I never thought the Universe was shrinking *that* fast!'

He relaxed on the couch and syphoned a double Martini.

'Yeah, that's it,' he murmured after a while. '*Whew*! I guess Vanning must have been the only guy who ever reached into the middle of next week and – killed himself! I think I'll get tight.'

And he did.

FICTION

GENERAL

☐ Chains	Justin Adams	£1.25
☐ Secrets	F. Lee Bailey	£1.25
☐ Skyship	John Brosnan	£1.65
☐ The Free Fishers	John Buchan	£1.50
☐ Huntingtower	John Buchan	£1.50
☐ Midwinter	John Buchan	£1.25
☐ A Prince of the Captivity	John Buchan	£1.25
☐ The Eve of St Venus	Anthony Burgess	£1.10
☐ Nothing Like the Sun	Anthony Burgess	£1.50
☐ The Memoirs of Maria Brown	John Cleland	£1.25
☐ The Last Liberator	John Clive	£1.25
☐ Wyndward Fury	Norman Daniels	£1.50
☐ Ladies in Waiting	Gwen Davis	£1.50
☐ The Money Wolves	Paul Erikson	£1.50
☐ Rich Little Poor Girl	Terence Feely	£1.50
☐ Fever Pitch	Betty Ferm	£1.50
☐ The Bride of Lowther Fell	Margaret Forster	£1.75
☐ Forced Feedings	Maxine Herman	£1.50
☐ Savannah Blue	William Harrison	£1.50
☐ Duncton Wood	William Horwood	£1.95
☐ Dingley Falls	Michael Malone	£1.95
☐ Gossip	Marc Olden	£1.25
☐ Buccaneer	Dudley Pope	£1.50
☐ An Inch of Fortune	Simon Raven	£1.25
☐ The Dream Makers	John Sherlock	£1.50
☐ The Reichling Affair	Jack Stoneley	£1.75
☐ Eclipse	Margaret Tabor	£1.35
☐ Pillars of the Establishment	Alexander Thynn	£1.50
☐ Cat Stories	Stella Whitelaw	£1.10

WESTERN — BLADE SERIES by Matt Chisholm

☐ No. 5 The Colorado Virgins	85p
☐ No. 6 The Mexican Proposition	85p
☐ No. 7 The Arizona Climax	85p
☐ No. 8 The Nevada Mustang	85p
☐ No. 9 The Montana Deadlock	95p
☐ No. 10 The Cheyenne Trap	95p
☐ No. 11 The Navaho Trail	95p
☐ No. 12 The Last Act	95p

WESTERN — McALLISTER SERIES by Matt Chisholm

☐ McAllister and the Spanish Gold	95p
☐ McAllister on the Commanche Crossing	95p
☐ McAllister Never Surrenders	95p
☐ McAllister and the Cheyenne Trap	95p

SCIENCE FICTION

☐ Times Without Number	John Brunner	£1.10
☐ The Dancers of Arun	Elizabeth A. Lynn	£1.50
☐ Watchtower	Elizabeth A. Lynn	£1.10

WAR

☐ The Andersen Assault	Peter Leslie	£1.25
☐ Killers under a Cruel Sky	Peter Leslie	£1.25
☐ The Serbian Triangle	Peter Saunders	£1.10
☐ Jenny's War	Jack Stoneley	£1.25

FICTION

HORROR/OCCULT/NASTY

☐ Death Walkers	Gary Brandner	£1.00
☐ Hellborn	Gary Brandner	£1.25
☐ The Howling	Gary Brandner	£1.00
☐ Return of the Howling	Gary Brandner	£1.25
☐ The Sanctuary	Glenn Chandler	£1.00
☐ The Tribe	Glenn Chandler	£1.10
☐ Croak	Robin Evans	£1.10
☐ Blood Island	James Farber	£1.35
☐ Curse	Daniel Farson	95p
☐ Transplant	Daniel Farson	£1.00
☐ Rattlers	Joseph L. Gilmore	£1.00
☐ Slither	John Halkin	£1.00
☐ The Wicker Man	Hardy & Shaffer	£1.25
☐ The Skull	Shaun Hutson	£1.25
☐ The Beast Within	Edward Levy	£1.25
☐ Parasite	Richard Lewis	£1.00
☐ Spiders	Richard Lewis	£1.00
☐ The Web	Richard Lewis	£1.10
☐ Gate of Fear	Lewis Mallory	£1.00
☐ The Nursery	Lewis Mallory	£1.10
☐ The Summoning	John Pintoro	95p
☐ Bloodthirst	Mark Ronson	£1.00
☐ Ghoul	Mark Ronson	95p
☐ Ogre	Mark Ronson	95p
☐ The Scourge	Nick Sharman	£1.00
☐ Deathbell	Guy N. Smith	£1.00
☐ Doomflight	Guy N. Smith	£1.10
☐ Entombed	Guy N. Smith	£1.25
☐ Locusts	Guy N. Smith	95p
☐ Manitou Doll	Guy N. Smith	£1.10
☐ Satan's Snowdrop	Guy N. Smith	£1.00
☐ The Specialist	Jasper Smith	£1.00
☐ The Offering	Gerald Suster	£1.25
☐ The Scar	Gerald Suster	£1.25

HAMLYN WHODUNNITS

☐ Some Die Eloquent	Catherine Aird	£1.25
☐ The Case of the Abominable Snowman	Nicholas Blake	£1.10
☐ The Widow's Cruise	Nicholas Blake	£1.25
☐ The Worm of Death	Nicholas Blake	95p
☐ Tour de Force	Christianna Brand	£1.10
☐ King and Joker	Peter Dickinson	£1.25
☐ A Lonely Place to Die	Wessle Ebersohn	£1.10
☐ Gold from Gemini	Jonathan Gash	£1.10
☐ The Judas Pair	Jonathan Gash	95p
☐ Spend Game	Jonathan Gash	£1.25
☐ Blood and Judgment	Michael Gilbert	£1.10
☐ Close Quarters	Michael Gilbert	£1.10
☐ The Etruscan Net	Michael Gilbert	£1.25
☐ Hare Sitting Up	Michael Innes	£1.10
☐ The Weight of the Evidence	Michael Innes	£1.10
☐ The Howard Hughes Affair	Stuart Kiminsky	£1.10
☐ Inspector Ghote Draws a Line	H. R. F. Keating	£1.10
☐ Inspector Ghote Plays a Joker	H. R. F. Keating	£1.25
☐ The Siamese Twin Mystery	Ellery Queen	95p
☐ The Spanish Cape Mystery	Ellery Queen	£1.10

NON-FICTION

GENERAL

☐ The Chinese Mafia	Fenton Bresler	£1.50
☐ The Piracy Business	Barbara Conway	£1.50
☐ Strange Deaths	John Dunning	£1.35
☐ Shocktrauma	John Franklin & Alan Doelp	£1.50
☐ The War Machine	James Avery Joyce	£1.50

BIOGRAPHY/AUTOBIOGRAPHY

☐ All You Needed Was Love	John Blake	£1.50
☐ Clues to the Unknown	Robert Cracknell	£1.50
☐ William Wordsworth	Hunter Davies	£1.95
☐ The Family Story	Lord Denning	£1.95
☐ The Borgias	Harry Edgington	£1.50
☐ Rachman	Shirley Green	£1.50
☐ Nancy Astor	John Grigg	£2.95
☐ Monty: The Making of a General 1887-1942	Nigel Hamilton	£4.95
☐ The Windsors in Exile	Michael Pye	£1.50
☐ 50 Years with Mountbatten	Charles Smith	£1.25
☐ Maria Callas	Arianna Stassinopoulos	£1.75
☐ Swanson on Swanson	Gloria Swanson	£2.50

HEALTH/SELF-HELP

☐ The Hamlyn Family First Aid Book	Dr Robert Andrew	£1.50
☐ Girls!	Brandenburger & Curry	£1.25
☐ The Good Health Guide for Women	Cooke & Dworkin	£2.95
☐ The Babysitter Book	Curry & Cunningham	£1.25
☐ Living Together	Dyer & Berlins	£1.50
☐ The Pick of Woman's Own Diets	Jo Foley	95p
☐ Coping With Redundancy	Fred Kemp	£1.50
☐ Cystitis: A Complete Self-help Guide	Angela Kilmartin	£1.00
☐ Fit for Life	Donald Norfolk	£1.35
☐ The Stress Factor	Donald Norfolk	£1.25
☐ Fat is a Feminist Issue	Susie Orbach	£1.25
☐ Fat is a Feminist Issue II	Susie Orbach	£3.50
☐ Living With Your New Baby	Rakowitz & Rubin	£1.50
☐ Related to Sex	Claire Rayner	£1.50
☐ Natural Sex	Mary Shivanandan	£1.25
☐ Woman's Own Birth Control	Dr Michael Smith	£1.25
☐ Overcoming Depression	Dr Andrew Stanway	£1.50
☐ Health Shock	Martin Weitz	£1.75

POCKET HEALTH GUIDES

☐ Depression and Anxiety	Dr Arthur Graham	85p
☐ Diabetes	Dr Alex D. G. Gunn	85p
☐ Heart Trouble	Dr Simon Joseph	85p
☐ High Blood Pressure	Dr James Knapton	85p
☐ The Menopause	Studd & Thom	85p
☐ Children's Illnesses	Dr Luke Zander	85p

NAME ....

ADDRESS ....

....

Write to Hamlyn Paperbacks Cash Sales, PO Box 11, Falmouth, Cornwall TR10 9EN.

Please indicate order and enclose remittance to the value of the cover price plus:

U.K.: Please allow 45p for the first book plus 20p for the second book and 14p for each additional book ordered, to a maximum charge of £1.63.

B.F.P.O. & EIRE: Please allow 45p for the first book 20p for the second book and 14p per copy for the next 7 books, thereafter 8p per book.

OVERSEAS: Please allow 75p for the first book and 21p per copy for each additional book.

Whilst every effort is made to keep prices low it is sometimes necessary to increase cover prices and also postage and packing rates at short notice. Hamlyn Paperbacks reserve the right to show new retail prices on covers which may differ from those previously advertised in the text or elsewhere.